PRAISE FOR

A Fatal Waltz

"[A] multitextured, beautifully written story."   —*Tucson Citizen*

"Alexander cleverly incorporates historical figures and events into a fictional story of European political intrigue, English society, Viennese culture, and plenty of genteel romantic chemistry. A wonderful choice for readers looking for a pleasant diversion from everyday troubles."   —*Library Journal*

"A breezy read with a depth of character and inventive plot. . . . Tasha Alexander has crafted another masterful piece of fiction. . . . She is a star on the rise."   —Blogcritics.org

"A captivating addition to the adventures of an irresistible Victorian iconoclast."   —*Booklist*

"A nineteenth-century amateur detective in a Worth gown . . . what's not to love? Lady Emily Ashton flirts, dances, and doesn't miss a thing. . . . Sprightly style and characters."
—Karleen Koen, *New York Times* bestselling author of *Through a Glass Darkly*

"Charming. . . . The book's entertaining voice and accurate period detail will seduce most readers."   —*Publishers Weekly*

Wolf Hoffman

About the Author

TASHA ALEXANDER attended the University of Notre Dame, where she signed on as an English major in order to have a legitimate excuse for spending all her time reading. She lived in Amsterdam, London, Wyoming, Vermont, Connecticut, and Tennessee before settling in Chicago. When not reading, she can be found hard at work on her next book.

A Fatal Waltz

ALSO BY TASHA ALEXANDER

Elizabeth: The Golden Age

A Poisoned Season

And Only to Deceive

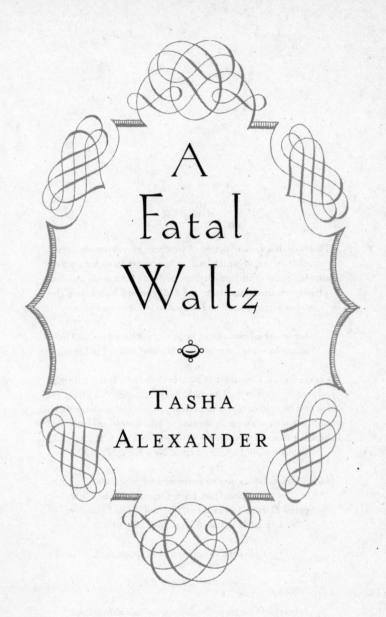

A Fatal Waltz

Tasha Alexander

HARPER

NEW YORK · LONDON · TORONTO · SYDNEY

HARPER

A hardcover edition of this book was published in 2008 by William Morrow, an imprint of HarperCollins Publishers.

HarperCollins books may be purchased for educational, business, or sales promotional use. For information please write: Special Markets Department, HarperCollins Publishers, 10 East 53rd Street, New York, NY 10022.

FIRST HARPER PAPERBACK PUBLISHED 2009.

Designed by Gretchen Achilles

Library of Congress Cataloging-in-Publication Data has been applied for.

ISBN 978-0-06-117423-0

10 11 12 13   OV/RRD   10 9 8 7 6 5 4

FOR ANASTASIA SERTL,
who I wish was here to see it

Anybody can be good in the country.
There are no temptations there.

OSCAR WILDE,
The Picture of Dorian Gray

Cast of Characters

EMILY, LADY ASHTON (KALLISTA): daughter of Earl Bromley, widow of the Viscount Ashton (Philip), and a scholar of Greek language and art.

COLIN HARGREAVES: a gentleman of independent means who is frequently called upon by Buckingham Palace to investigate matters requiring discretion.

CÉCILE DU LAC: a French woman of a certain age, iconoclast, patron of the arts.

IVY BRANDON: Emily's childhood friend, a perfect English rose.

ROBERT BRANDON: Ivy's husband, an up-and-coming politician and very traditional gentleman.

MARGARET SEWARD: daughter of an American railroad tycoon, she is a Bryn Mawr-educated Latinist who has little tolerance for society's rules.

CATHERINE, LADY BROMLEY: Emily's mother, wife of Earl Bromley, former lady-in-waiting to Queen Victoria.

JEREMY SHEFFIELD, DUKE OF BAINBRIDGE: childhood friend of Emily's whose twin goals are to avoid marriage and to be the most useless man in England.

BASIL, LORD FORTESCUE: Queen Victoria's most trusted political advisor, widely considered the most powerful man in the empire.

MRS. REYNOLD-PLYMPTON: a lady who takes great interest in politics; Lord Fortescue's longtime mistress.

MARY FORTESCUE: Lord Fortescue's third wife.

MR. HARRISON: a political ally of Lord Fortescue.

MR. MICHAELS: an Oxford don, Latinist.

KRISTIANA, COUNTESS VON LANGE: an extremely elegant Viennese lady.

GUSTAV SCHRÖDER: the leader of a group of Austrian anarchists.

ELISABETH, EMPRESS OF AUSTRIA: Sissi, Cécile's friend since they were girls. A famous beauty during her youth.

MEG: Emily's maid.

DAVIS: Emily's incomparable butler.

Chapter 1

I had not noticed it when she first arrived: the way she leaned too far towards him as he kissed her hand, the hint of surprised recognition in his eyes. But having spent an afternoon in the same room as them, watching the effortless manner in which they fell into familiar conversation—two striking individuals against an equally spectacular backdrop—I could not deny that they were more than casual acquaintances. Never had I suspected my fiancé was so close to another woman.

I was accustomed to, and often amused by, the parade of young ladies who flirted with Colin Hargreaves at every opportunity. The fact that he looked something like a Greek statue of ideal man—by Praxiteles, of course—made him irresistible to debutantes. His enormous fortune, family lineage that could be traced to the time of William the Conqueror, and well-tended estate ensured that he was equally attractive to their parents. But until today, I'd never seen him react to a woman the way he did to the Countess von Lange.

"And you know, *Schatz*, the Baroness Meinz thought that Tintoretto had done the doors of the Duomo in Florence. Can you imagine?" she asked. *Schatz?* I was shocked to hear her use a term of endearment in such an intimate tone of voice.

"Well, perhaps she's no scholar of art, but—," Colin began.

"Scholar? Darling, she's absolutely hopeless. Why, even you know who Tintoretto is, don't you, Lady Ashton?"

"Of course," I said, my lack of knowledge of Renaissance art making it impossible for me to add anything more.

"You understand, I hope, why Tintoretto couldn't have done the doors?" she asked, her green eyes dancing as she looked at me.

"My expertise is in classical art, countess," I said. "I'm afraid I'm unable to discuss the nuances of the Italian Renaissance."

"Nuance has nothing to do with it. Tintoretto was a painter. Ghiberti was a sculptor. He did the doors—Michelangelo called them 'gates of paradise.'" She pushed against Colin's arm playfully. "You are going to have to educate her. I can't have you married to someone who's as foolish as the baroness. It would be unconscionable."

"You've nothing to fear on that count," he said. "Emily's brilliant."

"Spoken like a man in love." She had turned so that her back was almost to me, cutting me out of the conversation.

"Will you excuse me?" I asked. There are moments when one is overwhelmed with a feeling of awkwardness, when grace and sophistication and even coherence are goals more remote than that of a woman in evening dress climbing Mount Kilimanjaro or of my mother convincing me to adopt her definition of a successful life. This was one of those moments, and I had no desire to prolong it. As I stood up, my heel caught the silk hem of my gown, and I tripped. Not daring to look at the countess, I mustered as much dignity as possible following what was a decidedly inelegant recovery and headed for the tea table.

Every inch of the mahogany surface was covered by dainty china platters heaped with sandwiches, biscuits, and cakes. Although I did not doubt for an instant that it was all delectable, none of it appealed to a stomach seared by embarrassment. I poured myself a cup of tea, my unsteady hands sloshing the golden liquid onto the saucer, and took a seat on the other side of the parlor.

"Stunning woman, the countess, wouldn't you say, Lady Ashton?" Lord Fortescue dropped onto the chair across from me, its delicate frame bowing under his weight. "Great friend of Hargreaves's. They've known each other for years. Inseparable when he's on the Continent."

I'd had the misfortune in the past year of drawing the attention and ire of Lord Fortescue, confidant of Queen Victoria and broadly considered to be the most powerful man in the empire. I despised him as much as he despised me, and wondered how I would survive for days on end trapped at Beaumont Towers, his extravagant estate in Yorkshire. Ignoring his question, I looked across the drawing room at a gentleman sprawled on a moss green velvet settee. "Is Sir Thomas asleep? That can't bode well for this party."

"So unfortunate that you had to postpone your wedding," Fortescue drawled. "But we needed Hargreaves in Russia. Couldn't be avoided." Colin and I had planned to be married as soon as possible after I'd accepted his proposal, but he was called away just two days before the wedding—no doubt by Lord Fortescue—to assist with a delicate situation in St. Petersburg. This had caused a considerable amount of gossip, as we'd bowed to family pressure to invite several hundred guests.

"Mrs. Brandon tells me that Sir Thomas has a terrible habit of dozing in Parliament. I marvel that his constituents continue to reelect him." I turned my head to stare out the window across the moors.

"I wouldn't expect Hargreaves to be in a hurry to marry you now that he's renewing his acquaintance with the countess." He tapped on the side of his empty glass, which a footman immediately refilled with scotch. As soon as the servant had stepped away, my adversary resumed his offensive. "I've no interest in protecting your feelings, Lady Ashton. You will never make an appropriate wife for him, and I shall do everything in my power to make sure that he never marries you."

"I wonder if I could fall asleep in Parliament," I said, refusing to engage him. "I shouldn't think the benches are that comfortable, though it's not difficult to believe many of the speeches are tedious enough to induce even the most hearty soul to slumber. But I'd wager the House of Commons is more lively than the House of Lords." Across the room, the countess had pulled her chair closer to Colin's, her hand draped elegantly over his armrest.

"You will not avoid conversation on this topic," Lord Fortescue said, his voice sharp, his already ruddy complexion taking on an even brighter hue.

"You're quite mistaken." At last I allowed my eyes to meet his. "Let me assure you that I have every intention of avoiding it entirely. My private life is exactly that: private." I was resolved to let this man see me as nothing but unflappable. "It's rather cold in here, isn't it? It can be so difficult to heat large houses."

"The sooner you learn your place, the better," he said.

"Lord Fortescue, there is little less appealing to me than having to pass even an hour in close quarters with you. But we're both here, and rather than spending the duration of this party bickering, I shall do all I can to be pleasant." I gave him my most charming smile. "Let's begin again. I was surprised to receive your invitation. It was good of you to acquiesce to Mr. Brandon's request." Robert Brandon, who was married to one of my dearest friends, Ivy, had recently entered politics. His quick mind and steady character appealed to Lord Fortescue, who decided to groom the younger man for greatness. It was Ivy who had wanted me at this party.

"Do you really think I agreed to invite you to amuse Brandon's wife? For a woman who claims an above-average intelligence, you are rather dim-witted."

There was no point in replying to this. Unfortunately the only thing I could focus on other than Lord Fortescue was not a welcome distraction: the intent look on Colin's face as he listened to his beautifully sophisticated companion. Thick, dark lashes framed eyes that sparkled when she spoke, with lips more red than should be found in nature. I bit my own, hoping to deepen their hue, then applied myself to my rapidly cooling tea. I was thankful when Flora Clavell sat next to me.

"Emily, Gerald decided to give the British Museum that Etruscan statue you found in our house." I had met Flora soon after her marriage to Sir Thomas's son, and though we were not much in each other's company, I had always enjoyed speaking with her. She and my friend Margaret Seward had attended the same school in New York when they were girls, but unlike Margaret, who had gone on to graduate from Bryn Mawr, Flora did not continue her education. Nonetheless, she was enlightened enough to have invited me to search her husband's estate when she'd heard about the project on which I'd embarked, a quest to locate and catalog significant works of art buried in country houses.

"How wonderful," I said. "Your family does a great service by making it permanently accessible to scholars. And I'm grateful beyond measure that you allowed me to record the rest of the objects in your collection."

"I've heard of your efforts regarding this." Mr. Harrison, who I had not met before he joined us that morning, approached us. Tall and wiry, he was all angles and bent down to give Lord Fortescue's hand a sharp shake before sitting next to him. "They are much to be commended."

"Thank you," I said.

"I can't imagine your meddling in private estates is much appreciated," Lord Fortescue said, finishing his scotch with a loud gulp and shooting Flora a strange sort of too-long look. The footman refilled the glass the moment it was drained. "Why must you harass people, Lady Ashton? Aloysius Bingham still rages about your inappropriate behavior."

"He may rage all he likes. I did nothing inappropriate. And he did, as I'm sure you well know, donate the silver libation bowl to the museum." I was still pleased with this triumph, which had taken more than an entire London season to achieve. Mr. Bingham had refused to part with the bowl, not because he admired it but because he did not approve of a lady pursuing any sort of academic agenda. I had no difficulty picturing him and Lord Fortescue as the closest of friends. If, that is, Lord Fortescue bothered to have friends.

"I didn't know. I shall have words with him."

"I'm sure he would welcome that," I said. The strained look on Flora's face reminded me that I ought to at least attempt to get along with this odious man, although I confess to being surprised that she showed such concern for Lord Fortescue. The expression on his face while he looked at her gave me further pause. He nodded almost imperceptibly, an admiring shine in his eyes as they met hers.

"Brilliant," Mr. Harrison said, giving me a broad smile. "It's been far too long since I've seen someone spar openly with you, Fortescue. Wouldn't have thought a lady could do it."

"Watch yourself, Harrison. I've no need for your nonsense."

"Gentlemen, please!" Flora said. "This is to be a sporting party, not a weekend of argument." Mr. Harrison apologized at once; Lord Fortescue held up his glass for still more scotch. At that moment Ivy, cutting an elegant figure in a gown of dark green brocade, entered the room. As always, she was dressed in the latest fashion, her waist impossibly small, the sleeves of her dress fuller than what had been popular the previous year. I was relieved at the opportunity to remove myself from the conversation and nearly knocked over my chair as I leapt out of it to rush to my friend, who greeted me with the warmest embrace.

"You look as if you've narrowly escaped from Lord Fortescue," she said in a low voice. We retreated to a window seat far across the room, away from the other guests. Had the weather been better, the view would have been spectacular: the estate overlooked the moors, and was considered by many to have the most sweepingly romantic location in England. As it was, a heavy mist had settled above the ground, limiting the distance one could see. This was not an entirely bad thing; I half expected to see Heathcliff striding purposefully towards the house.

Like the rest of Beaumont Towers, the drawing room was an exercise in ostentation, every piece of furniture upholstered in the finest silk or velvet, the parquet floor covered with an Axminster carpet. But quality and extravagance do not guarantee comfort. It was more like a state reception hall than a place to entertain friends. Rumor had it that Mrs. Reynold-Plympton, Lord Fortescue's long-time mistress, had overseen extensive redecoration of the house and that she considered this, the drawing room, her greatest triumph. The ceiling, all mauve, green, and gold, was at least twenty feet high, its plaster molded in an intricate pattern of entwined rosettes. The gilding continued in a diamond pattern against a taupe background down the top two-thirds of the walls, below which was paneling too dark for the room. On this, at regular intervals, characters from Shakespeare's *Merchant of Venice* had been painted.

"If only it were possible to escape," I said. "I wouldn't have agreed to come here for anyone but you, Ivy." The party was not to be a large one, populated by a select group of politicians and their wives. When the men were not buried in meetings, they would be out hunting the estate's birds, the ladies left with very little to do inside. A typical shooting weekend.

"I know he's awful, but he's so good to Robert. We owe him everything." Robert's ascent in politics had been hastened by Lord Fortescue's support, and in return, Robert was expected to give his mentor absolute loyalty.

"I wonder which is less pleasant, being Lord Fortescue's pro-tégé or his enemy?" I asked. "At least his enemies don't have to spend as much time with him."

"But they do. Lord Fortescue makes a point of keeping his enemies near. That's why Mr. Harrison is here this weekend."

"You mean I'm not the only unwelcome guest?"

"Oh, Emily, let's not talk politics. What do you know about the Countess von Lange? I'm told the attachés in Vienna speak of nothing but her. Her parties are infamous."

"Her existence had entirely escaped my notice until today," I said, frowning. "A statement Colin clearly could not make."

"They do look rather cozy. He must know her from his work on the Continent."

"Yes, Lord Fortescue was kind enough to let me know that."

"Oh, dear. We shan't talk about it," Ivy said, and dropped her voice to a whisper. "Lord Fortescue seems awfully friendly with Flora Clavell."

"I noticed the same thing. I thought he was devoted to Mrs. Reynold-Plympton?" For years she had acted almost as a wife, offering considerable assistance to him in political matters, particularly when he required personal information concerning his rivals. He was on his third marriage—his first wife had succumbed to fever when they were visiting the West Indies, the second to the rigors of childbirth. Like her predecessors, the current Lady Fortescue did not seem troubled in the least by her husband's mistress.

"*Devoted* is perhaps not the right word, but he certainly hasn't dropped her. I saw them together last weekend at Lady Ketter-baugh's in Kent. There was perhaps a coldness between them, but it was obvious that they're still very much attached. Have you been to the Ketterbaughs' estate? The house is gorgeous beyond belief."

"No, I haven't—"

"Her conservatory is absolutely unrivaled. I don't know when I've seen such an array of plants, and—"

I could see that Ivy was about to launch into a full description of the estate, and although no one could help being charmed when she waxed enthusiastic on any subject, I stopped her, not wanting to lose the thread of our conversation. "Surely Flora couldn't be . . . wouldn't . . . Lord Fortescue is so . . ."

"I couldn't agree more," Ivy said. "But I don't think the Clavell fortune is what it used to be. I've heard that at least half of his country house is shut, and all the rooms are in dire need of refurbishing. I think she's hoping to improve her husband's position. When Sir Thomas dies, there may not be much left for his son."

"I don't see how allying herself with Lord Fortescue is going to help her husband. Gerald isn't in politics."

"Perhaps he wishes to be," Ivy said, raising her delicate eyebrows.

I smiled. "You are enjoying the role of politician's wife, aren't you?"

"I am, Emily. Very much."

We both looked up at the sound of someone clearing his throat. A gentleman wearing the ribbon of some knightly order I did not recognize stood before us. "Lady Ashton, Mrs. Brandon, may I be so bold as to introduce myself? I've been waiting for our hostess, but she is blind to my plight, and I cannot bear to be kept from conversing with such beauties for even one moment longer. Surely at a party as intimate as this, formalities may be overlooked?"

"I don't see why not," I said, offering him my hand. He took it and raised it to his lips as he bowed deeply and clicked his heels together in a flawless Austrian *handküss*. "*Küss die Hand, gnädige Frau*. Or do you prefer English? I kiss your hand, gracious lady." He repeated this routine on Ivy, then stood still, perfectly erect, a shockingly tall man. "I am the Count von Lange, but I insist that you both call me Karl. I am not a sportsman, I'm afraid, so Lady Fortescue has given me the task of entertaining the ladies while the gentlemen shoot."

"I can assure you we'll be in dire need of entertainment," I said. His earnest manner made me warm to him at once, as did the fact that he was willing to dispense with social formalities. His smile could have charmed the coldest soul, but his eyes revealed nothing. He was more guarded than he wanted to appear.

"Nothing would give me greater pleasure than to provide it," he said, looking as if he were about to twirl the ends of his enormous dark mustache.

"What news have you from Vienna?" Ivy asked. "It was one of my favorite stops on my wedding trip." She blushed slightly as she said this and glanced across the room at her husband, who was speaking with Lord Fortescue.

"The city is as beautiful as ever. So far as I am concerned, nothing in Europe can match the Ringstrasse. And you English know nothing about waltzing."

"Is that so?" I asked. "Then I shall have to visit."

"You are fond of the waltz?" he asked.

"Immensely," I said. As if he could hear what I was saying, Colin looked towards me, and I felt bathed in warmth.

"Your fiancé is a lucky man," the count said.

"Well spoken." Ivy's eyes sparkled. "Do you know Mr. Hargreaves?"

"Very well. He's a frequent visitor when his work brings him to Austria."

I was about to ask the count how he and his distressingly elegant wife had wound up at Beaumont Towers on a dreary English weekend when I was distracted by Sir Thomas, who, upon awakening rather violently from his nap, managed to knock a towering vase off the table in front of him. His son grimaced, embarrassed on his father's behalf. I had always liked Gerald Clavell. He was well intentioned, if more than a little too eager, but even I had to admit that the prospect of spending more than two days in a row with him was exhausting. It was as if his father's lethargy had spurred him to become the polar opposite.

"I'm absolutely depending upon you this weekend, Lady Ashton," he said, coming to my side in a poorly disguised effort to divert my attention from his father. "Will you help me put together a theatrical entertainment? It will give you ladies something to do while we shoot. I can't bear the thought of you all sitting around wasting away."

"I—"

"You simply must. Perhaps something from the Greeks? You can choose whatever you'd like. I'm sure Lord Fortescue's library is at your disposal."

"If I may," the count interrupted, "I would be honored to assist you in finding an appropriate piece."

"How about something from *The Trojan Women*? We've more ladies than gentlemen who could be persuaded to take part," I said.

"I beg you, not a tragedy. Not a tragedy!" Gerald was turning beet red. "You must find something that will put us in a festive mood."

"Aristophanes?" I suggested.

"You know your Greek literature quite well, don't you, Lady Ashton?" I had not heard Mr. Harrison come up behind me, and started at the sound of his voice. "Not a woman to be underestimated, eh?" He looked at me carefully as he spoke.

"I find *Lysistrata* vastly diverting," I said.

"*Lysistrata*?" Gerald sounded a bit panicked. Rightly so, I suppose. The story of women joining together to withhold physical pleasures from their husbands in an attempt to thwart a war was, perhaps, not appropriate for our current gathering.

"Not to worry, Gerald," I said. "I'll find something that will delight us all."

"Right." The wrinkles between his eyebrows smoothed. "Please don't wait too long to get started. We should plan to be ready no later than Saturday, don't you think? Do you know where the library is? I could bring you there now." He took my arm and nodded at Ivy. "Mrs. Brandon, why don't you organize some cards while I'm delivering Lady Ashton. Whist? Yes? We could all meet in the game room in half an hour?"

Ivy stammered a reply as he steered me towards the door. Colin stood up to follow me, but was intercepted by Lord Fortescue. The countess watched all this, a glittering smile on her face, barely nodding at her husband as he rushed to join me.

"SHE IS AN ENCHANTING THING, Colin, but so young!"

I had gone to my bedroom after leaving the library and was about to return downstairs when I heard the countess's voice floating up from the main hall. I ducked behind a pillar.

"I will not discuss this with you," Colin said.

"Don't be silly. You can't expect that I—"

"Kristiana!" He spoke firmly, and I wished I could see them. The hall was an atrium, Gothic arches lining the second-floor balcony. If I were to stand two or three arches from where I was, I would be able to look down on them from behind a pillar. But if I moved, they might notice me.

"So you're abandoning your lifelong role as confirmed bachelor?" she asked.

"Yes, and I'm looking forward to it more than you can imagine."

"You underestimate my imagination, *Schatz*."

"Kristiana—"

"You had to know I'd be disappointed."

"I wrote you. This does not come as a surprise," he said.

"I confess that I did not take you seriously when you threw me over, though you were very stubborn about it."

"I've nothing more to say on the subject."

"I believed you when you said you'd fallen in love. It's an easy enough thing to do. But I never thought you'd marry her."

"She is everything to me."

"For the moment, perhaps. But I think we both know . . . Well, best not to consider that now."

"You're terrible," he said, and I could hear a smile creeping into his voice.

"That's why you've always adored me."

Stunned? Horrified? Frozen? If there were a word that might have captured my emotion at that moment, it was one I did not know. I realized I had been holding my breath, and when at last I drew air, it felt like icy knives in my throat.

"I may have held you in the highest esteem, Kristiana, but I never loved you, nor did you love me."

"We both know that's not true. But it was never your love that I wanted, *mein Schatz*. Wasn't that always our problem?" She was moving away from him, her heels clicking on the marble floor as she stepped into the hall under the balcony. Once her footsteps had faded, I tentatively peeked over the railing and saw Colin leaning against a pillar, arms crossed, countenance imperturbable. I counted to one hundred in Greek before speaking.

"There is a deplorable lack of fires in this house, don't you think?" I asked, calling down from above. "I've not been warm since I arrived."

"Don't move," he said, and crossed the hall to the Elizabethan staircase. When he reached the top, he took me by the arms and in one swift motion pressed me to the wall and kissed me with an urgent passion. Delicious though the moment should have been, I found myself distracted. Was he, in his usual charming manner, doing his best to keep me warm? Or was this display fueled by his encounter with Kristiana? *Kristiana*. Already I hated the name.

He pulled back and straightened his jacket, turning his head towards the stairs.

"Is something wrong?" I asked.

"Wait," he said. An instant later, I heard heavy, slow footsteps coming from the direction of the bedrooms.

"Hargreaves, let's go." Lord Fortescue, clutching a thick stack of papers to his chest, nodded sharply at him but ignored me. "I want to speak with you privately before Harrison and the rest descend upon us."

"I'm not quite done here," Colin said. Fortescue grunted and gave me a disparaging look before going back downstairs.

"You're not afraid of him?" I asked. "Everyone else in England is."

"I'm not afraid of anyone. And there's no one in Britain or elsewhere who is going to keep me away when I want to be with you." He kissed me again, and this time I did not think of the countess at all.

27 November 1891
Somerville Hall, Oxford

Dear Emily,

 *I'm timing the sending of this letter so that it will arrive during
your stay at Beaumont Towers, hoping that it may provide a fleeting
bright spot in what will no doubt be an otherwise dull weekend.
How I wish you were here at Oxford with me instead!*

 *Do you remember the don we heard lecture when you visited
at the beginning of term? Mr. Michaels? Who wouldn't deign to
so much as acknowledge our presence afterwards? Who pointedly
refused to answer my questions? After three weeks of hounding
him, he agreed to speak to me about my work on Ovid. Imagine
his astonishment when he found our views on the Metamorphosis
perfectly complementary.*

 *Now that another fortnight has passed, he's decided to take me
under his wing. I'll begin formally reading with him during
Hilary Term, but in the meantime he's doing all he can to advance
my studies, even though, in theory, he doesn't believe women should
be full members of the university. He will reconsider that position
before I'm through with him.*

 *I saw Jeremy last week. He's been cavorting with Lady
Templeton, but insists that he's more bored than ever. I told him
where you were spending the weekend and his face brightened—said
he was going to wangle an invitation to a neighboring house (the
Langstons', I think) so that he could descend upon you. If your
darling fiancé continues to postpone wedding plans, he may find
himself in the midst of a fierce competition.*

 *Have you ever met Gertrude Bell? She's planning a trip to
Persia, and it sounds absolutely marvelous. I think, Emily, that
you and I should embark on an exploration of the world before you
succumb once again to the bonds of marriage.*

 I am, as always, your most devoted and corrupt friend,
 Margaret Seward

Chapter 2

I was delighted to find that Margaret had sent me a note. The reading and writing of correspondence were some of the few activities available to ladies at a shooting party, and as we were only to be at Beaumont Towers for a short time, I had not expected to receive any letters. In the year we had known each other, Margaret and I had become closer than most friends after a lifetime. A mutual interest in the study of classics brought us together initially, but we soon discovered that our common ground was not limited to the intellectual. Her parents preferred to keep her at their home in New York—so far as I could tell, her father owned nearly every railroad in America—but she had convinced them to let her go to Oxford after finishing a degree at Bryn Mawr.

I folded her letter and paused. After the gentlemen, clad in tweed jackets and trousers, had gone outside to shoot, we ladies and the count had retired to the morning room, an oppressively gorgeous space. As with the drawing room, every object was of the best quality. The wallpaper was navy, its darkness relieved by a pattern of gold, but one did not see much of the walls, as a fine collection of old masters covered nearly every inch of them. The details of the paintings were lost against the midnight background, and the overall effect was claustrophobic. Palm trees, brought in from the sprawling winter garden, stood in three of the corners, and the amount of silk used to upholster couches and chairs made me wonder if any was left in China.

The count was doing an admirable job trying to keep the ladies occupied, and he proved a charming companion. He made a point of dividing his time as equally as possible among the ladies—although I noticed that he paid very little attention to his wife. While he, Flora, and Ivy looked at old stereoscope pictures of scenes of the English countryside, I wrote back to Margaret. The countess was reading a book whose title she kept hidden, and Lady Fortescue, who stayed so quiet that I'd nearly forgotten she was with us, was embroidering in the corner farthest from the fireplace, above which hung an enormous portrait of her husband.

It would have been difficult to find a woman more meek and unassuming—gray, really, despite her youth—than the new Lady Fortescue. She jumped, startled, whenever she was spoken to, not so much because she was shy as because she had grown accustomed to being ignored. Her husband was not openly cruel to her; that would have reflected badly on him. Instead, he treated her with an easy indifference, as if she were little more than a favored servant or a trinket he had received as a gift, but had never really wanted.

Ivy, who had grown tired of the stereoscope, came to me, leaning on the gilded table at which I sat. "I don't understand why he married her," she said, keeping her voice low enough that she would not be overheard.

"She does seem an unlikely choice for such a man," I said. "I should have thought he would want either a stunning beauty or someone with a significant fortune. And it's certainly safe to assume his motive wasn't love."

"She's practically penniless."

"All of society raved about how generous it was of him to marry her and bring her back to her ancestral home."

Poor Mary Fortescue. Her mother and father had died when she was very young, leaving her under the care of her elder brother, Albert Sanburne, who did not long survive his parents. After his death less than a year later there was no one left to inherit, and his barony, along with Beaumont Towers, the estate on which the girl had been raised, reverted back to the Crown. The queen, exercising her right to grant the title to someone else, bestowed it some years later upon her favorite political adviser, Lord Fortescue. Until his proposal, everyone assumed that Mary, who for ten years had been passed from distant relative to distant relative, would be forced to take a position as a governess. By marrying her, her husband appeared—for the first time in his life—a kindhearted, considerate, and selfless gentleman.

The engagement had enhanced his standing in society; for while he was a man to be feared, obeyed, perhaps even begrudgingly respected, it could not be said that Lord Fortescue was admired on a personal level by any but his staunchest supporters. I, for one, questioned even their sincerity. He was too powerful to be much concerned with being well liked, but if choosing the right bride might improve his reputation, he certainly didn't object to being lauded by the matrons of London.

"I thought the wedding was a bit ostentatious," Ivy said. "It was his third, after all. And she had seven bridesmaids."

"It's her first marriage," I said.

"You're right, of course. She ought to have had the sort of celebration she wanted to." Ivy's eyebrows shot together. "But I can't imagine it, can you? Being someone's third wife? Knowing that he'd adored two others before you?"

"You make the mistake of assuming that Lord Fortescue adored any of his wives."

"Still, I shouldn't like to think that my husband loved someone before me. It's . . . unseemly."

I knew not how to reply to this. I had loved my first husband before I loved Colin, and Colin obviously had been entangled with the countess before he'd met me. "It's . . ." I hesitated, not wanting to use the word "naïve." "It's lovely to think that one's first love will be one's last, but that's not always possible."

"Oh, Emily, I didn't mean—" She stopped at the sound of a commotion in the hallway that announced the return of the gentlemen, still dressed in tweeds from their afternoon activities. Kristiana watched, her eyes narrowing, as Colin crossed to me the moment he entered the room. Robert kissed Ivy's hand, and she leapt to his side, leaving me to my fiancé.

"Finished with your letter?" Colin looked over my shoulder.

"I've hardly begun," I said. "But I'll happily stop." I blotted the still wet ink before folding the paper in half.

"Come." He led me to a settee with a high, curved back, where we could sit close enough together that he could touch my hand without drawing anyone's attention. "This is absurd, you know. We're all but married, and I'm hardly allowed to touch you."

"This party would be much easier to bear if we were married," I said.

"If we were married, we wouldn't be at this party. We'd be in Greece." My late husband had left me a spectacular villa perched on a cliff on the Greek island Santorini, and it was there that I retreated whenever possible, there that Colin had twice proposed to me.

"Or Ephesus," I said, remembering a conversation we'd had in Paris about the Roman ruins found in Turkey.

"Egypt?"

"Anywhere." I smiled, and he rubbed his thumb against the back of my hand. It was all I could do not to sigh with delighted pleasure.

"I'm more sorry than I can say for having to postpone the wedding," he said.

"I've told you before, there's no need to apologize. It couldn't be helped."

"Now that my work's finished, there's no need for further delay. I see no reason why we couldn't be married within the next month."

"You'll hear no objections from me," I said. He squeezed my hand, and I wished I could fall into his arms. Our eyes met, full of longing, and we both knew that it would be best to change the direction of our conversation. I glanced around the room, my gaze resting on Sir Julian Knowles, owner of one of London's newspapers. "Why did Lord Fortescue invite Sir Julian? I shouldn't think he'd want the details of a political meeting exposed by the press."

"Lord Fortescue never does anything without a precise plan. There must be something he wants publicly known." He paused. "Hard to imagine, though, given the sensitivity of the issues we're discussing. He's been quite direct in insisting that this all remain quiet."

"Who opposes him on whatever this mysterious issue is? Could that person's position be undermined by some well-timed bad publicity? Scandals in the country aren't limited to the political, you know. Is anyone here on the brink of a personal disaster?"

"A very interesting idea, Emily," he said. We both turned at the sound of Sir Julian's voice booming with laughter. The newspaper man was sitting next to Lady Fortescue, close enough to Colin and me that it was impossible not to hear his words, spoken too loudly.

"Ah, there was something new every day then! Scandals enough to delight us all."

Lady Fortescue winced, her face pale, and rushed from the room. Her husband did not follow her; I don't think her absence registered with him in the least, particularly as he was sitting with Flora, who was glowing at his attention.

"She looks unwell. I should go to her," I said, removing my hand from Colin's and following her into the main hall. She was standing at the foot of the staircase, her knuckles white as she gripped an elaborately carved rail. "Are you all right?"

"Oh, yes, Lady Ashton, just a slight headache," she said, her voice barely above a whisper. "It's awfully warm in the morning room."

"Warm?" I asked. The fire had been so low it was in danger of going out. I touched her hand. It was ice cold.

"I see my husband coming. Will you excuse me?"

He was already upon us. "Thank you, Lady Ashton. That will be quite enough." He stood some distance from his spouse, hardly looking at her. "In the future, I would be much obliged if you would refrain from speaking to my wife unless absolutely necessary."

"I'm sure your wife is perfectly capable of deciding with whom she would like to speak."

"I will not have you take such a tone with me," he said. "It is intolerable. Any fool could see that she does not wish to talk to you."

"And I, sir, will not tolerate you speaking to me in such a manner. Perhaps it was a mistake to include me in this party if you feel that I'm an inappropriate companion for your wife."

"I do not make mistakes. I know you, Lady Ashton, and I know your kind. The best way to put a stop to your aspirations for marriage is to give you enough rope to hang yourself."

"What a thoroughly unoriginal thought, Lord Fortescue. I should have thought a man so well versed in vitriol could come up with something a bit more fresh. I'm rather disappointed."

"Learn to live with it, Lady Ashton. It's an emotion with which you will be spending a great deal of time in the future."

Seeing no point in replying to this sort of inanity, I started back to the morning room. I stopped when I heard Lord Fortescue burst into laughter, and could not help looking back at him. He had put his hands on his wife's shoulders and looked as if he were about to embrace her. Surprised and embarrassed, I turned away.

"Terrible man, Fortescue, don't you think?" Mr. Harrison stepped out from behind one of the pillars supporting the vaulted ceiling of the corridor that surrounded the hall. "I can't think of anyone worse." I wanted to agree, but something in his eyes—a coldness that was frightening in its lack of ambiguity—made me hesitate. "It's obvious that you don't care for him."

"I'm sure my feelings haven't the slightest impact on him," I said, quickening my pace. He caught up to me at once and put out a hand to stop me.

"He's never going to get along with you if you stay with Hargreaves."

"I'm well aware of his feelings on the subject. Fortunately, I've no desire to befriend him, and I certainly don't need his approval—especially as it pertains to my marriage plans."

"One of his daughters—Clara—has got it in her head that she should marry Hargreaves. They danced at a party some months ago, and she was enchanted by him. Hasn't stopped talking about him since. Fortescue will make sure she gets what she wants."

"I'm sure Mr. Hargreaves is perfectly capable of handling the situation. It is he, after all, who will decide whom he marries."

"Forgive me, Lady Ashton. I only meant to warn you. If Fortescue decides to put a stop to your wedding—" He stepped closer to me and placed a gentle hand on my arm. "It's not simply your wedding. He's an unsteady man. He puts us all at risk."

"I've not the slightest idea to what you are referring," I said, feeling a familiar swell of curiosity.

"I suppose you wouldn't, and that's unfortunate. A woman of your intelligence—" He stopped and squinted as he looked at me, a deep crease forming between his eyebrows. "May I speak freely?"

"I hope you will," I said.

"The manner in which you interact with Lord Fortescue has impressed me. You have the courage to push back when he tries to manipulate you. That takes a strength most men in England are lacking, and it makes me think you could assist me in a most vital matter."

"How?"

He stepped closer to me and continued in a low, gravelly voice. "I should like to continue this conversation in private. Will you follow me?"

I walked with him to a small chamber that could only be reached through the billiard room and appeared to have been commandeered for political purposes. A heavy table that must have dated from the medieval period filled much of the space, neatly stacked piles of paper sitting at each place. A map of continental Europe was pinned to the wall, and the air hung heavy with the lingering odor of cigars.

"How much do you know about why Fortescue has gathered us here?" he asked after he'd pulled the door partially closed behind us.

"Virtually nothing," I said.

"We haven't much time, so I can't give you full details at the moment. Fortescue is in possession of some papers that are crucial to my cause. I need you to engage him in conversation and keep him occupied long enough that I can locate them in his room."

"What sort of papers?"

"Ah, I can't share that," he said. "They are highly sensitive and political in nature . . ." He let his voice trail to silence. I waited for a moment, but he said nothing further, preferring, I suppose, to leave the rest to my imagination.

"Won't he notice if they are missing?" I asked.

"Eventually, yes. He keeps two copies of everything, storing the duplicates in a file somewhere in his dressing room, but they're just records. He doesn't *use* them, if that makes sense. The primary copy of the documents in question is in the sheath of papers he's refused to part with since we arrived here."

"And what is this cause you speak of?" I asked.

"To preserve the empire."

"Isn't that Lord Fortescue's cause as well?"

"Theoretically, yes. But I can't always agree with the strategies he uses to achieve that goal. There's a threat that has materialized in the past few weeks—a threat more nefarious than any you can conceive—and Fortescue has refused out of hand to take action against it."

"He must have his reasons," I said.

"Tell me, Lady Ashton, do you trust Fortescue? Do you think he's the best man to protect all that is dear to you? Have you faith in him?"

"Well." I paused. "Faith, Mr. Harrison, is a strong word." I tried to squelch my smile, but was unsuccessful.

"I've already complimented your intelligence. Can we agree that Lord Fortescue's is lacking?"

"I'm no supporter of his," I said.

"I suspected as much." He leaned against the table. "Your fiancé's work is dangerous. Fortescue's policies make it even more so. I'm asking a very small thing of you. A simple after-dinner conversation." Now he smiled. "Although I perhaps ought to acknowledge that the mere act of speaking to him is a dreadful chore."

"Yes, it is." Our eyes met, and I tried to hold back my laughter. It was more than a bit tempting to meddle with Lord Fortescue, particularly in a situation that didn't seem like much of a risk. Providing a distraction would be easy enough, and even if the rest of the plan imploded, no one would connect me to it. Furthermore, if Mr. Harrison was correct, I'd be helping Colin. "I suppose there's no harm in it. My part, at least. Any trouble you find is your own."

"Of course," he said. "You won't regret it, Lady Ashton."

"I don't do things I'll regret."

"I guessed as much. I have a great admiration for people who act with decisive purpose." He stared at me hard for a moment before continuing. "The timing of this is critical. I need the papers before the political discussions at this party begin in earnest."

"Tonight, then?"

"Yes. I think, Lady Ashton, that you and I could be very useful to one another." There was a hint of amusement in his voice, but then he grew serious. "I'll need at least half an hour, after dinner. I'll watch for you to engage him, and once it appears he's ensnared, I'll leave the room. Understand?"

I nodded.

"I'm beginning to trust you," he said.

"You would ask for my assistance without trusting me?"

"In my line of work, one is sometimes forced to make do with unfortunate circumstances. I'm sure your fiancé could enlighten you further." He pushed his hands deep into his jacket pockets. "But I have to ask that you not tell him what we're planning. Not quite yet."

"Why not?" I asked.

"Secrecy is essential. Telling one person, even someone you trust implicitly, can lead to unimagined troubles."

"But—" I hesitated.

"He'll know everything soon enough. I'm going to show him the papers in the morning. In fact"—he looked at me, a calculated smile on his weathered face—"why don't you join us? I believe this will not be the last time we can be of use to one another. Come to the library after breakfast."

"I look forward to it." I stood in front of him, awkward, feeling as if we ought to do something to acknowledge our agreement. I held out my hand in the manner of a gentleman, assuming he would shake it. Instead, he raised it to his lips.

"Very good, Lady Ashton. Until then, we shall not speak any further on the subject. Come now. Pretend we've been discussing antiquities."

We left the room, closing the door firmly behind us, and headed back towards the morning room, running into Colin, who was walking across the main hall as we crossed it.

"There you are, Emily," he said, taking my arm. "I've been looking for you."

"Your fiancée has a staggering knowledge of red figure vase painting," Mr. Harrison said, relinquishing my arm to my fiancé. This comment took me aback. How did he know I had a particular interest in Greek vases? It was no secret, certainly, but it struck me as odd that he'd picked up on it. Especially the red figure painting.

"How did you—" I stopped as Mr. Harrison turned and without a word walked away from us, disappearing down the corridor.

"Good of him to leave us alone." Colin stepped closer to me and touched my face. "Not that I wouldn't stand, rapt, for hours listening to you rhapsodize about ancient art. But aside from our inspiring encounter on the balcony, I've hardly seen you since you arrived."

"The countess seems to depend upon you for amusement."

"Apologies." He twined his fingers through mine. "I've known her for some time."

"So I've gathered. Lord Fortescue couldn't wait to let me know."

"He's a beast. I'm sorry. I would have rather told you myself."

"Told me what, precisely? He was a bit vague on details."

"Kristiana and I were . . . close . . . for some time, but that ended the moment I knew I loved you." His eyes held mine. "I wrote to her the night I escorted you back to the Meurice from Café Anglais in Paris last year. We talked on the Pont Neuf. Do you remember?"

"Very well," I said. "Although it was our subsequent encounter on the Pont Neuf that made more of an impression on me."

"I shouldn't have kissed you then."

"I'm glad you did." I should have been content standing there with him, but thoughts of the countess wouldn't stop tugging at me. "I never thought you were the sort to fall for a married woman."

"She wasn't married when we met."

"And after she was married?"

"Emily, I'm not going to impugn her reputation, even to you. It wouldn't be right. There's nothing between us any longer, and that is all that matters." Part of me admired his principles; the other part was rather too eager to hear anything that would portray the countess in a less-than-flattering light. "That's quite a wicked smile. I'm afraid to ask what you're thinking."

"Nothing that does me credit," I said.

"Then I shall have to redirect your imagination in a more acceptable direction." He started to kiss me, but pulled back at the sound of footsteps.

"You should be more careful with your fiancée's reputation, Colin," Kristiana said, her voice low and rich, seductive. "What would people say if they knew you two were skulking about hallways in country estates?"

"Very little, I'm sure," I said, meeting her stare. She smiled, the most dazzling, patronizing smile I had ever seen, and laid an elegant hand on Colin's arm.

"Enchanting, an enchanting little darling. I'm so glad you've found her. You really ought to bring her to Vienna sometime. The count is already excessively fond of her."

5 December 1891
Darnley House, Kent

My dear daughter,

    News as good as that which I have is worth sending express.

    Your father and I have just returned from spending several days at Balmoral with Her Majesty, and she has decided to bestow upon you and Mr. Hargreaves a great honor. She graciously offered to allow you to be married from St. George's Chapel at Windsor Palace. I, as you well know, was instrumental in facilitating the engagement between Prince Eddy and May of Teck, and the queen wishes to thank me for my service by taking particular note of your wedding.

    I told Her Majesty I think it best that the wedding take place during the Season, perhaps in June. This gives you plenty of time to make arrangements and organize your trousseau. The queen went so far as to suggest fireworks for the night before.

    Before I forget, I must mention that Lady Londonderry tells me you've written to ask her if you may catalog the art and antiquities at her husband's estate. Surely you know this is not the sort of activity in which you should be involved. I have no intention of addressing the issue again.

    I shall keep you abreast of plans for the wedding as they are made.

    Your very affectionate mother,
    C. Bromley

Chapter 3

M y mother's letter had arrived while I was dressing for dinner, and I spent much of the meal brooding over the thought of her taking over my wedding plans. Colin had been seated next to the countess at the opposite end of the table from me, so I'd not yet been able to give him the bad news. I did not doubt that he had even less interest in a society wedding than I did. Neither of us had wanted one in the first place, and the only bright spot in having to cancel the one we'd originally planned was that it gave us the chance to be married in a quiet, private fashion.

The count—Karl, as he kept insisting I call him—was my dinner partner, and I did my best to make the right sort of nonsensical noises of approval while I half listened to the stories he told to amuse me. Lord Fortescue and Flora were next to each other, heads bent close as they laughed over some private joke, something they would not have been able to do had Lady Fortescue been at the table. Her headache had grown worse, and she'd taken to her bed.

"Damn smart woman you married, Fortescue," Sir Thomas said. "I'd go to bed myself if I could. I'm exhausted. Bloody bore, sitting around like this."

"Yes, but you must eat, Father," said Gerald, who appeared to take no notice of his wife's friendliness towards our host. "And I think we can all agree that pleasant conversation while dining can only enhance—"

"That's quite enough, boy. Let's make it through dinner without prattling on about a lot of nonsense. Are we ready for the port, Fortescue? I don't think I can stay awake much longer."

This was the cue for the ladies to retire to the drawing room. Flora caught my eye, and I looked at Ivy, whose porcelain brow was furrowed. As I was the highest-ranking lady in the room, the rules of precedence dictated that I should leave first, but I didn't move. I looked above the fireplace at three golden statues of angels beneath Gothic canopies. They seemed to be staring down at me with looks of pained amusement. In my own house, I would never have left the gentlemen to the port, not only because it was my favorite beverage, but also because I disliked being excluded from what, typically, was the most interesting conversation of the evening. I glanced at Robert, who was incapable of masking the panic on his face, and decided that tonight, at least, I would join the ladies.

I rose from my chair and saw the countess smiling at me. "What a disappointment," she said. "I thought Lady Ashton was quite opposed to ladies being excluded from port. I shall have to soldier on without her, as I have no intention of being exiled to coffee in the sitting room."

My face grew hot. I stammered, trying and failing to form a pithy reply. Ivy took my arm. "Lady Ashton is kind enough to accompany me because she knows I cannot do without her."

"She is quick, then, to abandon her principles. Perhaps they only hold when she is in the familiar surroundings of her own home. But if one is to be an iconoclast, one must expect to live with some measure of discomfort."

"It is an admirable thing to put the needs of a friend before one's own personal agenda," Colin said, his gaze fixed on me.

"I find, Countess, that there are some things more important than blindly following one's principles. There are situations where the concerns of others ought to take precedence," I said.

"I couldn't agree more." She looked at Colin as she said this. Before I could reply, Ivy steered me through the door.

"I can't believe he ever cared for her," she whispered as we left. I did not reply, and instead silently wondered how deep his feelings for her had run.

We entered the great parlor, a room the family used only after dinner and, to my mind, the loveliest in the house. Somehow having escaped Mrs. Reynold-Plympton's attentions, it had been left in the style of the seventeenth century, curved wood beams crossing the ceiling, and white plaster on the walls at two ends. In the center of the roof was a charming frieze depicting the tragic story of Orpheus and Eurydice. The walls were lined with display cases of beautifully simple blue-and-white china. A soft Oriental carpet covered part of the wide, polished planks of the floor, and chandeliers emitted a soft, flattering light. The only failing was that the room was so cold I wondered if a window had inadvertently been left open. Many country estates are notorious for being drafty, but Beaumont Towers elevated what might have been a failing of architecture to the level of political statement.

An obliging footman had left on a table the stack of books I'd chosen from the library. I selected one of them and sat on a couch tucked into the inglenook, eager to be as close to the small fire as possible. Soon I was fully distracted by the wit of Aristophanes. I'd brought along my copy of Mary Elizabeth Braddon's *The Doctor's Wife* for Ivy. She sat opposite me, engrossed in the story of Isabel Gilbert, who, by marrying too early, missed having for her husband a man sprung from her dreams—dreams that had been fueled by novels. Robert, no fan of popular fiction, would have found both the premise and the execution unconscionable. A quarter of an hour passed in relative silence. Then another. Then, a commotion in the hall: raised voices—one obviously Lord Fortescue, the other more difficult to identify—the sound of someone striking the wall, and a door slamming.

Curious, I darted into the hallway, hoping to see who was the object of our host's ire, but there was no one there. I went back into the parlor, where I found it increasingly difficult to concentrate on Aristophanes.

Ten minutes later the gentlemen finally joined us. The countess entered with Lord Fortescue, who was all smiles. Apparently not all strong-willed women troubled him; his displeasure was selective. Mr. Harrison stood by himself in a corner; Colin was nowhere to be found.

"Have you settled on a scene?" the countess asked, looking over my shoulder at the book I was holding. The room had lit up around her, her evening gown fashioned from an iridescent silk that clung to the curves of her perfect hips.

"I think something from *The Frogs*."

"Greek, of course. You're like an eager schoolgirl. It's so sweet. But I think you should choose something more modern." The emerald choker around her neck drew out the green of her eyes.

"Funny you should suggest that. Do you know the story of *The Frogs*? The god Dionysus, the patron of theaters, has grown utterly disgusted with the current crop of tragedies being produced in Athens. He decides there's no hope for modern plays, and that the only thing to do is to go to Hades and bring back to earth one of the great playwrights from what he considers the golden days."

"And this is meant to be amusing?" the countess asked, idly twirling one of the dark curls that framed her face. Her hair shone like satin.

"It's vastly amusing. When he gets to Hades he sets up a competition between Aeschylus, Sophocles, and Euripides. They battle for the title of best tragedian. First—"

"Oh, please don't tell me, Lady Ashton. It will make it all the more difficult to sit and watch if I already know what is to happen."

"Watch? I'm counting on you to take part. I'd hoped you'd play Euripides," I said. Being this near to her, I felt utterly inadequate, washed out in the face of her brightness—too thin where she was curvy, my youth and inexperience paling next to her sophisticated wisdom.

"Is that so?" The corners of her mouth twitched. "Well, perhaps I've misjudged you. Even I know that Euripides is the greatest of the tragedians."

This brought a smile to my face. It was all I could do to resist pointing out that Euripides, in rather spectacular fashion, lost the contest. Feeling more than a little smug, I excused myself from her and crossed the room to Lord Fortescue, ready to embark on the task given to me by Mr. Harrison.

"Lovely dinner, didn't you think?" I asked. "Your wife has quite a flair for selecting menus. The venison was spectacular." He did not reply. "I've given a great deal of thought to what you said to me about marrying Colin."

"Have you?" he asked. I stepped towards him, forcing him to back into a corner, blocked from exiting unless I walked away. Mr. Harrison watched us for a moment, then left the room.

"I've heard it said that your daughter aspires to being his wife. If that's your motivation for trying to separate me from Colin, you should come straight out and say it rather than acting as if it's a matter of state security."

"You'll do well to keep out of Clara's business."

So Mr. Harrison was telling the truth. I should have known. It was unlikely that he'd conjured up by coincidence the correct name of one of Lord Fortescue's eight daughters. "And you'd do well to keep out of mine."

"Have you considered what I could do to Hargreaves if you continue to insist on marrying him?"

"I've heard it said that blackmail is your preferred method of controlling people. Colin is not the sort of man whose past is rife with fodder for that."

"You don't know him so well as you think. And don't forget about yourself. Imagine what I might do to you, and what seeing you destroyed would do to him."

"I know my own past well enough to feel certain that there is nothing you can hold over me."

"It's not your past that should concern you, but your present. You're very easily manipulated. Choosing to release Hargreaves from your engagement will be much less painful than the alternative."

"Do you mean to frighten me, Lord Fortescue? If so, I must tell you that you're failing dreadfully."

A menacing sound lurched from his throat. I only realized it was laughter when I saw the smile on his face. "You should be frightened," he said. "I can bring irreparable harm to you and those you care about. Your callous disregard for my power is dangerous."

"I'll try to remember that," I said, more glad than ever that I'd agreed to help Mr. Harrison. Still, I stepped back, uneasy at being so close to this loathsome man.

"I don't like your kind, Lady Ashton," Lord Fortescue said. "You're too forward, don't know your place, and refuse to behave like a decent woman. All the talk of modern women that circulates these days disgusts me, and I will do what I can to ensure that people like you do not get what they want. Furthermore, I won't have you distracting him from his work."

"Diplomats' wives are often as valuable as their husbands. Think of Lady Elgin—"

"Hargreaves is not a diplomat. Have you any idea what he does?"

"Of course I do. Not precise details, but I know that he—"

"You know nothing. His assignments require things of which a wife might not approve. Close relationships with female counterparts, for example." Fleshy lips pulled taut across his uneven teeth as he smiled.

"You mean the countess?" I laughed, but knew it sounded forced. "I'm not jealous, Lord Fortescue. I trust him implicitly."

"Do you?" His eyebrows shot up almost to his hairline, no small feat given how far the latter had receded. "Then perhaps you are naïve enough to play wife for him."

"I can only wonder, Lord Fortescue, if that's what you think of him, why you would want your daughter to marry him."

"That's quite enough, Lady Ashton. Just keep in mind that you are not safe with me. I know exactly how to deal with you." He kept talking, but I was hardly listening any longer, remembering instead his earlier comment that I was easily manipulated. Was I being manipulated now? Even though I knew I was doing nothing empirically wrong and that it was my partner in this scheme who had put himself in danger, I could not shake a nagging feeling that there was something I'd overlooked when I'd agreed to this task.

AIR RUSHED INTO MY LUNGS the moment my maid loosened my corset. "I don't know why I let you convince me to be laced so tightly," I said, drawing a much-needed deep breath.

"Because you know how lovely that gown looks, madam," Meg replied. "And it would never fit if you weren't tightly laced."

"Vanity is a terrible thing." I sighed. But who was I to resist such a delicious concoction of Mr. Worth's? The narrow silk taffeta skirt was a creamy ivory, the color deep enough to emanate an unmistakable warmth. A layer of the finest lace hung asymmetrically over it, forming a short train in the back. The low-cut neckline was draped with the same lace, topping off a bodice that required a tiny waist. The result was stunning, and further enhanced by a glittering diamond and sapphire necklace. I pulled the matching earrings off and handed them to Meg. "What an evening. How are things belowstairs? Any interesting gossip?"

"Well . . ." Meg always liked a dramatic pause before launching into details. "Lord Fortescue and his wife have separate rooms on separate floors. He's put Mrs. Clavell in the room directly across from his. Ordinarily, she and her husband share, but this time she asked for one of her own. She's afraid she's coming down with a cold and didn't want Mr. Clavell to catch it."

"Is that so? She seemed a picture of health all day." I couldn't help but smile at the serious look on Meg's face.

"You're across from the Count von Lange, another person who prefers a separate bedroom."

"Where's his wife?"

"Up on the second floor. The count's valet, Rolf, says their house in Vienna is in constant upheaval, what with all their lovers coming and going. Morally bankrupt, the Viennese, if you ask me. But Rolf is a very friendly sort of man. Gentlemanlike. Right handsome too."

"Where is Mr. Hargreaves?"

"He's up a floor, across from the countess." I raised my arms so Meg could drop a lacy nightgown over my head. "Do you need anything else tonight, madam? Some warm milk to help you sleep?"

"No, Meg, thank you. Get to bed yourself. Lord Fortescue expects us all to be up early in the morning."

After she left, I sat at the dressing table, brushing my hair. My mother insisted on a hundred strokes every night, and although I rebelled whenever possible against most of her rules, this was one over which we never argued. Not because I agreed with her firm belief that I should do everything in my power to enhance my appearance, but because I found the ritual relaxing, an effortless sort of activity that allowed my mind to wander. Tonight, however, I was agitated. Between the countess's sniping and Lord Fortescue's attacks, I was beginning to wish I'd stayed home, though I knew I couldn't have left Ivy to suffer through the weekend alone. Tomorrow offered little hope of improvement. The men would shoot all morning and then begin their political meetings late in the afternoon. I was wondering what I could do to best avoid the countess when I heard a soft tap at the door.

"What are you doing here?" I asked, pulling a robe over my nightgown and opening the door only a few inches. Colin was still in his evening kit.

"Are you going to let me in? Or am I to stand here in the hall waiting to be caught?"

Who was I to resist such temptation? I stepped aside so that he could slip into the room. "You're terrible to come here like this."

"I know." He took my face in his hands and kissed me, then buried his head in my neck. "I can't stay long. In another quarter of an hour the great room-swapping will begin, and it wouldn't do for me to be found coming out of here. But I couldn't resist seeing you, just for a moment." Another kiss, then he left me, dizzy, exhilarated, and quite unable to sleep.

MORPHEUS ELUDED ME for nearly the entire night, and I was exhausted the next morning, barely registering the change in light when Meg tugged at the heavy dark curtains that covered the windows, letting the sun fill the room. With effort, I raised myself to my elbows, squinting as I opened my eyes. Meg lifted the pillows behind me and I leaned back, accepting from her a steaming cup of tea.

"Lord Fortescue was awful disappointed by the ladies this morning," she said, brushing the dress she'd laid out for me to wear. "Mrs. Clavell was the only one of you to come down for breakfast."

"What time is it?" I asked. "Have the gentlemen already left to shoot?"

"They were getting ready to leave when I came upstairs. It's nearly ten o'clock."

"Help me get dressed, quickly."

Less than half an hour later I was rushing towards the library, where I hoped Mr. Harrison and Colin would still be waiting for me. The sight that greeted me when I opened the door took me aback, and I slowed my pace as I entered the room.

"Good morning, Lady Ashton," Lord Fortescue said. "Did you sleep well? A guilty conscience often makes peaceful rest difficult."

"I've no doubt you speak from experience," I said.

"I've had quite enough of your insolence. What were you doing in my room last night?"

"I wasn't in your room last night."

"It would be best if you didn't lie."

"I've no need to lie. Your room is the last place I would ever go."

He shook his head and smiled. "You are not good at this, Lady Ashton. How did this make its way to the floor by my bed?" He held up a bracelet: a simple gold bangle that I'd worn the day before.

"I don't know. It must have fallen off my wrist."

"While you were in my room."

"No—" The door opened, and Colin and Mr. Harrison entered the room.

"What did you find?" Lord Fortescue asked.

"All of them," Mr. Harrison said, holding up a neat stack of papers. "They were in her room underneath a copy of the collected works of Aristophanes."

"This is outrageous," I said. "I—"

Colin raised a hand to stop me, his eyes on Lord Fortescue. "This is nothing but the barest sort of circumstantial evidence.

Anyone could have put that bracelet on your floor, and anyone could have put the papers in her room."

"Perhaps, but I think the police would believe my version of the story. And I'm certain I could come up with at least one witness who saw her leaving my chamber. I wonder what Sir Julian would make of all this? I'm certain he'd want to run something about it in his paper."

"You've no more interest in involving the police or the newspapers than I do," Colin said.

"Quite right, as always, Hargreaves. Do you think Her Majesty would be interested in hearing my story? Would it cause her to lose faith in her favorite agent?"

"It's more likely to shake her faith in her favorite political advisor. The papers were in your possession. You should have seen to it that they were in a secure location."

"The queen would not approve of your marrying a woman suspected of theft."

"It does not become a man of your position to attack a lady. Save your venom for some other adversary," Colin said. Through all this, Mr. Harrison had remained silent, leaning against a bookshelf, inspecting his fingernails. His jacket hung open, and I saw that he was carrying a pistol under it.

"Ah." Lord Fortescue laughed. "So you don't view her as an equal, just as a mere lady? Can't imagine she'll be happy to hear that."

"She's my equal, but your superior. You degrade yourself by trying to insult her."

"A devastating observation. Think on it, though, Hargreaves. Can you afford a wife whose integrity is so easily compromised?"

"I've done nothing to compromise my integrity," I said, my voice strong. "Other than having the poor judgment to converse with you after dinner."

"I'm glad to see you're using the rope I've so generously left for you. You've let us all witness the danger of women trying to think for themselves. I've nothing further to say on this subject for now. But remember, Lady Ashton, that regardless of the opinion of your fiancé, I could use this incident against you. Do not try to cross me again. And when I need something from you, don't forget that this will become public should you refuse me." With that, he stalked out of the room, Mr. Harrison following close behind, a cold smile on his face.

I turned to Colin at once. "I'm so sorry," I said, and told him the details of my arrangement with Mr. Harrison.

"A clumsier plan than I would expect from Fortescue." He frowned and took my hand. "You must be more careful, though. What made you trust Harrison?"

"His story seemed reasonable; what he was asking of me, nominal."

"But what made you think he was trustworthy? It's simple to tell a reasonable story that is full of lies. Consider a man's character before you decide to believe him."

"Forgive me?" I asked, feeling like a child who'd been scolded for interfering with adults. It was unlikely that Kristiana had ever found herself in a comparable situation. She was Colin's colleague, his professional equal. I was the lowest sort of amateur. Was he drawing the comparison, too?

"Of course I forgive you. But you must promise that in the future you will be completely candid with me before you embark on anything like this."

"I promise." I hated that he had to ask this of me. "What was in the papers Mr. Harrison took?"

"He was correct when he told you they were politically sensitive. But that's all I can say. Don't worry any more about Fortescue. There's enough political trouble brewing that he'll soon have no time to worry about you. I fear there's more at stake than any of us realizes."

"Was there truth in what Mr. Harrison said to me?"

"Yes."

"I wish you could tell me more," I said.

"So do I. Because I suspect you wouldn't be daunted in the face of danger. There's something surprisingly appealing about you wanting to play spy." He took me firmly by the arms and kissed me, harder than usual. "You've always had a deleterious effect on my self-control, and I'm afraid this only makes it worse."

"I've never been particularly fond of your self-control," I said, returning his kisses and pulling him closer.

"How soon can we be married?" he asked.

"I'm free this afternoon, if you don't have other plans."

"If only," he said, kissing me deeper still. It was a very good thing we were not depending on my own self-control. At that moment, I knew I had none left.

6 December 1891
Berkeley Square, London

  Madam:
  I am forwarding via express the enclosed letter, as a missive I received from Madame du Lac's maid alerted me of her mistress's situation.

  —Davis

30 November 1891
Rue Saint Germain, Paris

Ma chère *Kallista,*

You know how much I have anticipated seeing you this Christmas. Aside from the pleasure I always take in your company, I had looked forward to at last seeing your country estate. Not, mind you, that I believe Ivy's claims that Ashton Hall could rival Versailles—size alone makes that impossible—but I think this will be your last year in possession of the house, and I would like to see it and your late husband's antiquities.

But I am afraid that I have to cancel our plans. I have received a most distressing telegram from my childhood friend, Sissi. Oui, that Sissi—Elisabeth, the empress of Austria. She is suffering from a deep depression and asks that I come visit her. She never recovered from the loss of her son to suicide—Do you know the story of the scandal at Mayerling? It happened soon after your own husband died, so you may not have heard the details.

The Crown Prince Rudolf and his mistress, a young woman named Mary Vetsera, were found dead at the prince's hunting lodge, both shot. Supposedly they had planned to die together—he killed her and then himself. I've never quite believed it. It was all hushed up at once, but of course that serves only to make rumors spread more quickly.

It seemed a straightforward case, but there are many people who believe the couple were murdered. Sissi is one of them. Unfortunately, she's no more likely to be told the truth about that night than you or I. One would think that she would be in a position of power, but some scandals are so great that they must be hidden from everyone.

I think if they weren't so very set on keeping the truth hidden, I would be more inclined to believe the official story.

I cannot ignore my friend's pleas to visit her—but still very much want to see you, too. Consider coming with me. The city is stunning at Christmas, incomparable for New Year's, and after that, the Fasching carnival will be at its peak. For a connoisseur of the waltz, there is no better place.

I realize it would be impossible for you to get away until after Christmas, but will hope to see you soon after the New Year, once your other guests have returned to their own homes.

Odette continues her unbearable moping and is cheered only momentarily when letters arrive from Davis. I had no idea your butler was such a romantic. I believe he is sending her poetry. What a pity I can't convince you to move to Paris. I fear that one of us is bound to lose a treasured servant before long.

I am your most devoted friend,
Cécile du Lac

Chapter 4

I was terribly disappointed to read Cécile's letter. I understood, of course, why she could not come to me at Christmas, but I would miss her keenly. The idea of meeting her later in Vienna was appealing and something that merited serious consideration, but it would be difficult to get away until late January—my parents planned to stay at Ashton Hall most of the month. After that, however, I would be more than ready for a flurry of waltzes.

Lord Fortescue would not have liked it in the least, but at the risk of courting more of his displeasure, I planned to spend the remainder of the day cataloging the art that filled Beaumont Towers. If I was careful to limit this activity to times when the gentlemen were out shooting, it was unlikely in the extreme that he would notice what I was doing. Unfortunately, I found very little of interest. A wooden box caught my notice—smooth mahogany inlaid with a circle of mother-of-pearl in the center—and I opened it, hoping to find treasure inside. Instead, I saw one slender dueling pistol with silver mountings that bore the symbol of the Baron of Beaumont: a griffin in profile.

The inside of the case was fitted to hold two guns, cradled in crushed velvet, but the second space held no weapon. Fabric tabs protruded from both edges of the lining, and when I pulled on them, the interior fitting lifted out of the box. Underneath, against bare wood, were the charred remains of a burnt piece of paper that crumbled when I tried to examine them. Frustrated, I closed the box and moved upstairs to unoccupied bedrooms. As I walked into a small anteroom on the second floor, I saw a woman sitting, one hand over her eyes, her shoulders shaking.

"Lady Fortescue?" I crossed to the windows and pulled open the heavy drapes to let some light into the room, which was a charming space: cozy, warm, comfortable. Quite unlike the rest of the house. "Are you all right?"

"I—I—oh, Lady Ashton, forgive me." She wiped her eyes with the back of her hand. "I'm rather overwhelmed at the thought of tonight's dinner. I prefer a quiet life to political entertaining." The prime minister as well as several cabinet ministers were due to arrive after lunch, when the day's meetings would begin.

"There's no cause for worry. Lord Salisbury is perfectly amiable. But surely you've met him before?"

"No, Lord Fortescue knows I am happier when I can stay at home and only rarely asks me to socialize with him. We've a very comfortable arrangement. But one can't very well bow out of a party one is hosting."

"You're fortunate to have such an understanding spouse," I said, resolved not to make a cynical comment about marriages and arrangements.

"I'm loath to refuse him anything. He's returned me to my family's estate after many miserable years."

"I can't imagine the difficulties you've been through," I said. She looked away, then wiped her eyes again. "Forgive me, I shouldn't bring up unpleasant subjects."

"Some things, Lady Ashton, are simply too painful to revisit, no matter how much time has passed. It is most distressing when one is forced to. Will you excuse me? I'll need to change my dress before we walk out to join the gentlemen for lunch." She gave me what might be construed as a semismile, then left the room.

When I saw her that afternoon she was perfectly composed, standing quietly by herself, hands neatly folded in front of her. She had not walked with the other ladies and was waiting near a large pavilion that would shield us from the slightest hint of inclement weather. Ivy and I arrived with the count and his wife, who somehow managed to look elegant in the ankle-length tweed skirt and sturdy shoes that were de rigueur for trekking from the house to the field. The morning's bag had been lined up for us to admire before we ate, and we all did our best to muster appropriate enthusiasm over the bounty.

"How many of them are yours?" I asked Colin.

"I didn't count," he said, giving me his arm and steering me away from the group.

"It's rather obscene, don't you think? There must be fifteen hundred birds here."

"At least. But I spent a weekend in Buckinghamshire, where we shot nearly four thousand. Even Bertie speculated that perhaps we'd overdone it."

"Obscene, particularly as the Prince of Wales is not known for his moderation. If he thought—" I stopped at the sound of raised voices coming from the edge of the field.

"That's quite enough, Brandon." Lord Fortescue's face was a brighter-than-usual shade of red as he walked towards the rest of the group.

"Sir, I'm—" Robert's reply was interrupted at once.

"What you are is not trustworthy." His voice strained as it grew louder. "You had no business speaking to Gladstone."

"I only thought—"

"I don't remember giving you permission to think. Get out of my sight." He threw down the shotgun he was holding and stalked towards the pavilion, turning back once to look at Robert. "Go!"

Robert hesitated for a moment, nodded at his wife, and set off in the direction of the house. Ivy started to follow him, but a quick shake of his head told her to stop, which she did, wavering as she stood. Colin moved to her side at once and steadied her.

"What happened?" I asked, joining them as the rest of the party looked on in shocked silence.

"They've been arguing all morning. Your husband and Lord Fortescue don't share the same views on the Irish situation. Evidently Mr. Gladstone learned that and approached Brandon looking for support for a Home Rule bill. Fortescue, as you might imagine, does not approve of his allies speaking to the opposition."

"What a dreadful scene," Ivy said, her face blanched, hands trembling. "Everyone's staring."

"Fortescue shouldn't have reprimanded him in public," Colin said.

"He shouldn't have reprimanded him at all. I don't see that Robert's done anything wrong," I said. The count approached us, smiling.

"My dear Mrs. Brandon, Lord Fortescue's temper is notorious. Think nothing of this little incident. Come, join me for lunch. This will all blow over in no time."

Ivy took his arm and gave a brave smile. "You're right, of course," she said. They walked ahead of Colin and me.

"Is he right? Will this blow over?" I asked.

"Fortescue's not the sort to forgive what he views as a lapse in loyalty. Robert's career will face a serious obstacle if he loses his mentor's support."

A luncheon following such an event could not be pleasant, despite the fact that the spread before us was lovely. The pavilion itself was rustic, formed from unhewn logs, but the tables inside were decorated with every bit of finery: bright flowers cascaded from tall silver vases, and the flatware that surrounded each set of porcelain plates was polished to a nearly blinding shine. But all the beauty in the world could not cut through the tension engulfing us. Which was fitting, considering that I planned to take the opportunity to confront Mr. Harrison.

"Why did you do it?" I asked, sitting in a chair next to his.

"Do what?" His smile took away none of the coldness from his eyes.

"I suppose you're just another of Lord Fortescue's lackeys," I said. "I should have known better than to believe that you would be here if you weren't in his good graces. You were invited to help him in his quest to destroy me."

He laughed. "Destroy you? How pre-Copernican! The universe does not, in fact, revolve around you, Lady Ashton. It revolves around the sun. You give yourself too much importance. Fortescue's merely trying to free Hargreaves for his daughter—a crime no worse than those plotted daily by mothers in drawing rooms across England."

"Why did you steal my bracelet and leave it in Lord Fortescue's room?"

"I couldn't risk letting him know that I'm the one who wanted the papers."

"But you don't have the papers. You gave them back to him."

"I copied all the essential information from them. Our plan worked flawlessly."

"For you, perhaps," I said. "I'm somewhat less pleased. Don't try to involve me in another of your schemes."

"My dear Lady Ashton, if I need your assistance, I'll have no trouble persuading you to help me."

"You could not be more wrong, Mr. Harrison."

The remainder of the luncheon break did not improve. Our host snapped at everyone, guests and servants alike, and eventually we were all left sitting in uncomfortable silence. The food itself was spectacular—no beer and sandwiches here. A man of Lord Fortescue's girth required regular and substantial meals, and we were treated to service that rivaled that inside the house. I did not, how-ever, feel entirely right eating pheasant stuffed with truffles after seeing how many of the birds' brethren had rained out of the sky that morning. And there was more shooting to come. Once we had finished eating, the ladies dutifully watched the gentlemen return to their sport, Ivy standing with me at Colin's side.

"Shall I prove my devotion to you by staying for a second drive?" I asked as he reloaded his gun.

"I'd much prefer it if you'd allow me to prove my devotion by insisting that you return to the house."

"You're very kind," Ivy said.

"Nonsense. I can see that Emily's already duly impressed with my shooting skills," he said. "So there's no point keeping the two of you here any longer. It looks like it's going to rain, and at any rate, we'll only be out for another hour or so. The prime minister will be arriving soon."

"I should have liked to see Robert shoot," Ivy said.

"Tomorrow." Colin gave her a reassuring smile. "Now get back inside before you both catch cold."

IVY EXCUSED HERSELF as soon as we entered the house and went off in search of her husband while I skulked about continuing to catalog art. Beaumont Towers was full of spectacular paintings—many from the late Renaissance, but also a handful of glorious Turners—yet almost nothing in the way of antiquities. As a result, I gasped with delight when I found a small statue, not even half a foot in height, tucked away in a cabinet in the drawing room. It was fashioned in bronze, a charming depiction of a young man reclin-ing at a banquet. The smoothness of the finish astonished me, as did the piece's elegant lines. I began to sketch it, slowing my hand, careful not to sacrifice accuracy for speed. I had nearly finished when I startled at the sound of the door opening.

"There you are." The countess glided over and stood in front of me. "I've been so looking forward to a private chat with you."

"I'm all astonishment," I said, not looking up from my paper.

"I never thought I'd see the day that Colin would be married. Of course, that day hasn't yet come, but—" She smiled, looking down at me. "I suppose we're to believe it will. You're very lucky. He is wonderful beyond measure." She spoke with too much relish, her diction exaggerated, and I gathered her meaning at once.

"I would expect nothing else," I said. "Should I offer you my pity, as the loss is entirely yours?"

"I never lose, Lady Ashton. Never. Don't presume that I am going to step aside for you."

"From what I understand, there's no need for you to do any such thing. Colin already has."

"Is that what he told you?" She laughed. I was trying to conjure up the right sort of mildly biting but not wholly inappropriate reply when the door opened again.

"Why are you ladies hiding in here?" Colin came towards us, a cautious amusement in his eyes.

"Your fiancée is all charm," the countess said, her gaze lingering on him the way mine was wont to in unguarded moments. Did he compare the way we looked at him?

"Has Lord Salisbury arrived?" I asked, searching for any distraction from my sophisticated nemesis.

"He's had to cancel his visit because of a threat of violence. A telegram arrived half an hour ago."

"You don't mean—" Kristiana stopped, then muttered something in German. She spoke too quietly for me to make out the words, but whatever she said caused Colin to look at her askance.

"Don't even think it," he said.

"It's possible," she said.

"Not here."

"Colin?" I asked. "What is it?"

He hardly looked at me. "I'm sorry, my dear. This is extremely urgent. I had no idea things could take such a rapid turn for the worse. I must speak to Fortescue at once."

I RETIRED EARLY THAT EVENING. Robert and Ivy had remained sequestered in their room, not coming down even for dinner, and I'd seen nothing of Colin since he disappeared in search of Lord Fortescue. I was reading in bed—*The Picture of Dorian Gray*—considering whether the countess might have a similar portrait hidden away in her house when I heard a knock. Colin! I leapt from the bed, not bothering to cover my filmy nightgown with a robe, and opened the door, my heart racing.

"Expecting someone else, Lady Ashton?" Lord Fortescue pushed past me into the room, closing the door behind him. "Very inappropriate. Have you no sense of decency?" He picked up the dressing gown I'd draped over a chair and threw it at me.

"I ought to pose the same question to you," I said, holding the robe, all lace and frills, to my chest as a deep blush stained my cheeks. "How dare you burst into my room like this?"

"I shouldn't bother to wait for your fiancé tonight. He won't be coming. And I wouldn't recommend going to him. He wouldn't welcome the interruption."

"What is that supposed to mean?"

"He's not alone in his room." He leered at me, made a sound that could only be described as a growl, and left, closing the door behind him.

I was trembling, angry that he would come to me like this. Colin would never betray me; to do so would go against the very grain of his character. Even if the countess came to his room, he would never have opened the door to her. And surely not even she would force her way in. Would she? If she tried, he would stop her. Yes. He would stop her. I did not doubt him even for an instant. At least not for more than an instant. Sitting on the edge of my bed, I breathed very slowly, summoning a feeling of calm. And for a moment, it seemed to work.

I was about to congratulate myself for being so mature when I realized that I was nothing of the sort. For the first time since I'd arrived at Beaumont Towers, I felt uncomfortably warm. I pulled on my dressing gown and went up the stairs to Colin's room. As I was about to knock, an unmistakable sound came from the other side of the door: the countess's laughter.

Chapter 5

M y hand froze inches from the door, and I stepped closer, straining to hear. The laughter had stopped, and Colin was talking now, his voice too low for me to distinguish the words. It was apparent, however, that whatever he was saying, it was not in a tone that suggested he was trying to forcibly remove his visitor from the room. Surely there was an innocent explanation for her coming to him so late at night. She might have been distraught, finding it difficult to accept that he had thrown her over for me. He would be loath to turn her away in such a state, and would offer what comfort he could in an entirely appropriate fashion.

Yet his voice sounded just a bit too soothing to me, and her laughter didn't suggest she was upset. I leaned against the wall across from his room and stared at the flame of the candle I was carrying, my eyes barely able to focus on the light. Then I heard another sound, this one even more unwelcome than the countess's laughter: a low, throaty chuckle. Lord Fortescue was watching me.

"Trust him, do you?" he asked.

"Yes, I do," I said, not believing the words even as I spoke them.

"I'm sorry, Lady Ashton, I couldn't hear you. Could you speak more loudly?"

"How dare you?" I asked, keeping my voice the barest whisper. He said nothing in reply; I turned on my heel and ran back to my room.

So began my second sleepless night at Beaumont Towers, this one far less pleasant than its predecessor. To lie awake for hours, consumed by the memory of a particularly satisfying kiss, can be nearly as intoxicating as the kiss itself. But to lie awake for hours wondering if the gentleman who bestowed said kiss was now giving one to someone else was a very different thing. I vacillated between lauding Colin for his steadfast fidelity and worrying that the countess was just the sort of woman who could tempt even a man of his resolve to abandon his principles.

As the light of dawn began to creep through the cracks in the curtains of my room, I finally succumbed to slumber, only to have Meg wake me a few restless hours later, telling me that our host was insisting that we all come down for breakfast. We were a bleary group at the table, but everyone save the countess appeared as requested. I could only conclude that the activity of the previous evening had been too much for her, a thought that somehow led me to realize I had no appetite. Colin, who sat across from me, applied himself to an enormous plate of food. Late nights, apparently, made him ravenous.

Robert and Ivy sat side by side, both silent. Ivy made a careful study of her food, not meeting the eyes of the other guests, none of whom bothered to speak to her beyond a rote greeting.

"The count and I are desperate for your help, Ivy," I said, sprinkling salt on eggs I had no intention of eating. The small flowers that were painted on every inch of the walls and ceiling had begun to give me a headache. "We're having a terrible time organizing our scene from Aristophanes."

"Mrs. Brandon will not be able to help you with your little

drama, Lady Ashton." Lord Fortescue's face clouded as he looked at Robert. "She and her husband are returning home this afternoon." Robert's expression did not change, but his shoulders snapped back and his fork clattered against his plate. "And as we've had to cancel our meeting with the prime minister, the rest of the gentlemen will leave to shoot in an hour." He threw his napkin on the table and stomped out of the room, pausing when he reached the door. "I want you out of my house by noon, Brandon."

None of us breathed for a full minute after he'd left. Sir Julian picked up his coffee cup, his large hand nearly crushing the thin china. "Does this have something to do with Home Rule? What say you to that, Hargreaves? Are the Irish threatening Lord Salisbury?"

"Unlikely," Colin replied.

"Is that what I should report in the paper?" Sir Julian asked, a lopsided grin splitting his face.

"I don't see that any of this merits the public's attention." Colin continued to devour his breakfast. "The less said, the better." He looked pointedly at Robert and Ivy, and Sir Julian nodded.

"No good can come of creating scandal where none exists," Lady Fortescue said, her thin voice straining to fill the room. "I don't want any of my guests to feel that their presence at this party will lead to embarrassment."

"Quite right, madam," Sir Julian said. "But as there aren't any Irishmen here—"

"We all know I'm not speaking of the Irish." No one replied, and without another word, she returned to eating her breakfast. Soon thereafter, Robert rose from his chair and excused himself, Ivy following close behind. I all but ran after them, grabbing Ivy's arm to stop her once I'd caught up to them in the main hall.

"Ivy—"

"This is so awful I hardly know what to do."

"How can I help?" I asked. "Are you going to Halton House?"

Robert's estate was in southern Yorkshire, a moderate drive from Beaumont Towers.

"No, London. Robert wants to talk to Lord Salisbury."

"I'll go with you."

"Thank you, Emily, but it's not necessary. I'm afraid your presence would make Robert feel even more awkward than he already does. He needs privacy more than anything right now."

"Then I'll leave you alone." I hugged her, and my heart broke when I felt the tension in her slim body. "Send for me if you need anything."

"I must go to him." She rushed after her husband. I leaned against the wall, looking up at stone vaulting that would have fit in perfectly at an Oxbridge college. Unsure of what to do, I was relieved when Colin came to me moments later.

"Brandon will manage," he said. "Politics is a dirty business, but he knew that going in."

"What's going to happen?" I asked.

"He'll lay low for a while and then either reinvent himself or decide he's content with the life of a gentleman."

"He didn't do anything wrong."

"He made a poor choice of mentor," Colin said. "We all know the sort of man Fortescue is. He took a risk allying himself with him."

"Did he have a choice?"

"We always have a choice, Emily. But come, let's not dwell on unpleasantries. Am I to get no kiss before I'm forced to spend another day shooting?" He caught my hand and pulled me into a small room, full of dusty furniture. "Safe to assume we won't be disturbed here, I think. I'm sorry I didn't see you last night."

"As am I." I bit my lip. "But you were working."

"Yes."

"With the countess?"

"She's one of my primary contacts in Austria."

"Are all your contacts so beautiful?"

"Unfortunately not." He held my hands. "You've no need to worry."

"I trust you," I said. "But I can't say the same for her. I'm not naïve enough to think she's content with being merely your colleague."

"For a long time she was more. I can't apologize for that, Emily. But you don't know Kristiana. She's not pining for me—she's not the sort to give her heart to anyone. She likes to flirt, likes the game of it. Everything's a waltz to her. And she knows that many men would not view marriage as an impediment to continuing a relationship with her."

I didn't believe she hadn't pined for him. But that did not bother me so much as the fact that he didn't say he had never pined for her. I stifled a sigh. "The world is so different from what young ladies are led to believe," I said.

"I'm certain the subterfuge does no good." He frowned. "People do better when they have the truth before them. I've never understood why a man would want a wife who'd been set up for nothing but disappointment."

"You're more cynical than I thought."

"No, I've just no use for hypocrisy."

"I share your opinion on the subject, but many would not. There are those who prefer a happy ignorance," I said.

"If you marry for purely practical reasons—to preserve a title, an estate, gain a fortune—there's no reason to be sentimental about the arrangement. Get an heir and a spare, your duty's done, and at last you can pursue someone who sparks a passion in you. So long as all parties are discreet and neither husband nor wife is hurt in the process, what's the harm?"

"I imagine there is none in such a case. But it seems a most unsatisfactory way to live. I'd rather be alone."

"Being alone has its drawbacks too. How did we stumble on such a morose topic?"

"Your good friend, Kristiana. And so long as we're on the subject of all things morose, I received a letter from my mother yesterday. She wrote to inform me that the queen would like us to be married at Windsor. Next summer."

"Next summer? Why would we want to wait so long?"

"I don't believe our desires factored into the equation. My mother and Her Majesty are rather taken with the month of June. It's to be quite an event."

"An event?"

"Yes. Fireworks were mentioned."

"I see." There was laughter behind his eyes.

"After our aborted attempt at an English wedding, I was rather hoping we could be married in Greece," I said.

"Just the two of us, the necessary witnesses, and one of Mrs. Katevatis's feasts afterwards?" The cook at my villa had unparalleled culinary talents, and the thought of the sun on Santorini and a platter of spanakopita was more than a little tempting, particularly when I was trapped on a dank English estate.

"Precisely," I said.

"Lots of ouzo toasts and a rather late night."

"One that extends all the way to morning." Our eyes met.

"I don't see how we can go against the queen's wishes," he said.

"I was afraid you'd say that. I admire your loyalty and sense of duty to your country, Colin, but you go too far. I can't bear the thought of waiting so long."

"You were perfectly willing to put me off yourself for more months than I care to count." His smile warmed every inch of me.

"I was dreadful."

"You weren't. I understand perfectly why you waited to accept me. If you did not value your independence so well, I wouldn't have wanted to marry you in the first place."

"We're disgustingly well suited to each other." I raised my lips to his, but he did not kiss me.

"Regardless, we shall have to wait. It wouldn't do to displease Her Majesty."

"I don't suppose there's even a hint of sarcasm in that statement?"

"Perhaps just a touch."

"I do adore you," I said. He pressed my hand to his lips. "But there will be no changing her mind. She's offering Windsor to thank my mother for her assistance in machinating the engagement between Prince Eddy and May of Teck. Everyone's convinced the girl will make an excellent queen."

"If only Eddy would make an excellent king," Colin said. The Prince of Wales's eldest son had a reputation for being rather slow-witted and had been embroiled in any number of scandals, each worse than the last.

"Speaking against the royal family, Colin? If you're already this disaffected, there's hope that I may be able to persuade you to go against the queen's wishes. I shall do all in my power to tempt you."

He put his hand on my cheek. "My dear girl, resisting you will take all of my will."

"I wonder if you have quite so much will as you think?" I stood on my toes and kissed him, slowly, once on each cheek. "What a pity you have to go shoot today. I can think of much more pleasant ways to pass a morning."

As it was, there was very little about the morning that could be called pleasant. We had all expected an influx of guests the previous day—the prime minister and others would have brought their wives—giving us ladies someone new with whom to converse. Ivy was still upstairs overseeing her packing, the countess and Lady Fortescue were nowhere to be found, so Flora and I were left with the count, finding almost nothing in the way of amusement.

"I don't understand why we can't shoot," Flora said.

"It's never made sense to me," I said, looking up from the letter—already six pages long—that I was writing to Margaret. "We're allowed to foxhunt. I suppose directly killing a bird is unladylike, but pursuing a fox and leaving him to be torn to bits by dogs is not."

"Have you abandoned Aristophanes?" the count asked.

"So far as performance goes, yes," I replied. "I don't think any of us is in the mood for theatrical entertainment."

"I am!" Jeremy Sheffield, Duke of Bainbridge, who'd been a dear friend since we were children and now as resplendent as a man could be in tweeds, strolled into the drawing room.

"Jeremy!" I leapt up to greet him. "What a surprise! Where have you come from?"

"Highwater, not five miles from here. I headed for Beaumont Towers the moment I heard you were here."

"Yes, Margaret warned me to look out for you."

"She's a terrible girl. Tell me this party's not as tedious as the one I've escaped."

"Tedious is perhaps not the right word," I said.

"Pleasantly soporific?" he suggested.

I smiled. "Mildly diverting."

"We didn't have it even that good. Langston, our host, wouldn't let all of us shoot at once—insisted that we go out in small groups, which meant hours of sitting around doing nothing. But I suppose you ladies are used to that, and I now feel your pain keenly. Mrs. Reynold-Plympton was the most amusing person at Highwater, and she was in such a dreadful mood I was afraid to speak to her."

"Really?" I asked. "I'm surprised she's not here."

"As am I," he said, lowering his voice. "What a relief to be able to gossip with you."

"I'm equally delighted to see you," I said.

His voice returned to normal. "I've come to ask you to walk with me," he said. "If your friends can do without your company?"

"Lady Ashton will be missed, but we shall bear it as best we can." The count's smile was rather more familiar than I would have liked. I took Jeremy's arm and escaped with him as soon as I'd put on a coat and hat.

"I'm more pleased to see you than you can imagine," I said as we walked, glad to turn my back on Beaumont Towers' multitudinous turrets and chimneys. The weather was far from fine; the air was chill, and the wind bit through my coat, but it was a relief to be cold outside, where one expected it, rather than in the house.

"You've no idea how it affects me to hear you say that." His smile was as winning as it had been when, as a little boy, he'd begged my forgiveness for any number of juvenile offenses, most of which involved frogs or snakes. "I don't suppose you've decided to throw over Hargreaves."

"Really, Jeremy. You're awful."

"Always. But a chap can hope, right?"

"Who am I to deny you amusement? Particularly as we've no unattached ladies at this party with whom you can flirt."

"I've always preferred attached ones. They're much less demanding."

"Oh, Jeremy, it is good to see you. I can always count on you to make me laugh."

"If only you knew how serious I am. I've every intention of making a bid for your affections the moment you're married."

"And I look forward to spurning your every advance."

"Where's Ivy? I thought she's the one who dragged you here for this miserable gathering."

"She's preparing to go home."

I had just started to explain to him what had transpired between Robert and Lord Fortescue when Flora, no coat covering her dress, tears staining her face, came running out of the house.

"Emily, I must speak to you at once!" Her voice sounded torn as she screamed. "Something dreadful has happened!"

Chapter 6

W hat is it?" I asked, running towards her.

"Perhaps we should go inside," Jeremy said, shrugging off his topcoat and putting it around Flora's shaking shoulders.

"Thank you, Your Grace. I'm most obliged, but I think it's best that we speak out here." The contrast between her formal mode of speech and her ragged voice was frightening. She clung to my arm, and I wondered if the gesture was meant to steel her or me. "There's been a terrible accident."

"Tell us!" I said. "Is someone hurt?"

She took three deep breaths. "Lord Fortescue is dead."

I was stunned. "Dead?" As I watched Flora's shoulders tremble, I remembered it was probable that she was one of the dead man's mistresses. If she cared for him, she must be crushed, but would not be able to grieve openly, and for this, I felt sorry for her. "How?"

"I don't know." Her tears would not stop. "He must have been shot."

"Bird shot isn't going to kill a man," Jeremy said, handing her a handkerchief and placing a strong arm around her.

"I don't know what else it could have been."

"Did he fall ill?" I asked. "Collapse?"

"No. The police are coming," she said.

"Was anyone else hurt?" I asked.

"No." The handkerchief was already soaked. "I don't think so."

"Does Lady Fortescue know?" Jeremy asked.

"No. That's why I came to find you. The Groom of the Chambers told me the news and asked me to inform her, but I don't think I can bear to tell her. Will you, Lady Ashton?"

"I'm happy to assist in any way possible," Jeremy said, "but I imagine it would be best for her to hear such grim news from another lady."

"Of course I'll tell her." The words flew from my mouth. I couldn't imagine a more dreadful situation than having to tell your lover's wife that her husband was dead. "Don't worry. Do you know where can I find her?"

"She was in the drawing room with us," Flora said. "Embroidering a cushion."

"I hadn't noticed her. She has a remarkable ability to fade away."

"I'll go to her at once," I said. "And while I do, you let Jeremy take care of you." Her tears had slowed somewhat, and she'd rested her head on his shoulder. She was in control enough to return to the house. As for me, I felt shocked, confused, and surprisingly sad.

Back inside, Flora and Jeremy discreetly gathered up the count and countess while I searched out Lady Fortescue, who had abandoned her embroidery for a stroll in the conservatory. I looked at her for a moment before I started to speak, knowing that her life would forever be divided between the time before and after the conversation that was to come. I can't recall what I said, but in situations where irrevocable news changes everything in an instant, the words used to deliver it are irrelevant. She stared straight ahead, her body absolutely still. I reached for her hand, but she pulled it away, blinked, and then all at once her eyes filled with tears, and she began to sob. I stayed next to her, considering the possibility that a man, no matter how dreadful he seems to others, may be something quite different to those close to him.

An artificial silence enshrouded us as the news spread through the house. Both Lady Fortescue and Flora had taken to their rooms, and the rest of us were speaking in whispers, as if our words could be carried along lengthy hallways and disturb the mourners' grief. Jeremy had sent a servant to collect his things from Highwater, not wanting to leave in the midst of the confusion. Not that leaving would have been allowed.

Lord Fortescue's death had been no accident; he had been shot, a single bullet through the head. No bird shot and hunting rifles; the weapon in question was a dueling pistol, and had been found beneath a tree some yards from where the guns had stood, shooting for sport. The police had arrived shortly thereafter, and questioned each of us, including Robert and Ivy, whose departure had been postponed.

"Have you noticed anything suspicious since your arrival at Beaumont Towers?" a very young and very eager inspector asked me when it was my turn to face the inquisition.

"I was surprised to see that Mr. Harrison carries a pistol under his jacket. Lord Fortescue is—was—an enemy of his. It's possible—"

"Mr. Harrison's gun was not used in the murder. Have you seen this weapon before, Lady Ashton?" He held it out for me to see.

"Yes, yes, I have." Without thinking, I reached out for it.

He colored slightly and shifted his weight from foot to foot as he pulled it away from me. "When was that, ma'am?"

"Oh, heavens, I didn't kill Lord Fortescue. I saw the gun in its case in the library when I was . . ." I paused, unsure if I ought to admit that I'd been rifling through the dead man's possessions. "I was cataloging the art in the house."

"Yes, well, I'm not quite certain how that would lead you to opening a pistol case."

"I didn't know what it was. I thought it might hold an artifact of some sort."

"Is that right?"

"Yes." I looked at him, holding my gaze steady. "But there was only one gun in the case. Its mate was missing. I can only assume this is it."

"The case is empty now," he said.

"Do you think that—"

He cut me off at once. "I won't need anything further from you at the moment, Lady Ashton. Thank you for being so candid in answering my questions."

Some hours later, three gentlemen from the Foreign Affairs Office and two of Lord Salisbury's aides descended upon the house, having traveled by special train from London. They, along with Colin, Mr. Harrison, and Sir Thomas, sequestered themselves in the room that was to have been used for their political meeting. None of them had emerged since.

"I hate feeling so useless," Mr. Clavell said, pacing the room in an agitated manner. I wondered if this was because his wife's grief was making him face head-on her relationship with Lord Fortescue, or if it was because he worried that the affair might make him a suspect in the murder.

"Between the police and all the interested members of the government, the matter is well in hand," I said. "You needn't worry."

"One of us must have seen something," he said.

"The inspector is a competent bloke. He'll sort it out," Jeremy said.

"Ah, I see the countess is back. Excuse me—she may have noticed something out of the ordinary."

Jeremy laughed softly while we watched Mr. Clavell approach the countess. "He is determined to keep busy, isn't he?"

Robert had not appeared downstairs since the police had finished with him, but Ivy was with us, twisting her handkerchief, looking out the window. "This is too dreadful," she said. I hesitated to reply, assuming that she was expressing concern for her husband. We had all witnessed the strife between him and Lord Fortescue. His position could not be a good one. "None of us liked him, but now we all feel terrible that he's dead."

"I don't think anyone in this room feels the slightest regret at his death, and it's the resulting guilt that's filled us with gloom," I said.

"Don't speak ill of the dead, Emily," she said.

"I didn't. But you can't tell me that you were fond of him."

Jeremy took Ivy's hand as he sat next to her. "He was awful, now he's dead, and for once I have the opportunity to impress your dear friend with my knowledge of Homer. 'It is not right to glory in the slain.'"

"The *Odyssey*. I'm impressed, Jeremy." Our eyes met, and I felt a surprisingly strong connection with him. "When did you start reading?"

"Oh, I don't read. I skulk about in search of quotations that might make me appear educated." This succeeded in making Ivy laugh. "Excellent. You're lovely when you smile, Ivy. Don't stop." The concern in his eyes as he flashed me a glance told me that he was at least as worried as I about Robert.

I didn't notice that Colin had entered the room until he touched my arm. "I need to speak with you. Will you come with me?" He kept his voice low.

"Of course."

We excused ourselves and walked to the library, no words passing between us on the way. Only when he had closed the door and looked about the room, as if to ensure that no one else was with us, did he speak. "I'm afraid things have taken a rather serious turn. It's obvious that Fortescue was murdered by someone at this party, and Ivy's husband is the chief suspect."

"He would never kill anyone!"

"I'm inclined to agree with you, but we all saw Fortescue verbally assault him and threaten to destroy his career."

"But what about Gerald Clavell? If he knew his wife was having an affair with Lord Fortescue, he certainly has a motive for wanting him dead."

"You're certain they were having an affair?"

"Well, I can't prove it, if that's what you mean, but—"

"You'd have to be able to prove it. Yes, it might give him motive, but he did not have opportunity. He was shooting with us at the time of the murder. Robert is the only member of our party whose whereabouts cannot be confirmed at the time of Fortescue's death."

"He was with Ivy."

"She was in their bedroom with her maid. He says he'd gone to collect some papers from the billiard room. No one saw him there."

"Could he offer no further explanation?"

"He insists that Fortescue had received a warning in the past few days, threatening violence. Brandon's convinced he was assassinated. But we've found no copy of any such letter, and no one else can corroborate the story."

"Who sent it?"

"He doesn't know."

"What about Mr. Harrison?" I asked. "We've already established that he can't be trusted."

"He was standing next to me at the time of the murder."

"Is there nothing you can do for Robert?"

"I wish there were, but I'm being sent to Berlin at once."

"Because of this?"

"Yes. Fortescue's death will have political implications, particularly as it relates to some trouble that's been festering on the Continent. I can't say more than that, except that I will miss you, so very much."

"How long do you expect to be gone?"

"Indefinitely."

"Doesn't bode well for my plan to tempt you into marrying me before the summer," I said.

"Then I won't have to worry about falling from the queen's good graces."

"Unless you've time before you go. I'm free this afternoon."

"If only," he said, smiling.

I saw in his eyes all my own longing reflected, but instead of stepping towards him, I pulled away. "How is it that despite what you've just told me, despite the fact that a murder occurred here today, I'm overwhelmed at finding myself alone with you? I shouldn't be capable of having these feelings at such a moment."

"We don't always have control over our desires," he said.

"Hardly an encouraging thing to hear on the eve of your leaving me." I tugged at his lapels. "What can I do to help Robert?"

"I don't know, Emily. The situation's grave. But if anyone's capable of ferreting out what actually happened, it would be you." It had been only a few months since I'd solved the murder of David Francis, and nearly a year since I'd discovered the truth about my husband's death.

"The police would tell me nothing when they were questioning me," I said.

"When has that ever stopped you? I'll tell them to speak freely to you if you'd like, but honestly, Emily, I don't think they've much to say. The case is purely circumstantial."

"They've obviously overlooked something."

"Yes, but at the moment, I think that you should perhaps focus on Ivy. Her world is about to come crashing down. Take care of her. Then you'll be able to focus on the rest. I hate that I must leave you now."

The kiss he gave me was hurried, rough, and left my lips feeling bruised. Catching my breath was difficult.

"I shall write to you as soon as I can," he said.

I DID NOT MAKE IT back to the drawing room. Ivy was in the main hall, sitting on the bottom step, her small hands clenched in tight fists, her eyes unblinking. I knelt in front of her.

"They took Robert," she said. "They're going through our luggage now. They think—"

The rustle of silk and a glimpse of red skirt caught my attention; the countess was standing in a doorway, close enough that she could hear every word. "Don't say any more here. Come upstairs." We went to my room, where she collapsed, tears soaking her face. I held her until she succumbed to an uneasy sleep, tossing restlessly, small sobs escaping as she dreamed. Careful not to wake her, I rang for Meg and waited for her outside the bedroom door, directing her to prepare to return home and to fetch Jeremy for me.

"They're hauling Brandon to London. Apparently Scotland Yard are taking an interest in the case because there are whispers of treason," he said when he came to me in the hallway. "Are you going to take Ivy to London?"

"Yes. She can't stay here."

"Of course not. I'll arrange everything and accompany you. I'm sorry about all this, Em." There was a kindness in his eyes I'd not often seen. "I can't imagine how difficult this is for you."

"Reserve your sympathy for Ivy."

"I've plenty for her as well. But I don't envy you the position of trying to help a friend who's in such dire straits."

"Robert is innocent."

"I believe you, darling, but Scotland Yard may be more difficult to convince." He touched my shoulder, then dropped his hand. "I'll let you know as soon as we're ready to leave."

Jeremy was never the sort of man from whom one would expect much efficiency, but in this case he outdid himself, and within the span of a few hours we were speeding away from Yorkshire. I hoped I would never see Beaumont Towers again.

Parliament was not yet in session, so London was a shadow of its usual self. My house in Berkeley Square had been closed since the Season ended, all the furniture covered with cloths to keep the dust from it, most of the staff sent to my late husband's estate in Derbyshire, where I had planned to spend Christmas. My butler, Davis, had left Ashton Hall as soon as he received a telegram from Jeremy, and arrived early enough to organize the few servants who remained at the house when I wasn't in residence.

It was after midnight when we reached home. Davis greeted us at the door. "I wired Halton House as soon as I learned Mrs. Brandon would be joining us, and they'll be sending several trunks for her on the first train tomorrow morning." He turned to Ivy. "In the meantime, we've laid out some things for you in the yellow bedroom. Mrs. Ockley will show you the way and bring you something to help you sleep."

"Thank you, Davis," Ivy said, following my housekeeper up the baroque staircase without a glance back in my direction.

"We've prepared the library for you, madam," Davis said. "I decanted a '47 Warre and had a cold supper sent over from the Savoy in case you're hungry. Cook will be here in the morning."

I had nearly forgotten that Jeremy was standing next to me until he took my arm and leaned close to me as we started for the library. "Your butler knows you too well. He didn't bother to try to pack you off to bed. I'll come with you to discuss the murder, but if you pull out any Greek, I shall leave at once."

"I save my Greek for Colin," I murmured back to him, not wanting Davis to hear.

"You nearly make me regret not paying better attention at university. Nearly."

The warmth of the library enveloped me the moment I entered the room, soft light bouncing off the high, curved ceiling, the rows of books seeming to greet me like old friends. I slumped into a favorite chair and rubbed my temples.

"What's to be done, Jeremy?" I asked when Davis had left us.

"You're the one with a history of solving crimes. I'm of no use."

"You're not quite so useless as you'd like the general public to believe, my friend. You've done marvelous things today."

"Well, don't go telling people. You'll ruin my reputation. I work hard to appear the idlest man in England. It's more exhausting than it looks."

5 December 1891
Somerville Hall, Oxford

Dear Emily,

The most extraordinary thing has happened. I'm to dine with
Mr. Michaels tomorrow—can you imagine? I'd shown him some
translations of rather obscure bits of Latin poetry, and he was so
taken with what he called "my delicate hand" that he invited me to
join three of his colleagues at dinner.

The amusing part, my dear, is that the poetry was rather
risqué—Sappho has nothing on this—and if anything, my hand was
precisely the opposite of delicate. I plunged in with nothing short of
wild abandon. I'd rather expected him to be shocked and scold me.

But apparently, my efforts had quite the opposite effect, and I'm
not sure what to make of it. I shall have to try harder to outrage
him next time.

I think that I will insist on smoking after dinner.

In the meantime, I'm sending all wishes that you're not terribly
bored in Yorkshire.

I am yrs., etc.,
Margaret

Chapter 7

Margaret's letter had arrived only a few hours before I'd left Beaumont Towers, but I didn't read it until the following morning. The weather in London was atrocious, a dense yellow fog settling on the town and paralyzing its inhabitants as it crept into every corner of the city. This was not the transparent, floating sort of fog that artists adored. It was a killing fog, one that would lead to an increase in deaths in the poorer parts of the capital, where people were already suffering respiratory ailments. When I was a girl, one such incident had killed hundreds, if not thousands, in a handful of days—the story was on the front page the first time I read a newspaper. My horrified mother had ripped it from my hands and flung it into the fireplace the moment she'd seen I was looking at it.

"May I speak freely, madam?" Davis asked, filling my cup with steaming tea. It was not customary for one's butler to assist in the serving of breakfast, but Davis had fallen into the habit of doing just that. He would read the paper as he ironed it before giving it to me, and liked to make pithy comments about the day's news while I ate. I smiled at the thought of what my mother's response would be should she ever discover how my relationship with this man had evolved. He had become much more than a servant to me; he was an indispensable friend.

"Of course." I poured milk in my tea.

"You may want to finish with the paper quickly this morning. Mrs. Brandon is already awake and should be down shortly. There's a scathing story about Mr. Brandon on the front page."

I had not yet turned my attention to the news, but grabbed the paper and read the offending article at once. It contained the expected sensational account of Lord Fortescue's murder and barely stopped short of lamenting that there were no more public executions in Britain. The only useful bit of information I read was an explanation of why Robert had been brought to London—information that caused me to worry more than ever. According to the paper's unnamed source, Robert was suspected of not only murder but treason, as sensitive political documents had disappeared from Beaumont Towers.

"This borders on libel," I said, folding the paper and tossing it to Davis. "You may as well burn it. And don't bring me tomorrow's edition." I paused and rubbed my hand across my forehead. "No. Ignoring it won't help. It's better that I know what's being said."

The door opened, and one of the parlor maids stepped into the room, curtsying neatly in front of me. "The Duke of Bainbridge is here, madam. Would you like me to bring him to the drawing room?"

"Please do." Knowing it was unlikely he bore any glad tidings, I wanted to speak with him without Ivy. "Davis, ask Mrs. Brandon to wait for me in the library when she's finished her breakfast. The duke and I will come to her as soon as we can."

I had never before given much thought to the drawing room at Berkeley Square, but as I walked into it today, its warmth struck me. Walls draped in red silk, Venetian marble mantel framing a blazing fire, chairs meant to be comfortable, their curved backs and soft leather like a gentle embrace. Despite its palatial proportions, it felt like a snug, welcoming home. The precise opposite of Beaumont Towers. Jeremy was idly slouching in a seat near the fireplace, but leapt to his feet when he saw me.

"I can't remember the last time you received me in a drawing room. You treat me more like a favored suitor with every passing day."

"You're a dreadful flirt and know perfectly well that the way to my heart is through my library. The drawing room is a vapid and soulless place." I smiled as he kissed my hand.

"Soulless. Perfect for me." He sat down. "I've just come from Newgate."

"Newgate?" There was not a person in England unaware of the horrors associated with London's most notorious prison. "Of course. That's where they would have taken Robert."

"I've just visited him. He asked if you would come to him."

"Of course. I'll get Ivy at once."

"No. He doesn't want her to see him in his present circumstances. He was very clear on this point."

JEREMY INSISTED ON accompanying me to the prison, and I was grateful for this. The drive, filled with nervous discomfort, seemed to stretch to eternity. My stomach was uneasy, and I couldn't keep my hands still. When at last we arrived, I was horrified to find Newgate more appalling than I could have imagined. Whitewashed walls did nothing to hide the filth and stench that filled the place. Jeremy spoke to the warden near the entrance and in short order convinced him to have Robert brought to me.

"I don't like giving prisoners special privileges, Your Grace."

"It's not for him, sir, it's for her. Do you really expect her to go all the way inside?"

The warden looked at me through narrowed eyes and grunted. "Very well. Wait here." This was one moment where I did not object to being treated like a lady; I had little desire to see firsthand just how awful the depths of the prison would be. He returned ten minutes later and led us up a maze of stairs to a small office. "You may speak to Mr. Brandon for ten minutes, but I will have to remain in the room with you." He unlocked the door and swung it open.

Robert was standing with his back to us, facing windows that looked out on the Old Bailey, where his trial would take place. The buildings of the prison and London's Central Criminal Court were joined by a series of dismal passages; I wondered if Robert was considering what it would be like when he was led through them to face his prosecutors. The warden locked the door after he'd closed it behind us and returned the key to his pocket. It was an odd feeling to know that I could not leave the room without his assistance.

I crossed the room to Robert, who was still staring out the window, despite the fact that he must have heard us enter, and spoke to him in a low voice. "It would be ridiculous to ask if you're all right, but I don't know where else to begin."

He turned to me, his face drawn and pale, dark smudges beneath vacant, frightened eyes. "I'm relieved that you're not fluent in the language of conversing with prisoners. If you were, I'd have to forbid Ivy from speaking to you." He nodded at Jeremy, who was hanging back near the warden.

"I'm a bad enough influence as it is," I said.

"I know that you and I have not always agreed when it comes to subjects on which you hold firm opinions. I'm a traditional man, Emily. I believe there is a natural order to things, and that, as a gentleman, one of my primary responsibilities is to shield ladies from the uglier sides of life."

"It is sometimes better to see the truth."

"Not necessarily." He glanced towards the warden, who had sat on a chair and was pretending to be engrossed in a newspaper as Jeremy looked over his shoulder. "But at present, I find myself in the unhappy position of having no one to whom I can turn other than you."

"How can they believe you killed Lord Fortescue?" I whispered.

"They've no other reasonable suspect."

"At least half the population of England is rejoicing to see him dead," I said, careful to keep my voice low. "And you don't stand to benefit from the death of your mentor. Why would you have killed him?"

"He publicly insulted me in a manner certain to destroy any hopes I'd have of a political life. It's well known that I'm an excellent shot and would have had no difficulty in carrying out the murder."

"Perhaps not the technical aspects of it, but I know you're not capable of killing a man."

"But I am, Emily. I have," he whispered.

I was stunned. "But . . . surely not . . ."

"No, not Fortescue. It was ages ago. A duel."

"A duel?" I could not image mild-mannered Robert agreeing to duel.

"Ivy does not know this, of course, and you are not to tell her. It would only cause her further anxiety."

"I don't see that it matters regardless. You didn't kill Fortescue."

"No. But the gun used to kill him was a dueling pistol."

"I don't understand why this matters," I said, frowning.

"Fortescue knew about the duel and has a file that proves my involvement."

"Why would he want such a thing?"

"To hold over me, Emily."

"Hardly seems like grounds for blackmail," I said. "Repugnant though it is, dueling is still considered by some gentlemen an honorable activity."

"Not for cabinet ministers." He stared out the window. "But that's out of the realm of possibility for me now."

"Why did you ask to see me, Robert?"

"I don't know who killed Fortescue, but I'm convinced that he was assassinated. He told me that he'd received a warning while we were at Beaumont Towers."

"From whom?"

"I'm not sure. All I know is that it came from Vienna, that he was personally threatened in it, and that it contained information about a planned attack against a high-ranking political figure."

"Who?"

"I don't know."

"Did you tell the police this?"

"Yes. But they found nothing to corroborate my story at Fortescue's house."

"I read that there were papers missing. Surely this could be among those stolen."

"That's exactly what I think," he said. "But I can't convince anyone else."

"We have to find out who sent the message," I said.

"That's why I asked to see you." He took a deep breath before continuing. "My father was just here with his solicitor and has vowed to spare no expense in mounting my defense, but all his pretty words couldn't hide the fear in his eyes. It was perfectly clear that neither of them holds out much hope that I will be acquitted."

"But surely your solicitor—your barrister—someone will be able to discover who sent the message to Fortescue."

"The only way to do that would be to send someone to Vienna, and no one aside from myself seems to think that's a worthwhile endeavor. I realize that it is wrong of me to impose upon your friendship with my wife. With Hargreaves out of the country and my colleagues turning against me with dizzying speed, I've no one left with proven abilities to handle any sort of investigation but you. I asked Bainbridge, but . . ."

"He didn't know what to do."

"Precisely. But he did suggest that I speak with you. It is unconscionable to ask a lady to embroil herself in such a thing, but I can't deny the fact that you've succeeded"—he sighed—"rather spectacularly when you've taken up cases in the past."

"What would you have me do?"

"As little as possible. I don't want to place you in any danger. If you could go to Austria and find out who sent the warning and get that person to talk—perhaps to Sir Augustus Paget at the embassy in Vienna—then the authorities here might be persuaded to believe me."

"Do you know anything else that might be of use?"

"Only that Fortescue was concerned about a group of anarchists there, headed by a man called Schröder. But I don't know if they are connected to any of this."

"I will do everything I can," I said.

"I am indebted to you beyond measure."

"No, you're not. I haven't succeeded in helping you yet. But I hope, soon, to be able to say that you owe me your life."

"I look forward to the day." He managed a slight smile.

"I've something for you," I said, and pulled out from behind my back a book. "It wasn't easy to convince your jailer to let me bring it, but Jeremy's wallet is very persuasive. I know your views on popular fiction, and can't resist taking the opportunity to persuade you that sensational novels do, in fact, have some merits."

He looked at the cover. "*Lady Audley's Secret?* I've heard more than enough about this atrocious story."

"Even my late husband enjoyed it, and you know how seriously he took his academic pursuits." Philip's reputation as a gentleman scholar was unparalleled.

"I will read it, but only because there's nothing else here for me to do."

"Precisely why I thought now the perfect time to corrupt you."

"First ladies drinking port, now this. Is there no end to your debauchery?" He was trying too hard to take a light tone.

"I will do everything in my power to secure your release." Our eyes met only briefly, both of us all too aware that any power I might have was negligible at best. I squeezed his hand.

The warden coughed. "No touching the prisoner, madam."

"I WANT TO GO TO VIENNA." Ivy's delicate complexion had lost all its glow. She'd hardly flinched when I told her she couldn't come to Newgate, but her eyes were swollen and red when we returned.

"You must stay here. What if Robert asks to see you?" I was more concerned with what I could not say to her: If I failed to uncover anything in Vienna he might be executed before I returned to England. "And if he does, you can update him on anything I've discovered. It's a pity they won't let you touch him. Much can be said during a prolonged embrace."

"Emily!" She looked at Jeremy.

"Let me assure you that I've heard far worse, Ivy," he said. "I've been in the middle of far worse."

"You're very kind," Ivy said, blushing.

"Good. I've made you smile again. There's no use giving into melancholy, no matter how desperate the situation. It will all turn out in the end."

"Thank you, Jeremy."

"I wired Margaret. She sent a reply back express and is coming in from Oxford as soon as she can, so you won't be alone. I want you both to stay at Berkeley Square while I'm gone." After I'd sent a wire to Cécile informing her that I hoped to travel with her to Vienna at once, I'd dashed off quick letters to Colin's brother and sister-in-law as well as my parents, all of whom were expecting to spend Christmas with me at Ashton Hall. Although William and Sophie would accept the change of plans with grace—they were accustomed to Colin's work causing similar disruptions—my mother would not react well.

"Robert's parents are already in town. I'm afraid they'll want me to stay with them."

"If you don't want to, you don't have to. Margaret will take care of everything," I said.

"And what about me? You can't cut me out of the excitement now," Jeremy said.

"Are you planning to stay in London or return to the country?" I asked.

"Neither," he said, eyes full of mischief. "I'm coming to Vienna. You, darling, need someone to keep you out of trouble, and I am just the man for the job."

"I don't imagine Cécile will object to traveling with you, though she's sure to remind you at regular intervals that you're not as handsome as Colin," I said.

"Looks aren't everything, my dear girl."

8 December 1891
Somerville Hall, Oxford

My dear Emily,
    I received your wire and am sending my reply express, as what I
want to tell you is too long for a wire. First, inform Ivy to expect me
in London at once.
    Second, you'll find it impossible to believe, but Mr. Michaels offers
whatever assistance he can give. I informed him in no uncertain
terms that he would be completely out of his element in this
situation.
    But I will confess to being pleasantly surprised that he offered.
And though now is perhaps not the most appropriate time to
mention it, he accepted my smoking at his dinner party with nothing
more than a single raised eyebrow.

    I am yrs., etc.,
    Margaret

Chapter 8

Traveling with Jeremy was like nothing I'd ever experienced. Our mission was a grim one, difficult and daunting. But my friend patently refused to be morose, insisting that I would be in a better position to pursue my work in Vienna if I arrived relaxed. He goaded me, flirted with me, and if I so much as sighed, he read aloud to me from the script of Oscar Wilde's new play, *Lady Windermere's Fan*, which was set to open in the West End in February. Try though I might, I could not convince him to tell me how he managed to persuade the author to give him a copy.

Cécile met us at the Gare de l'Est when we arrived in Paris, and together we boarded the Orient Express. Along with an inordinate number of trunks and her minuscule dogs, Brutus and Caesar, Cécile had brought a picnic for us to share, preferring to dine in the privacy of our compartment so that we could speak freely about the plight of the Brandons. Although the food in the dining car would no doubt have been spectacular—we were on board the most luxurious train in Europe—we did not much suffer. Cécile's basket was filled with magnificent treats, all of which were served on china and silver by an attentive member of the wagons-lits staff. Jeremy retired soon after we'd finished eating, though I suspect he did not stay alone long. The lure of the smoking car and the company he'd find there would have been too much for him to resist.

The stress of the previous days left me exhausted. The valet had made up the bed in my compartment, which was snug and cozy and reminiscent of the most comfortable rooms in a country estate. Very small rooms, of course, but the effect—achieved with a combination of wood paneling and dark paint with gilt trim—was lovely. When I crawled into my surprisingly soft bed, the lull of the car's movement on the track sent me to sleep almost at once. Jeremy's theory proved sound: By the time we reached the Westbanhof station in Vienna the next evening, my mind was clear and focused.

I'd never been to Vienna before, but had always imagined it to be an ornately beautiful place. The reality of it did not disappoint. The Ringstrasse, which Emperor Franz Joseph had ordered built over the remains of the city's ancient walls, was a series of wide, circular boulevards lined with grand buildings: the Kunsthistorisches Museum, which housed the imperial art collection, the Naturhistorisches Museum, one of the world's finest natural history museums, and the opera, among others. Now, in winter, with snow covering them, they all looked like prettily decorated cakes set among parks on a tree-lined cobbled street.

We'd reserved suites at the exquisite Hotel Imperial, which had been constructed some years earlier by the Prince of Württemberg as his palace. He sold it when he decided to leave Vienna, and the buyers converted it into a hotel. The prince's private apartments on the *belle étage* had been turned into an enormous suite, and it was here that Cécile and I ensconced ourselves, surrounded by every luxurious thing. We had two bathrooms, beds dressed in the finest linens, and multiple sitting rooms, walls covered in pale blue silk that highlighted elaborately carved moldings. Electric chandeliers lit the room, but candles had been placed strategically throughout, in magnificent silver holders, in case the suite's occupants desired softer light.

Even the route to our rooms was spectacular, up the grand staircase, fashioned from gleaming, pale marble. The high ceiling, smooth columns, and classically styled statues on the landing were worthy of Versailles, although Cécile was quick to point out that the scale was far too small to be part of the Sun King's palace. Still, it was difficult not to feel royal in such impressive surroundings.

It was too late in the evening to make an unannounced visit, so I instead sent a note to the countess telling her to expect me in the morning. I hoped her contacts with the British intelligence community might prove useful to me. After Meg helped me into a favorite gown—crimson silk covered with intricate beadwork—I joined my friends for dinner in the hotel's dining room, where the food, all of it delicious, was more French than I would have expected. The next morning, the concierge gave me directions to the von Langes' house, and I left the Imperial by eight o'clock, feeling not the slightest concern that I might be calling too early. Though I should be loath to admit it, I rather liked the idea of disturbing Kristiana. Regardless, I'd given her fair warning.

I'd expected that Cécile would not be able to come with me. She was here, after all, to see her friend, the empress. But although she left the hotel at the same time I did, her destination was not the imperial palace. Instead, she headed for the studio of an artist whose work I greatly admired: Gustav Klimt. He was to paint her portrait. When I asked her if the empress would mind that she did not come to her first, Cécile smiled, and there was a wicked gleam in her eye.

"No one would understand better than Sissi," she said, stepping into a carriage and leaving me at the curb.

The Viennese were early risers. Already, people bundled in furs were streaming in and out of shops, bakeries, and coffee-houses, rushing across the narrow snow-covered streets that cut through the city like a spider's web. My feet were wet, my unlined leather boots no match for the snow, and by the time I reached the countess's imposing residence, it felt as if the very fabric of my coat was frozen. The von Langes' house was palatial, its baroque grandeur dwarfing the very street on which it stood. The interior, full of stuccowork—cherubs and scenes from mythology everywhere I turned—overwhelmed me with its intricate beauty. As a servant in formal livery led me to an impossibly warm drawing room, my opinion of Kristiana thawed along with my toes.

For a moment, that is.

She kept me waiting nearly half an hour before she glided into the room and sat directly across from me. "You poor child. You look positively frigid," she said. "Something warm to drink?"

"No, thank you. I'm perfectly comfortable."

"I didn't expect Colin to bring you to Vienna so soon."

"He's in Berlin. I came on my own, and am hoping that you can assist me."

"Berlin?" She smiled, laughter in her bright eyes. "Is that what he told you?"

"I'm here because Robert Brandon thought you might know something about a message Lord Fortescue received while we were at Beaumont Towers."

She laughed. "Oh, dear, you shouldn't involve yourself in these things. It's unseemly."

"For me but not for you?" My limbs were beginning to throb as the numbness faded from them. "I don't like you any more than you like me. But the fact is, we may be able to assist each other. It would be foolish to let our personal—"

"Assist each other? How do you plan on assisting me, Lady Ashton? I can't imagine any way in which you could do so."

"I'm discreet and able to keep a secret. No doubt at some point in your own work, you might benefit from an ally."

"Do not flatter yourself by thinking you could ever be my professional equal." She was resting her elbow on the arm of the sofa and raised a single finger to hold up her chin as she scrutinized every detail of my face. "There is only one thing you have that I want."

I met her gaze and held it with my own. "Colin?"

She nodded. "Release him to me, and I will tell you what you desire to know."

"I don't have him on a chain, Countess, and I'm not the one who decided to leave you."

"Of course not. He would never stand being on a chain. But if you were to change your behavior—flirt in a more serious manner with other gentlemen, for example—he might be more inclined to see me again. If you took a lover, he would too."

"I won't do that," I said.

She shrugged. "Then Mr. Brandon's life is worth very little to you."

"I'll find out who sent the message on my own."

"Not before they hang your friend." She laughed again, and I had to restrain myself from reaching out to slap her.

"Frankly, I'm shocked that you would stoop to seek my assistance to seduce your former lover," I said. "I assume he was your lover? Wouldn't you be humiliated to have me hand him back to you?"

"You've no idea the depth of pain that comes when you are forced to accept that you will never have the man you love."

"I didn't think it was love that was between you."

"Then why did he beg me to marry him?" Her smug smile taunted me.

"I'm the wrong person to answer that question," I said, feeling a burning heat rushing to my face. Was she telling the truth? Colin had admitted a relationship with her, but had said nothing that suggested this level of seriousness. I was overwhelmed with discomfort.

"My husband is rather fond of you. Perhaps you'd find him entertaining. He and his most recent mistress had a falling-out a few weeks ago. You should talk to him."

I stood to leave the room. "I'm sorry for you. You must be deeply unhappy."

As I left the von Langes' house, I was stopped briefly by the count, who effused delight at finding me in Vienna. Charming though he was, I found it difficult to speak with him after the conversation I'd had with his wife, so I stepped outside, feeling as battered as the snow crushed under the fiacres traveling up and down the street. Unsure of what to do, I started to walk aimlessly, not wanting to return yet to the Imperial. It was growing colder, and snow had begun to fall, but no graceful soft flakes. Icy edges strengthened by the wind slashed at my cheeks.

My mind was uneasy, though I knew I had no right to the feelings consuming me. I could not fault Colin for loving someone before he'd met me. But faced with the woman who came before, I felt wholly inadequate. She and I were so different. How could he have loved us both? Would he find in the end that I was a poor substitute for what he'd known in the past?

I was walking along the Michaeler-Platz, looking over at the sprawling Hofburg, residence of the Imperial family, when a gentleman slammed into me. He apologized quickly and walked on. I watched him cross the street towards Schauflergasse and duck into a café. The golden light escaping through the windows looked inviting; I followed him.

Inside, round tables filled a room with an arched stone ceiling. Newspapers hung on wooden racks or were scattered in front of gentlemen bent over them with eager eyes, many of them scribbling frantic notes in the margins. I took a seat in the back of the room, and the man I'd followed turned and glared at me. I ignored him, smiled at the waiter who'd appeared next to me, and ordered a coffee *mehr weiss*. He brought it almost at once, along with a glass of water. My friend was still scowling at me. Despite the milk in it, the coffee was too hot to drink, so I walked to the nearest newspaper rack and pulled down a copy of *Weiner Literaturzeitung*. A man at the table next to it smiled at me.

"A disgruntled former lover?" he asked.

"Excuse me?" I answered in German, wishing, not for the first time, that I spoke it as fluently as I did French.

"Forgive me, I did not mean to offend." He jumped to his feet and bowed. "I am Friedrich Henkler."

"Lady Emily Ashton," I said, hesitating, never before having encountered someone bold enough to introduce himself to a total stranger. I backed away, slinking to my table and sitting down. I spread the paper in front of me, hoping I looked engrossed, then tasted my drink and cringed.

"You do not like your coffee?" Herr Henkler called from his seat.

"No, it's not the coffee. Not this specific coffee, that is. I don't like any coffee."

"So why did you order it, Lady Emily Ashton? You are English? You want tea?"

"I didn't come to Vienna to drink tea," I said.

"I like you." He crossed over to me and flung himself into one of the vacant chairs at my table. "We speak English?"

"My German's terrible."

"Not at all. But I must practice my English." He waved an arm in the direction of the waiter. "Viktor! *Holen sie ihre heiße schokolade mit gepeitschter creme.*"

"Thank you," I said.

"Can I have your coffee?"

"I—I suppose so."

"*Danke.*" He drained the cup before Viktor returned with my chocolate. "So if he's not a spurned lover, who is he?"

"Who?" I asked.

"Your friend." He nodded at the man who'd bumped into me.

"I've not the slightest idea."

"I like a woman who can offend without even realizing it. Shows a supreme lack of awareness."

"I can assure you I did nothing to offend him!"

"I'm teasing. May I draw you?" he asked.

"Draw me?"

"I'm an excellent artist." He leapt from the chair, went back to his table, and returned with a large sketchbook that he handed to me.

"These are magnificent," I said, looking at his work, each sketch so full of energy it seemed it could spring from the page. He took the book from me.

"So I may draw as we talk?"

"I—I suppose so." I scooped up a mound of whipped cream from my cup of chocolate. "What are we to talk about?"

"Well, Lady Emily Ashton, what has led you to grace Vienna with your royal presence?"

"I'm not royal, and you must stop calling me by my full name."

"All right, Lady Emily."

"It's Lady Ashton, actually."

"I'm not much fond of either. Do you have anything else?"

"Herr Henkler, I—"

"*Nein*. You must call me Friedrich. I insist."

It was impossible not to find this man endearing. His dark hair was a tousled mess, his suit so wrinkled it was nothing short of a disaster. He must have been about my age, perhaps a bit older, and his hands were rough, as if they knew hard work.

"Some friends call me Kallista," I said.

"'Most beautiful'? That I can enthusiastically support."

"You know Greek?"

"I'm not wholly uneducated." He hardly looked up from his

sketchbook as he spoke. "You've not told me why you've come to Austria."

"I'm searching for someone."

"The lost lover?"

"No. Someone I've never met."

"That makes things considerably more difficult, but I have faith. Everyone comes into the Café Griensteidl eventually. Do you see that man over there? With the dark hair and mustache? He's handsome, isn't he?"

"Yes, rather," I said.

"That's Gustav Mahler. You know his music?"

"Of course I do. Is it really him?"

"*Ja.* You want me to introduce you?"

"Oh, I wouldn't know what to say."

"Another time perhaps. But I think you will find the man you seek here. You'll simply have to join the rest of us, holding vigil all day, every day, week after week."

"I can't afford to waste any time," I said.

"I wouldn't have thought there was anything a woman like you couldn't afford."

Suddenly I felt self-conscious. "I understand that you might think such a thing, but—"

"Again, I do not mean to offend."

"You need not apologize."

"Why the urgency to find this man?"

"My friend's husband stands to lose his life if I'm not quick enough."

Friedrich whistled and leaned back in his chair. "Who's after him? It's impossible to keep track of who's assassinating who these days."

"It is?" I asked.

"I'm beginning to think the anarchists are right."

"The anarchists?"

"Enough spurts of violence will cause the state to collapse, leaving us in blissful anarchy. Or so they'd have you believe."

"Are they plotting something now?"

"They're always plotting something." He smiled. "You know nothing about any of this?"

"No," I said. "But the man I seek has some connection to anarchists. I've got to figure out how to find him."

"It's not so easy, or so difficult, for that matter. There are lots of anarchists here. Lots of groups. Some are easy to find, but I don't see how you'd ever track down one nameless individual."

"His name—" I stopped myself. I knew nothing about Friedrich; it might not be wise to identify Schröder.

"You don't need to tell me," he said. "It's perfectly understandable." He put down his charcoal and held up his sketchbook.

I gasped. "It's as if I'm looking in the mirror!"

"Very well done." I started at the sound of a familiar voice, and looked behind me to find Mr. Harrison, whose gray eyes were fixed on Friedrich. "Will you excuse us?"

"*Selbstverständlich*." He went back to his own table, taking the sketchbook with him.

Mr. Harrison leaned close to me. "Coming here was a mistake."

"You prefer a different café?" I asked. "I find that I've already grown quite fond of the Griensteidl."

"You should not have come to Vienna."

I raised an eyebrow. "Is that so?"

"I know why you're here. You can't help him, and trying to do so will put in jeopardy not only yourself, but the man whom you hold most dear."

"And who is it that I should be afraid of?" I asked.

"Me." He reached into an inside pocket of his jacket, and I saw that he still carried the gun he'd had at Beaumont Towers.

"Take this, and remember every time you see one like it that I've been there. I can get to you, Lady Ashton, and those you love, whenever the fancy strikes me." He rolled something across the table, a small object that I did not identify until it had stopped moving: a bullet.

15 December 1891
Berkeley Square, London

My dear Emily,

 I hope all is well with you in Vienna and that you will be able to return to England soon. I miss you so very much. I can't stand the thought of Christmas this year. My parents have wired to say they would return from India at once, but I can't bear to face them and begged them to stay away. How quickly our fortunes have changed.

 I have news that should be joyous, but in the present circumstances brings angst rather than pleasure. I'm sure you can guess what it is. How cruel that such a thing—something Robert and I have wanted for so long—should happen now. I've told no one else, Robert included, though I think Margaret may be suspicious. It would be difficult for her not to be. I can't bear the sight of breakfast.

 Robert's mother calls on me daily, but we do little more than sit in grim silence. She used to give me cheery updates on the plans for Robert's defense, but she's had nothing positive to say for many days in a row now. I'm afraid that if she discovers my condition, she'll insist that I go to her house, and I don't want to do that.

 Every day there's another story in the paper, each one more wild than the last. Margaret and Davis try to hide them from me, but I manage to find them nonetheless. Today it was suggested that Robert is a German spy. Can you imagine? I don't know how they can print such baseless accusations. But apparently Lord Fortescue had sensitive documents that went missing from Beaumont Towers. Do you know anything about this? How could anyone think Robert had taken them?

 There is so little at present that I can tell you to offer a bit of joy. But you should know this: Margaret's friend, Mr. Michaels, has been sending letters to her with alarming frequency, and I caught her blushing as she read one. What a pity he is an Oxford don instead of a peer of the realm—and don't scold me for saying that,

Emily. It's only that I fear her parents would not approve of the match.

But I don't know Margaret so well as you do. Perhaps it is only an academic correspondence. I may be entirely misjudging the situation.

I miss you very, very much and am your most devoted friend,
Ivy

Chapter 9

Cécile and I were snug under heaps of blankets in a carriage, slowing as it reached the Amalienhof wing of the Hofburg Palace, where we were to call on the empress. It was our second full day in Vienna, and already I could see how easy it would be to get caught up in the lovely frivolity of the city. In many ways, it reminded me of the London Season: balls, parties, concerts, the opera. But added to that was the café culture, with which I was much taken, the postcard-perfect architecture of the Ringstrasse, and a lively community of artists. Notably absent, of course, were the matrons of London society. The Viennese had their own rules, but as a foreigner, I found it deliciously simple to do what I wanted without being the target of withering glares on a regular basis.

It had taken me longer than usual to dress for our trip to the palace, a fact that disappointed me, as I liked to believe that I was utterly undaunted by royalty. In the end, I settled on one of Mr. Worth's creations, a striking gown on which gold embroidery covered a dark burgundy underskirt. Fastened over the high-necked bodice was a trim jacket and overskirt made from soft golden velvet. Flounces at the hips were gathered to reveal the rich burgundy below, and the material from the underskirt, with its lovely embroidery, featured again on wide lapels and fitted cuffs. Meg had taken extra pains with my hair, taming my curls in an upswept knot and pinning a darling hat trimmed with wispy feathers to my head. She would not let me leave the hotel until she was confident I could impress the empress.

In contrast, Cécile was nonchalant when choosing a gown. She knew full well that she would be all striking elegance no matter what she wore. Despite her age, her face was still beautiful, her silver hair shone, and her every movement was filled with grace. Furthermore, there was not a single item in her wardrobe unfit for a queen.

She and Sissi had met when they were girls and Cécile was visiting Bavaria. From that time, they corresponded, although they saw each other infrequently. The connection between them, she had told me, was strong, and in difficult times, each turned to the other.

The empress's eccentricities were as infamous as her beauty was legendary. It was said she maintained her figure with a never-ending series of extreme diets: oranges and violet-flavored ice cream, raw eggs and salt, substituting meat juice or milk for meals. She pampered her face with masks of strawberries or raw meat (although I never quite understood how raw meat fit with pampering), and bathed in water mixed with olive oil or milk and honey.

I had never seen her in person, but when we were girls, Ivy had a postcard that pictured her, and we'd lamented that our own queen was not nearly so lovely. Empress Elisabeth was a vision of royal perfection: a fairy tale. But the woman who greeted Cécile and me after we'd been settled into a formal salon in the Amalienhof bore little resemblance to the figure from the postcard.

"My darling Cécile, I have so longed for you." She was shockingly thin and swathed from head to toe in black, still mourning the loss of her son, Rudolf, whose death at the imperial hunting lodge at Mayerling had shocked the Austrian nation.

"You should have sent for me sooner. I am distressed to find you in such a condition."

"Don't scold me. I can't bear it. Things are more dreadful here than ever. I don't know why I ever come back to Vienna. I wish we were still girls, playing in the Alps."

"How are the horses?" Cécile asked, and the empress's face brightened at once. They embarked on a spirited discussion of the animals (one of whom was called Nihilist, an excellent name) that lasted nearly a quarter of an hour, neither of them paying me the slightest attention. At last, Sissi sighed and looked at me with eyes void of energy.

"Perhaps you would like to read so Cécile and I do not bore you with tales of our squandered youths." She waved a slim hand in the direction of a desk in the far corner of the room. "I've all sorts of books. Take whatever you'd like."

"Thank you," I said. The books piled in neat stacks on the desk caught my interest at once: two volumes of Greek mythology, a copy of Plato's *Republic*, six volumes of rather sensational poetry, and a copy of the *Odyssey* in the original Greek. The empress was no vapid royal. I flipped through the poetry first, assuming I would not be spending much time reading.

I underestimated how much Sissi had to say to Cécile.

Three-quarters of an hour later, I had come to the conclusion that I'd always underrated the Romantic poets. I was just about to pick up *The Republic* when the conversation on the opposite end of the room grew louder. By *louder*, I mean slightly less inaudible than it had been. I couldn't understand much of what was being said beyond the word "Mayerling," and that caught my attention not only because it was a topic Cécile had warned me to avoid, but also because it was also written on a letter that was sitting on the desk.

I—like everyone else in Europe—had read the story of Crown Prince's Rudolf's death nearly three years earlier. It was originally reported that he'd died of heart failure, but rumors of a very different ending were rampant. His mistress, young Mary Vetsera, had died the same night, and although the young lady's name was not mentioned in any papers in Austria, the news I had read in London was full of stories of a lovers' suicide pact.

Ordinarily, I would not dream of reading someone else's correspondence, but I found myself leaning forward across the desk, straining to make out the words of the letter while keeping an uneasy eye on Cécile and the empress. I did not want to pick up the letter and risk being caught doing the literary equivalent of eavesdropping. In it, someone was reporting to Sissi that there had been many shots fired at the hunting lodge the night Rudolf died. Trailing at the bottom of the page was the beginning of an intriguing sentence about the motivations of the French and their English compatriots. I longed to turn it over to read the rest, but was not bold enough. What had the French or English to do with Mayerling?

"We've ignored you long enough," Cécile said. "Rejoin us. Kallista is a kindred spirit to you, Sissi. She studies Greek and spends much of her time on Santorini."

"You are a fortunate girl," the empress said. "I've a castle on Corfu. If I were wise, I'd never venture from its safety."

"Surely you're safe in Vienna." I sat on a chair across from them.

"No one is safe in Vienna."

I believed her when she said this and agreed even more strongly when, after we left the palace, I saw Mr. Harrison standing across the street, watching our carriage as it pulled away.

"THEY'RE A LIVELY GROUP," I said as Viktor placed in front of me a cup of hot chocolate mounded with whipped cream. A crowd of gentlemen were passing a stack of loose papers around a table across the room from me, taking turns reading with mock dramatic emphasis, erupting into frequent laughter.

"*Junges Wien*," the waiter said. "Young Vienna."

"Avant-garde writers, all of them," Friedrich said. "They practically live here."

"The young one—sitting on the far right—has already started publishing poems. I don't think he's yet eighteen," Viktor said. "Hugo von Hofmannsthal."

"I'd love to read them," I said. He bowed and disappeared, not responding. I opened a newspaper.

"Hugo von Hofmannsthal is a remarkable talent," Friedrich said, picking up his sketchbook and setting to work drawing a woman who was sitting at the table next to us, wearing a bonnet of astonishing height. "He's sure to be an enormous success. If I didn't like him so much, I'd have to hate him."

We passed a content half hour. "Do you know this man?" I asked, showing Friedrich a letter to the editor written by Gustav Schröder, whom I suspected at once was the Schröder mentioned to me by Robert. The piece was well written and articulate; if one were debating whether to embrace the principles of anarchy, Herr Schröder's piece would serve as a deft push towards his side. I was shocked that his views could sound so reasonable.

"*Ja*," he said. "I know Schröder."

"Does he come here often?"

"To the Griendsteidl? *Nein*." Friedrich slouched in his chair across from me. "Are you a budding anarchist?"

"Far from it," I said.

"No. A person in your position would hardly want to lose her status."

"*A person in my position?*" I flung the paper onto the table. "What, precisely, do you think my position is?"

"Your wealth affords you a great deal of freedom."

"Yes, it does." I met his stare.

"And you suffer not from the inconvenience of having to work to support yourself."

"Granted. But my financial situation does not liberate me from the bonds that restrict a woman's activities."

"You've far more liberty than the poorer members of your sex."

"Do I? Or is my prison merely more comfortable?"

"No. You've infinitely more opportunity. You can travel, pursue an education, socialize with whomever you please."

"So long as I don't go too far from the bounds of what is generally acceptable to my peers."

"And if you went too far? And they ostracized you? You could retreat into your luxurious cocoon and continue to amuse yourself however you wished. I grant you that a woman who measures her self-worth through the eyes of her equals is held captive by society. But you, I think, are not such a woman. You do not crave acceptance, so rejection would not be disaster."

"Are you an anarchist?"

"No." He opened his sketchbook and passed it to me. "This is Schröder."

The face that stared out at me was a hard one, all scowls and lines.

"How can I meet him?" I asked.

"It's unlikely that he'd come to you at the Imperial," he said, stirring his coffee.

"I'll meet him wherever he likes. Can you put me in touch with him?"

"I'll see what I can arrange and let you know tomorrow."

"Thank you."

Friedrich sighed and sunk farther down in his chair.

"What's the matter? You don't approve of my frolicking with anarchists?"

"Anarchists do not frolic."

I smiled. "Then what's the matter?"

"Anna's here. With her mother."

"Anna?" I followed his gaze to a young lady seated on the opposite end of the café. Soft brown curls framed her dimpled face, and her cheeks were flushed pink from the cold. Her mother did not share her daughter's easy good looks. At the moment her eyes, no wider than slits, were focused on Friedrich with violent intensity. She shook her head, stood up, and jerked Anna to her feet, marching her straight out the door.

"Frau Eckoldt detests me," Friedrich said.

"Why?"

"Because I had the audacity to win her daughter's love."

"She objects to the match?"

"To put it politely. My shortcomings are too many to list, although my dubious profession alone is enough to make me unacceptable."

"She objects to an artist?"

"To a largely unsuccessful, often unemployed one, yes."

"But if you were employed?"

"I'd still be Jewish."

"Ignorance and prejudice." Now it was my turn to sigh. "I'm cynical enough to believe that rampant success would overcome anything she views as a shortcoming."

He shrugged. "I had hoped to get a commission to paint murals in some of the Ringstrasse buildings, but have had no success."

"I'll commission something from you."

"I don't want favors."

"No favors, then. But if I can assist you, you must let me." I was determined to find some way to help him. "It's the least I can do to thank you for arranging a meeting with Herr Schröder."

"Fine, Kallista, so long as you promise not to secretly fund my success as an artist."

"I wouldn't dream of it. You've the talent to manufacture your own success. But it never hurts to let a friend help with your luck."

17 December 1891
Berkeley Square, London

Dear Emily,

Much is happening here. None of it good.

Perhaps a little good. But the bad first. Today I persuaded Ivy she ought to get some air—and we thought it would be fun to find Davis a Christmas gift.

At least, I thought it would be amusing. Ivy was a bit horrified, but rallied to the idea once we'd set out. We had just walked into Harrods when we saw Mrs. Hearst, a dreadful woman and acquaintance of the Taylors, my parents' friends. Do you remember them? The horrible family I stayed with during last Season? Mrs. Hearst was in town shopping with one of her vapid, utterly uninteresting daughters—I can't remember her name, not that it matters, they're all interchangeably dull. As soon as she spotted Ivy, she steered her daughter away and then—can you believe it?—she came to me, pulled me away from Ivy, and told me in a loud voice that it would do me no good to associate with murderers.

I admit that perhaps—just perhaps—my reaction was a bit dramatic. I wrenched my arm from hers and reprimanded her loudly, using some choice words that were, in hindsight, not perhaps the most appropriate for the situation.

Still, I don't regret it. She's a toad, and I will not stand by and see Ivy bullied by people like her.

We had to hold our own afterwards, although I'm certain poor Ivy would have liked nothing better than to return home, preferably under the cover of night in a closed carriage. I made her shop instead and bought your butler a gold cigar cutter on which I'm having his initials engraved. I do hope he likes it.

As for the good, it's not much. Only that Mr. Michaels has asked for my assistance—yes, assistance—on his current project. I told *him I would be happy to help, so long as he publicly acknowledges that women should be allowed to be full members of the university. He turned red and tugged at his collar, but he agreed. Primarily, I think, because he knows I have a flair for translation.*

I hope your work in Vienna is going well. We are so very much depending upon you.

I am, as always, your most corrupt friend, perhaps becoming more corrupt daily,
Margaret

Chapter 10

After days and days the snow had stopped falling, but the sky was gray, matching the slush as it grew dirty beneath the wheels of fiacres. The paltry light that seeped through lingering clouds was absorbed by the city's buildings; nothing glimmered. Even the electric lights that filled the new Court Theater looked dull to me. Another week gone, and no evidence to exonerate Robert.

Cécile, Jeremy, and I spent the morning at the third-floor studio on Sandwirtgasse that Klimt shared with his brother, Ernst, and Franz Matsch. The three men made up the Känstlercompanie, and together worked on murals for public buildings, many on the Ringstrasse. Cécile sat for her portrait while Jeremy and I watched in awe the artist at work. He wore a long smock, and his thick beard stood stiff as he mixed paints and scrutinized his subject, occasionally reaching up to scratch the brindled cat that sat on his shoulder. I was somewhat distracted, watching the time, because although Friedrich may have said that anarchists do not frolic, Herr Schröder had sent a note inviting me to ice-skate with him. We planned to go to the turreted Eislaufverein, Vienna's new skating palace, straight from the studio, but my friends would leave half an

hour before I did, so they could watch the meeting without drawing any suspicion. None of us felt comfortable with me meeting
this stranger alone, even in such a public place.

"You are an exquisite woman, Kallista," the artist said once
Cécile and Jeremy had left. He, like most of Cécile's friends, had
adopted her use of my late husband's nickname for me. "I wish
you'd let me paint you."

"I've no time for it," I said. "Someday, perhaps."

"I have a strong feeling you will never sit for me. I will have to
memorize your grace, your eyes."

"Your work is so very different from anything else I've seen.
Your brushstrokes are so intricate, yet they reveal the passionate
depths of your subjects with such elegance. I wonder if they recognize themselves. Their faces, their bodies, yes. But do they see in
themselves what you do?"

"I couldn't begin to answer your question. I have no talent for
speaking, especially about my work. You will find, if you get to
know me, that I am remarkably uninteresting."

"If that were true, Cécile would have no time for you. I think
you're pretending to be modest," I said, circling the room, feeling
myself come alive in the face of the paintings and drawings that
covered the walls, tables, every available surface. It was such a comfortable feeling to be surrounded by art. I breathed in the smell of
the oil paints, headier than perfume. "It's quite a talent to be able
to see so deeply into others. Have you ever done a portrait of the
Countess von Lange?"

"Kristiana? Yes. It's at her house. You have not seen it?"

"We're not particular friends."

"That is a surprise. You're so similar." He pulled a stack of
drawings out of a portfolio and began paging through them.

"Similar? I don't agree at all," I said.

"She's more cynical and more worldly, yes, but she's older than
you. Give yourself a few years. You both have the same sort of spirit,

the same stubbornness." He handed me a large piece of paper. "This is a study for her portrait." She was beautiful; that I knew already. But Klimt had captured, even just in pencil, her strength, her elegance, and her heartbreak. There was a profound sadness in her eyes. "And you both love the same man."

"I—"

"It is time for you to meet your friends," he said, taking the sketch back from me.

I left at once, glad to be away from the drawing, not liking in the least the thought that I might be like this woman—my rival—at all. And once again, I was wondering how deep Colin's feelings for her had been. All this left me utterly morose as I made my way to the park. When I arrived, Jeremy and Cécile were on the ice, making their way effortlessly around the rink, arm in arm.

I strapped on my skates. A brass band began to play a delightful march, and for a moment I allowed myself to be caught up in excitement and anticipation. I stepped out, ready to join the parade of gliding skaters, realizing immediately that I did not have even an ounce of their grace. My ankles bent hideously, and I would have fallen flat on my back were it not for the quick reflexes of a nearby gentleman.

"Your friend is an excellent skater," he said, and as soon as I saw his face, I recognized Herr Schröder from Friedrich's sketch. But his eyes took me by surprise. They were dark, with flecks of gold that rendered them entirely mesmerizing. "Is she here to protect you from me? Or is that the role of her amiable and useless companion?"

Undaunted, I took his arm, and we began to slowly circle the rink. "I'm not foolish enough to have come here alone."

"Your German is appalling. Speak English."

"My German is nothing of the sort," I answered, refusing to switch to English. "And it's leagues better than your English."

"Why have you sought my company?" he asked.

"I'm here on a . . . diplomatic . . . mission. A man was murdered in England shortly after receiving a warning that came from Vienna. I want to know who sent it."

"What makes you think I would know anything about it? Because I am an anarchist, I'm likely to be a murderer?"

"I did not accuse you of murder. But you think freedom can be obtained through violence, so, yes, I think you're likely to be connected in some way."

The muscles in his arm tensed. "You know nothing about anarchism."

"There's no need to get upset. I sought you out not simply because you are an anarchist, but because your name was mentioned to me by a friend. As it is, I'm not particularly concerned with what you do, so long as you help me identify the person who sent this information to England." He said nothing. "If he is a member of your, well, I suppose 'organization' wouldn't be a proper word to describe a group of people opposed to order. What would be?"

Now he laughed. "Organization will do. We'll agree that the irony is deliberate."

My laughter joined his. "Will you help me?"

"I don't like being charmed by someone who embodies everything I despise," he said.

"I'm hardly to blame for anything you despise, particularly where politics are concerned. I'm not allowed to vote, after all."

"Voting is a useless exercise. No matter who is elected, no one wins but the government."

"So as a person who does not vote, I should earn your anarchist approval."

"Faulty logic, Kallista."

"I did not give you permission to call me that." As I struggled to keep my balance, Herr Schröder tightened his hold on my arm, steadying me.

"Friedrich told me it's your name, and I don't see why I need permission to use it."

"I won't argue the point. We both stand to benefit by finding this informer."

"I don't see how I benefit."

"It was not merely a vague warning that was sent to England. It included detailed information about a plot with which you are intimately acquainted." I was bluffing a bit, but saw no other option. "I'd think you'd want to know if someone in your 'organization' is sharing that sort of thing. Particularly if you have any desire to see your plan executed."

"Why would you have even the slightest knowledge of such things?"

"Because I have worked with Mr. Harrison." I watched his face, but it revealed nothing.

"There are few people I trust less than Harrison."

"I couldn't agree more."

"I don't trust you either," he said.

"Let me assure you, Herr Schröder, the feeling is entirely mutual. But it's also irrelevant. As I said, we both stand to benefit."

"I can uncover this person on my own," he said. "Why bother to share the information with you?"

"Because you're an anarchist. You believe in equality. My right to this information is equal to yours."

"More flawed logic, but I appreciate the sentiment. And because I find you inexplicably beguiling, I will see what I can discover. Meet me at the Griensteidl in three days. I'll come in the morning, but I don't know what time."

"Thank you."

"Be careful of Harrison. He'll know that we've met."

"Why should that matter?" I asked.

"Everything matters to him. He is a dangerous man because he has his government's unqualified support despite the fact that he is more ruthless than they know, and pursues agendas of which they would not approve. You should be careful." He dropped my arm, skated away from me, and left the rink.

I realized at once that I was in danger of falling. I began to slowly move my feet, but this was a mistake. There are circumstances when speed is in fact steadier than caution; this was one of them. With no momentum, I lost my balance almost at once, my feet flying out from under me, and fell flat on my back. I tried to get up, but fell again. This time, my hat flew off my head and slid across the ice.

Jeremy appeared from nowhere and bent over me. "Are you hurt?"

"Nothing more serious than wounded dignity. Though I will confess to wishing bustles hadn't fallen out of fashion. At the moment I'd welcome the extra padding." I brushed snow off my slim-fitting chocolate brown coat, trimmed with mink and tortoiseshell buttons.

With a strong hand, he pulled me to my feet, then retrieved my hat and placed it on my head. "It's rather fun rescuing you."

"This does not constitute a rescue, Jeremy," I said, smiling and securing the hat as firmly as possible with its untrustworthy pin. "Had Herr Schröder thrown me over his shoulder and attempted to abduct me, then you might have managed a rescue."

"*Might have?* You doubt my abilities?"

"Not in the least. It's the circumstances that I find unlikely." I looped my arm through Jeremy's, buried my hands in my fur muff, and soon we were circling the rink at a leisurely pace.

"Isn't that your dear friend, the Countess von Lange?" Jeremy asked, directing my attention to an elegant figure executing a series of perfect spins at the center of the ice. When she finished, she saw us staring at her and waved, looking more sophisticated than ever in a gorgeous green velvet skating costume.

"What a treat to find the two of you together," she said, her narrowed eyes belying the smile on her face. "Have you heard from your devoted fiancé?"

"Of course," I said, wishing it was not a lie. "We correspond regularly whenever he's away." In fact, I'd had no word from him since he left Beaumont Towers. The letters I'd sent him in Berlin to inform of my trip had gone unanswered.

"Really? How very curious. I shouldn't have thought it possible."

"Are we gentlemen such cads?" Jeremy asked. "I am, certainly, but Hargreaves is disgustingly good."

"I didn't think he'd know where to find you," the countess said, her voice full of laughter. "And there's been no point sending a letter to him since his departure from Berlin."

"Is that what you think?" I asked, not wanting her to know that, so far as I knew, he was still in Berlin. "It's been my experience that he always manages to get my letters, no matter where he is. But then, he's particular about having them forwarded to wherever he goes."

"So he knows you're in Vienna?"

"Of course," I said, clutching Jeremy's arm awkwardly, hoping that I would not fall.

"You know, Lady Ashton, you are a very bad liar." She twirled in a circle again, then skated off, the sound of her laughter bouncing after her.

Chapter 11

N o, I don't think I can tolerate any more chocolate," I said, waving Viktor away. I'd been sitting for nearly two hours at what had become my regular table at the Griensteidl waiting for Herr Schröder and was beginning to regret the extra whipped cream I'd had on my three cups of cocoa. He whisked away an empty cup and refilled my glass of water, then handed me a piece of paper.

"One of von Hofmannsthal's poems," he said, nodding towards the table the *Junges Wien* seemed to occupy permanently.

"Thank you," I said, scanning the lines. "'The longing branches / Rustled by the night wind / In your little garden . . . / How sweet it is to only / Think of such little things.' It's quite good. Do you want more coffee, Friedrich?"

"I shouldn't," he said.

This meant that he had neither money nor credit left and planned to drink water for the remainder of the day. "Please bring more coffee, Viktor," I said.

"No—," Friedrich began.

"I admire the fact that you do not wish me to hand you money or commissions to support your career. You want to forge your own success. But to deny yourself a twenty-kreuzer coffee on principle is ridiculous."

He did not argue.

I was finding, as I spent more time in Vienna, that the cafés were centers for culture unlike any others to which I'd been exposed. The city's artists treated them like second homes. First homes, really. I'd visited the cafés Central, Schrangl, Bauer, and Heinrichshof (where I saw Johannes Brahms), but none appealed to me so well as the Griensteidl. Here I could watch playwrights argue the dynamics of a bit of dialogue, poets curse their search for an elusive word, and painters deep in games of billiards, their eyes hardly focused, thinking more about how to mix their colors to the perfect hue than whether the right ball would drop in the right pocket.

The city's wealthy frequented the cafés as well, and though there was not perhaps as much mingling as Herr Schröder would strive to obtain, it was leagues from anything that I'd seen in London. Here, within a quarter of an hour, one could find a like-minded soul to discuss nearly any academic subject.

"Have you seen Fraulein Eckoldt again?" I asked Friedrich after Viktor had brought him another coffee.

"Her mother has forbidden all contact between us. And now that she knows I frequent the Griensteidl, Anna isn't allowed to come here again."

"I'm sorry."

"I never expected a different outcome. We are neither of the same class nor the same religion. It was always a hopeless love."

"So you give up?"

"*Nein.* I will find a way to win her. I am applying to paint murals at the university. It's a commission that would bring me both prestige and enough money to support a wife."

"Enough for her mother?"

"Not even close," he said, grinning. "But enough for Anna, and that is all that matters."

"Friedrich, I like you more with every passing moment." I thought of the innumerable instances I knew of in which a gentleman had stepped aside to give the lady he loved a chance to find someone of more desirable financial status—regardless of her thoughts on the matter. "It's unlikely that I'd be able to convince Frau Eckoldt you're a suitable match for her daughter, but I'm quite capable of arranging meetings for you and Anna."

"You would do that?"

"It would be my pleasure." I smiled.

"How—" He stopped the moment he saw Herr Schröder approach our table. "I'll leave you to him," he said, gathering up his drawing materials and disappearing to the other side of the café.

"Kallista," Herr Schröder said, shaking the hand I'd given him.

"No *handküss*?" I asked.

"Don't be ludicrous," he said, his lips pulled taut, eyes squinting as he looked down at me.

"Forgive me. I've become accustomed to Austrian gallantry and wasn't aware that anarchism requires the death of manners." He grunted in reply, then flagged down Viktor and ordered a decadent hazelnut torte. "Have you any information for me?" I asked.

"You have a powerful enemy in Kristiana von Lange," he said.

"I know all I care to about the countess. Have you identified the person who sent information to England?"

"There is no one in my"—he paused and smiled—" . . . 'organization' who is dealing with the British."

"You're certain?"

"Beyond all doubt."

"Perhaps someone has told a spouse or a lover, and that person—"

"Impossible."

"Of course it's possible." I bit my lip and forced myself to keep from rolling my eyes. Men and their confidence.

"I do not think you grasp the seriousness of what I do. I have no choice but to surround myself with people whom I trust."

"No one is immune from betrayal," I said. "And while you've told me you don't trust Mr. Harrison, you obviously have a connection with him."

"I would not be alive, Kallista, if I were not immune to betrayal. I take stringent measures to ensure it."

"But you did not deny the possibility of an informer existing within your group when I first spoke with you about it."

"I can be certain of my safety because I never overlook a threat. And my cohorts are in no doubt of their fate should they betray me in even the smallest way. Vienna is plagued with suicides. An extra one on any given day wouldn't draw attention."

It felt as if the air around me had turned to water, and my lungs were filling at a rapid and irreversible pace.

"You've never had coffee with a murderer before?" he asked, raising the cup Viktor had brought him.

"Tea, yes, but never coffee." My face was hot. I could not control the color rushing to it, but forced composure into every other part of me.

"There is much more to Vienna than the Ringstrasse and Fasching balls. But it would be best, perhaps, if you chose to ignore the darker side of the city."

"A luxury, Herr Schröder, that I do not have. I want to interview every person who knows the details of your plan. One of them must have some connection with Lord Fortescue."

"Fortescue?" He laughed. "There's no chance any of my associates was involved with him."

"You may have missed something. I don't know these people, so when speaking to them I'd bring no preconceived notions."

"You will not talk to them."

"But—"

"You will never know who they are. This is not some amusing game, a diversion to let you feel useful. You do not belong here. I'm sorry I was not able to help you. If your friend does not escape his fate, well, take comfort in the knowledge that his death may go far in bringing a better life to the masses."

"I will not let Robert be hanged for a crime he did not commit."

Herr Schröder shrugged and rose from the table. "Not all goals are attainable." He walked out of the café. I pulled on my coat and slipped my hands into my pockets, where I felt something cold and hard: one of Mr. Harrison's bullets. I could not help but shudder. So far as I knew, I hadn't been in his presence since that day at the café, and I was certain that I hadn't left the bullet he'd given me that day in my coat. How had he managed to slip this into my pocket?

Consumed with unease, I looked out the window and saw Herr Schröder starting across the street. I waited two beats, then followed.

COLIN HAD TAUGHT ME the art of trailing someone. Granted, he'd done it not so that I might follow a murderous anarchist, but so that I would be aware if someone were following me. Nonetheless, I was thrilled to make use of my training. I did well at first, crossing the street and staying far behind my quarry, keeping him in my sight as he made his way around the Hofburg and through the Volksgarten to the Grillparzer Monument, erected to honor Austria's finest dramatist and poet. I hung back, knowing that it would be difficult to stay out of view on the park's wide paths, but I was not cautious enough. Herr Schröder brushed the snow off one of the benches that flanked a large sculpture of the writer, sat down, and waved at me.

Mortified, I steeled myself and approached him.

"I wasn't finished with you," I said.

"So I gathered several blocks ago."

"You should have let me know you'd seen me."

"And ruin your fun? Hardly sporting." He kicked at the snow in front of him. "What do you want?"

I was not about to tell him that I hoped to follow him to his home, to skulk about after him until I'd discovered where he met with his compatriots. "Give me an honest answer. If you had discovered the identity of the informer, would you have told me?"

"No."

"Neither his name nor the fact that you'd found him?"

"Neither." He paused, still kicking the snow. "But I am rather taken with your persistence, so I will say again: I did not find him. I did not need to lie to you in the Griensteidl."

"How can I possibly believe you?"

"You can't." He smiled. "Don't follow me anymore, Kallista. There is no reason for us to speak again."

I took his place on the stone bench and watched him walk away. I would follow him again, but not while he was expecting it.

A familiar voice drifted through the freezing air. "That's a miserable place to sit on such a cold day."

"Colin?" I leapt to my feet as he grabbed my hands and pulled me towards him. "How—I—you—Berlin—"

"Don't speak. Not just yet." His kisses warmed me better than the summer sun could have, and I basked in his embrace. "Come. Let's get inside." He led me through the park, his arm tight around my waist. "We'll go to the Kunsthistorisches Museum. Have you been yet?"

"No. I'm not here on a pleasure trip."

"So I've gathered. But I do love finding you unchaperoned." He stopped walking and kissed me again. "I'd never before contemplated the advantages of coming to parks in the depths of winter. Wonderfully private places, don't you think?"

"I don't think you understand the gravity of the current situation," I said.

"Don't underestimate me. I know exactly what I'm doing." We reached the front of the museum. "What will it be? Greek sculpture?"

"Please," I said, a smile escaping against my will. He took me by the arm in the most proper sort of fashion, and we entered the building. We said nothing further until we'd reached a gallery that contained a statue of Artemis from the second century B.C., done in the style of Praxiteles.

"Harrison was following you. I think we've convinced him there's nothing to see but a romantic encounter between a man and his fiancée."

"He was following me, too?" I looked up at the ceiling and sighed, clenching my hands into hard fists. "I'm hopeless at this. I can't believe—"

"No, darling, you're not hopeless. You just need more practice. And now, just in case he's still watching, let's look at the art. What do you think of this Artemis?" he asked, squeezing my gloved hand.

"Magnificent." The goddess leaned gracefully on another statue, a smaller image of herself.

"Why are you meeting with Gustav Schröder?"

"First tell me when you arrived in Vienna," I said.

"I've been here for some time. I'd no idea you were here."

"I wrote to you," I said.

"Your letter's undoubtedly waiting for me in Berlin. I was there only for a few days, and I've had no time to write you. I'm sorry."

"It's fine," I said. "You know I understand."

"You're a dear girl," he said. "Now tell me about Schröder."

"I think we'd better sit." We found an empty bench, and I told him all about Robert and Lord Fortescue's mysterious informer.

"You've done well, Emily. And with very little to go on."

"You don't object to my doing this?"

"My usual caveat applies: Do not put yourself in any unnecessary danger. If I find out that you have, I'll carry you back to England myself." There was something in his eyes. A calm pride, perhaps, coupled with the sparkle that I saw nearly every time we were alone. But there was something different, too. Their darkness was deeper, warmer.

"Sounds like a pleasant way to travel. If I'm good now, will you carry me?"

"If you're good, I'll do anything you want."

"Including marry me before the date set by the queen?"

"That's being bad, Emily, very bad." How I longed to kiss him! I was blind to the art that surrounded us, intoxicated by his presence. He stood up and looked at me with such intensity, I felt my skin begin to ache.

"I shan't force the issue in such a public place," I said.

"Thank you."

"How did you find me?" I asked.

"Sheer luck. I was coming from an appointment and saw you on the other side of the street. I could tell at once that you were following someone."

I frowned. "And I thought I was being so discreet. It's bad enough that both you and Herr Schröder were on to me, but even worse that I didn't notice Harrison tailing me, too."

"That's because you weren't suspecting it."

I recounted for him what had passed between Mr. Harrison and me and showed him the bullet I'd found in my pocket. Concern filled his eyes, and he took my hand.

"From now on you must be better aware of your surroundings. I don't like you being pursued by someone whose motives are so distinctly not innocent."

"I wouldn't object should your motives become less innocent," I said.

"You, my dear, are certain to send me to an early grave."

"Not if we're married."

"No, not if we're married."

"I'm free tomorrow," I said. "You?"

"If only," he replied.

"Where are you staying? Are you at the Imperial?"

"No, I come here so often I've rooms close to the Stephansdom."

"Near the von Langes' house," I said.

"Yes. How do you know where they live? Have you been there?"

"I called on the countess as soon as I'd arrived. She was singularly unhelpful."

"Kristiana knows you're in Vienna?" he asked.

"I've seen her twice."

"She didn't tell me," he said. "I wish—"

"You've seen her as well?" I asked.

"I'm working with her."

"I see." I did my best to exhibit not the smallest sign of jealousy, but in truth, I decided at that moment to abandon the guarded disdain I'd felt for the woman and let myself openly despise her.

"Emily—"

I waved my hand in the air in what I hoped was a sophisticated dismissal. "She's of no consequence to me."

"Is that so?"

I did not like the way he was smiling.

"None whatsoever." I stood, composure itself.

"And you've nothing further to say on the subject?"

"Heavens, no. Tedious, tedious, tedious."

"Good girl. Though I will say I'm aggravated that she didn't tell me you were here all this time. It's not like her to be deceptive."

"No, I would imagine most sources of covert intelligence aren't deceptive in the least."

"Emily—"

"Don't scold me. I won't stand for it. Perhaps you don't know your friend quite so well as you thought. At any rate, it doesn't matter. You've found me."

"And now that we're both in Vienna, we'll have to waltz," he said, an obviously forced smile on his face. There was no question that he wanted to move our conversation in any direction so long as it was away from his erstwhile lover.

"After Robert is exonerated."

"You can't work all the time, my dear. Every covert investigator needs periodic breaks. Besides, you never know where you might learn something that will prove to be useful. There's a ball tonight at the Sofiensaäle. Strauss's orchestra is playing. I'll expect to see you there."

THERE WERE AN IMPOSSIBLE NUMBER of balls in Vienna during the winter: masked balls, state balls, debutante balls, and court balls, where five hundred bottles of Moët et Chandon, the emperor's favorite champagne, would be consumed in an evening. The most dedicated person could not manage to attend even a quarter of them. But the crush of people inside the Sofiensaäle, one of the city's famous public ballrooms, made me wonder if the entire population of the city had decided to dance that night. Cécile and I had arrived late, bringing Jeremy with us.

The atmosphere was incomparable: spectacular dancing, effervescent music, beauty in every direction. We'd stepped out of winter into a summer garden, flowers spilling everywhere, swans swimming in a pool whose water reflected sparkling electric lights. The dance floor was so crowded it was difficult to waltz, but with effort, and a single-minded partner, it was possible to carve out enough space to turn.

"You're certain to find someone who can amuse you here," Cécile said, leaning close to Jeremy as soon as we'd ducked inside. "I don't know a single person in Vienna who is not having an affair. If you don't have a paramour by the end of the evening, you'll have no one to blame but yourself."

"I've decided to become a paragon of virtue in what will un-doubtedly be a futile attempt to impress Emily," he said, a broad grin on his face.

"Futile indeed. You may as well dance with me," Cécile replied, and they disappeared onto the floor. I made my way to a refresh-ment table and took a glass of champagne, then looked around for somewhere to sit.

"Lady Ashton! Can it be you?"

"Lady Paget," I said. "How good to see you." Walburga, Lady Paget, was the wife of the British ambassador to Austria. I'd met her on several occasions—she and my mother were friends—and she was one of England's most respected ladies.

"Have you been in Vienna long? Are you managing the weather?"

"Only a fortnight, and I must confess to being utterly charmed by the snow."

"No! It's hideous. When I first came here, I wondered daily to what purpose such a climate exists. The wind is extraordinary. One can hardly breathe. But I suppose you are young enough to tolerate it. Did Worth design your dress? It's exquisite—the perfect shade of blue. No one here has worn anything but pink for the past year. I wonder if it even occurs to them there is another color."

Lady Paget was perhaps a bit hard on the ladies of Vienna. Yes, many wore pink, but the room was filled with every other color a person could want. My own gown, pale ice blue with shots of silver embroidery through the silk, had a skirt with enough fullness that it begged to be spun while dancing. The bodice was décolleté, the sleeves the barest caps. Meg had placed diamond pins through my hair and clasped over long, white gloves a wide platinum and diamond bracelet that matched the choker around my neck.

"The music is magnificent. I don't know how I'll bear anything short of Strauss himself at a ball again. I can't wait to dance," I said.

"Ladies, greetings." Mr. Harrison stood in front of us, bowing.

"Oh! It's so good to see you." Lady Paget gave him her hand. "You, of course, know Lady Ashton?"

"All too well," he said.

"A perfect choice of words." I did not hold out my hand.

"Mr. Harrison is absolutely indispensable to the ambassador," Lady Paget said. "I don't know what we would do without him."

"You're too kind," he said.

I should very much have liked to reply, but forced a thin smile instead.

"Lady Ashton was just telling me how she's longing to dance. You really ought to—"

"That's not necessary," I said. "I—I—"

"I'm afraid I've no time for you this evening, Lady Ashton, and, regardless, I've already promised the next dance." He kissed Lady Paget's hand again, and disappeared. Lady Paget raised an eyebrow and turned to me, about to speak. Thankfully, just at that moment Colin approached us. He bowed neatly to me and bestowed on Lady Paget a perfect *handküss*.

"How Austrian of you, Mr. Hargreaves," she said. "Please assure me that you haven't completely abandoned your Englishness."

"Not at all, Lady Paget. I'm merely embracing the local culture."

"If I see you adopting the dreadful manners that I see in the Hapsburg court, I shall insist that you be returned to London at once."

"Then I shall limit my emulation of the Viennese to the ballroom. It is there where one finds the souls of our Austrian hosts."

"You are quite mistaken, sir. It is the copious libation of beer and the inordinate consumption of schnitzel and *Kaiserschmarren* that chains the Austrian souls to this earth." Lady Paget closed her eyes and shook her head with an air of elegant hopelessness as she spoke.

"You have spent more time here than any of us, Lady Paget, so I shall defer to your superior knowledge. But I will say that I am rather fond of *Kaiserschmarren*."

"Dear Mr. Hargreaves, I worry for you. If you insist on being Austrian this evening, dance with your fiancée."

"You have anticipated me, Lady Paget." He took my hand.

"Do call on me soon, Lady Ashton," she said. "I'll make sure you've invitations to all the best parties while you're here." I thanked her without noticing the words I used. The moment Colin's hand touched mine, my heart began to race, and the skin beneath my glove tingled at his touch.

"*Kaiserschmarren*?" I asked as we began to dance.

"I've no interest in discussing pancakes with you." He held me close and led me around the floor with a marvelous grace; I could hardly breathe. Our eyes held each other's gaze as the room flew by us in a blur. Guiding me firmly, he spun us around and around more quickly than I would have thought possible. The Viennese waltz moved at a much quicker pace than anything I'd danced before. I do not think my feet touched the ground; it was intoxicating. An ordinary waltz would be a disappointment after this.

As we swirled again and again, a pair of figures caught my attention, snapping out of the haze and into focus: Mr. Harrison and the Countess von Lange, standing far too close together in the corner of the room.

22 December 1891
Berkeley Square, London

Dear Emily,

I am enclosing all the most recent articles from the London
papers that include references to Robert's plight. Aside from everyone
believing he's guilty of murder, people have begun speaking openly of
treason and financial ruin. The papers are careful to avoid charges
of libel, but the gossips share no such worries. It's surprising, really,
when you consider the fact that everyone despised Lord Fortescue.
I wouldn't have thought people would take such an interest in his
murder—at least not in a way that involves viciously attacking an
innocent man. But apparently suffering a violent death has made
the victim likable. All anyone remembers now are the people he
helped. No one dares mention those he ruined, his propensity for
blackmail, his disgusting behavior, ill manners, well . . . I need not
go on. You know perfectly well what I mean.

And I need hardly tell you how great the toll has been on Ivy.
I tried to visit Robert yesterday, but he wouldn't see me, and he
continues to refuse to see his wife. She's disconsolate. You can see how
dire are his straits. You can't merely prove him not guilty, Emily,
you've got to find out who committed the crime. Otherwise I fear
that no one will ever believe his innocence, and there will always be
a cloud of uncertainty hanging over him.

On a less serious note, my dear Mr. Michaels is overwrought
that I've not returned to Oxford and wrote me a passionate note
reprimanding me for abandoning my studies. In the course of my
reply to him, I disagreed with him about certain analogies in Ovid's
Ars Amatoria. This so disgruntled him that he sent his own reply by
express.

I confess to finding that unexpectedly exciting.

Finally, Davis is moping. It's been three days since he's had a

*letter from Cécile's maid. Tell Odette to send one posthaste. Your
butler is no fun when he's morose. He's hidden Philip's cigars, and I
can't find them anywhere. I'm so irritated with him that I think I
would return his Christmas gift if I hadn't had it engraved. What a
pity I know no one else with the same initials.*

> *I am yr. most devoted, etc., friend,*
> Margaret

Chapter 12

I awoke the next morning full of satisfaction, pulled on my dressing gown, and flung open the curtains in my suite. Snow was falling again, huge flakes that made it impossible to see across the street. It was a lovely sight. Lovely, that is, until I looked down at the windowsill and saw a bullet sitting on it. Mr. Harrison had been in my room.

I picked it up, but my trembling hands could not hold on to its cold smoothness, and it flew to the ground, striking the parquet floor with a ping that sounded far too innocent. Had he come in while I was sleeping? Or when I wasn't here? The distressing feeling of violation that was pressing, unwelcome, on my chest was familiar. I'd been the target of a cat burglar in London only a few months ago. In the end, however, that had turned out harmless. This time, my intruder was unquestionably an enemy. I retrieved the bullet, my head spinning as I bent over.

Meg opened the door a sliver. "Madame du Lac and the duke are already breakfasting, milady. That painter was here, too, but he's already left." She wrinkled her nose, disapproving of Klimt's presence so early in the morning. I, on the other hand, welcomed the distraction and considered shoving the bullet into my nightstand drawer. I willed away my feeling of unease and wondered when Klimt had appeared at the Imperial—he hadn't been at the ball or the café afterwards, and I thought it unlikely that he'd come for breakfast. Unfortunately, I'd have to wait until I had Cécile alone to find out any details.

"Are you ready to get dressed, ma'am?" Meg asked.

I was in no mood to rush, and took my time selecting a gown of the softest midnight blue wool. Its bodice crossed in a deep *v* in front, blue paisleys embroidered along the edges. Underneath was a matching high collar, trimmed with dainty Venetian lace identical to that peeking out from the bottoms of the sleeves. The color brought out the blue of my eyes, and my cheeks were flushed with the memory of dancing with Colin the night before. I was succeeding, at least for the moment, in distracting my mind from Mr. Harrison's bullet.

I went out to the sitting room, where Cécile was pouring coffee for Jeremy.

"Em, it's not right for you to be so alluring this early in the morning," Jeremy said, adding no fewer than four lumps of sugar to his coffee.

"Apologies," I said, taking a cup of tea. I put the bullet on the table and told my friends where I'd found it.

"*Mon dieu*," Cécile said. "This is unacceptable."

"We shall have to ask the hotel to provide us better security," I said. "I cannot have this man in our rooms."

"Let me speak to the manager for you," Jeremy said.

"I'd appreciate that. If he could perhaps station someone at the top of the steps, watching the hallway, I'd feel much better."

"I can't imagine there will be any difficulties in arranging that."

I picked up an apricot pastry. "You look exhausted."

"Dancing until four and rising at eight is taking its toll on me," Jeremy said.

"Perhaps you're getting too old to stay out so late," I said. I felt something tugging on my skirt. "Brutus! Stop!" I picked up the dog and handed him to Cécile, who glared at him and fed Caesar a biscuit.

"That's unfair, Emily. I'm in the prime of life and intend on staying there." He took a long drink of coffee, frowned, and started adding more sugar. "I've already decided to never admit to being older than thirty-two. That is, once I reach thirty-two."

"Darling, you forget that I know exactly how old you are," I said. "I'll do whatever I must to keep you honest."

"You do know, I hope, that no man under the age of forty can even approach fascinating," Cécile said.

"I've no interest in being fascinating, Madame, merely young," Jeremy said.

"Such a mistake." Cécile shook her head. "You'll learn eventually."

"I wouldn't want to set you up for disappointment. I rarely learn anything." Satisfied that his coffee was at last sweet enough, he drained the cup and filled it again at once.

"So am I to believe that Klimt is not yet fascinating?" I asked.

"He will be in time. For now, he's merely amusing."

"And brilliant," I said.

"Yes, brilliant, too," Cécile said.

"So a chap can be brilliant without being fascinating?" Jeremy asked.

"Yes," Cécile and I answered in chorus, then started to laugh.

"You ladies are brutal," Jeremy said, spooning up more sugar, then dropping it back into the bowl. He scowled and pushed his coffee away from him. "Where are we off to this morning, Em?"

"The count asked to meet me here," I said. "But I didn't want him to come to our rooms. So we're to see him at the Griensteidl."

"I take it he won't be expecting me?" Jeremy asked.

"No," I said.

"Capital."

"How is the empress, Cécile?" I asked.

"Melancholy, depressed. I worry for her. She's beginning to re-mind me of Hamlet, which is *toujours* disappointing in a friend."

"Will you have time to see her this morning?" I asked.

"Not before my guests arrive." At the ball the previous evening, we'd had Lady Paget introduce us to Frau Eckoldt and her daughter. Cécile, who had heard all about Friedrich's plight, had convinced Anna's mother that she was in dire need of someone to help her with conversational German. This was nonsense, of course. Cécile's command of the language was flawless; she'd even mastered Wiene-risch, the Viennese dialect. Furthermore, everyone at the Hapsburg court spoke French. But Frau Eckoldt was easily deceived, and I had no doubt that Cécile would face little if any difficulty in persuading her that Anna was the perfect person to coach her on idioms.

I glanced at the clock on the mantel. "We'd better hurry, or we'll be late."

"I'll go find us a carriage," Jeremy said, abandoning his coffee.

"We're walking," I said. Meg helped me with my coat and I slipped my hands into a fur muff as Jeremy moaned.

"Walking? In the snow?"

"It'll be fun." I had purchased new boots several days earlier and was confident that my feet, protected by thick leather, fur lin-ing, and sturdy soles, would remain warm and dry for the duration of our stroll. We bade farewell to Cécile and headed outside. Jer-emy frowned at me as he lifted the hat from his head and knocked off the snow that was quickly piling on it, but he gave me his arm and we set off along the Kärntner Ring towards the opera, where we turned onto Operngasse and then Augustiner Straße. The fresh snow was soft, piling on top of the frozen sidewalks and cushioning our steps. Jeremy started to slide through it rather than walk as we made our way along the Hofburg.

"Easier than ice skating," he said. "And it gives me an excuse to hang on your arm in an entirely inappropriate manner."

"If you grab me much harder, I'm going to fling you into the street."

"I might enjoy that." His smile brightened his entire face. "Do you really think it's a good idea to encourage your young friend Anna in her forbidden romance?" he asked.

"Why would you ask such a thing?"

"The Viennese are worse even than we English when it comes to class. At least we stick together, more or less, as a group. They're divided into little cliques."

"I'd no idea you were a scholar of the culture."

"I met a charming woman who told me all about it a few nights ago. She married a man of higher rank and is ignored by his peers. Apparently marrying up is only acceptable if the spouse of lower position is a foreigner."

"I do hope you were able to offer her a modicum of comfort."

"Unfortunately I was not. My affections are otherwise engaged." Snow was stuck all along his eyelashes.

"Who's the lucky girl? And who's her unfortunate husband?"

"I'll never tell."

"You are a dear boy," I said, squeezing his arm and dropping my head against his shoulder. "I do hope she appreciates you." We did not speak again until we had shrugged off our coats inside the Griensteidl.

"Come," I said. "My table is in the back."

"Your own table?"

"At least I'm not receiving my mail here. Friedrich does, as do most of his friends."

"Very like a nonexclusive London gentlemen's club," Jeremy said, pulling out a chair for me.

"I wouldn't know," I said. "But I'd wager that Vienna's cafés are far superior, if for no reason other than that they are open to ladies."

"You'll get no argument from me." Viktor took our orders and returned almost at once with our drinks.

"I mentioned to von Hofmannsthal that you liked his poem. He was quite pleased," Viktor said.

"I'm glad," I replied, looking around but not seeing the poet. "One of these days I shall have to meet him."

"I've no doubt that would please him. Do either of you require anything further?"

"No, thank you, Viktor," I said. He bowed and left us.

"Are you searching for a poet, Em? What would Colin say?"

"He wouldn't say a thing. I admire Herr von Hofmannsthal's work and nothing else. And at any rate, I've no time for the pursuit of poetry at the moment."

"Good, because I've no interest in discussing it." Jeremy wrapped his hands around his cup. "I don't know when I've been so happy to have hot coffee. How can you bear walking around in this city when it's so cold?"

"I rather like it. The air snaps me to attention. It's invigorating."

The count arrived as I was saying this. He raised an eyebrow when he saw Jeremy, but forced a smile on his face and greeted me with his usual *handküss*. "*Küss die Hand, gnädige Frau.* You have brought a protector with you?"

"She's in trouble if she's looking to me for protection," Jeremy said, crossing his legs and tipping back in his chair.

"I know I'd never need protection from you," I said, smiling sweetly at the count. "Particularly after you so generously offered to help me."

"You are an exquisite dancer, Lady Ashton. I was quite overwhelmed last night."

Jeremy choked on his coffee, then descended into a coughing fit. "Pardon me. It's extremely . . . hot."

I glared at him. "The Viennese waltz is the pinnacle of dance."

"You must stay for the Fasching," the count said.

"I'd love to, more than anything. But if I've not cleared my friend's name . . ."

"She can't abandon him," Jeremy said.

"Of course not. That is why I've extended to you my assistance. I apologize that my wife declined hers."

"I understand."

He leaned close to me and whispered so that Jeremy, who was pretending to read a newspaper, would not hear. "She does not want to let Hargreaves go." He tugged at his mustache. "Everyone here has a lover, Lady Ashton. It may offend your English sensibilities, but there is no use in pretending otherwise."

I needed to tread carefully now, and found doing so something of a challenge. I was not accustomed to this level of candor, particularly when it came to another woman's affection for my fiancée. "I'm not used to it, that's all."

"They've worked closely together for many years. It is hardly surprising that they were more than friends."

I wanted to ask him if he knew whether Colin had really proposed to her, and if so, when. Did he know how long the affair had lasted? I bit my lip. What I really longed to know, only Colin himself could tell me: Had he loved her? Why had he stopped? What did he feel for her now? My brief marriage had taught me very little about love. I hadn't felt even the slightest affection for my husband until after his death, yet I still sometimes felt an uncomfortable tug when I thought about Philip, knowing that I was now engaged to his best friend. In the end, when it was too late, I had grown to love him dearly.

But how much stranger would it be to have loved someone and stopped, not because of death, but because of something else? How would it feel to pass him on the street? To see him with another woman? When I thought about my love for Colin, it was inconceivable to me that one could have such strong emotions for a person only to have them fade away completely. Surely some tenderness lingered. And if it did . . . I hated to even think about it.

I pushed the thought from my mind. "Were you able to find anything?"

He pulled an envelope out of his coat pocket and placed it in my hands. "Schröder's associates. You did not get this from me. I included a small note, should anyone press you to tell what I handed you."

"*Danke vielmals*," I said. "No doubt we shall see each other again soon."

He kissed my hand. "I look forward with great intensity to our next meeting." And with that, he left the café.

"Shall I press you to tell?" Jeremy asked, dropping the newspaper onto the table. "I'd hate for his small note to go to waste. Pitiful excuse, Em. I'm not sure I approve of any of this, and I certainly don't trust him. He's the sort who gives us rakes a bad name."

"I won't let him cross any inappropriate boundaries." I ripped opened the envelope and pulled out two sheets of paper. The first, as promised, had a list of names and addresses. The second, a quote from Goethe's famous work *The Sorrows of Young Werther*:

> *Never have I moved so lightly. I was no longer a human being.*
> *To hold the most adorable creature in one's arms and fly around*
> *with her like the wind, so that everything around us fades*
> *away.*

Jeremy took the pages from me and read, then rolled his eyes. "Appalling, Em, appalling. The man is a disgrace. But at least he gave you addresses. Just make sure he doesn't try to extract any additional thanks from you."

"There's no need to worry. I danced with him five times last night. That's thanks enough."

"There's always cause to worry when you involve yourself with a man who is so quick to betray his wife."

"A rich criticism coming from you," I said. "I think he considers himself the wronged party," I said. "And as I'm Colin's fiancée, flirting with me is easy revenge."

"I suppose I'm only jealous, but still, I don't approve."

"When did you develop morals, Jeremy? I'm not sure I like it."

"Then I shall abandon them at once." His eyes sparkled. "With your permission, of course."

Friedrich walked into the café, a swirl of snow following him through the door. I waved him over at once. "Who is your friend?" he asked.

"Friedrich Henkler, meet Jeremy Sheffield, Duke of Bainbridge, Earl of Northam, Viscount Bridgewater. Am I forgetting any of your titles?"

"Scores of them," Jeremy said, shaking Friedrich's outstretched hand. "A pleasure. Coffee?" He flagged down Viktor, who brought Friedrich's usual beverage and a torte without having to be asked.

"I'm surprised there are so many people here today," I said. "I thought no one would want to fight the weather."

"No one wants to heat his apartment," Friedrich said, devouring his pastry.

"I understand you are soon to be the beneficiary of Lady Ashton's machinations," Jeremy said.

"Lady . . . oh, *ja*, Kallista." Jeremy raised an eyebrow as Friedrich nodded at me. "You promised not to set up a commission."

"This has nothing to do with art." I explained to him the plan Cécile and I had concocted. "She's meeting with Anna and her mother right now. If all goes as planned, you should be able to see her at the Imperial in another day or two."

"I cannot begin to express my gratitude," Friedrich said.

"Please don't try," Jeremy said. "I haven't the stomach for fawning this morning. Are you an artist?"

Friedrich nodded and passed his sketchbook across the table. Jeremy started to flip through it in his usual casual manner, but stopped after the first few pages.

"These are striking. So alive. I'm not much for art, you know. But this—this I like. Do you paint as well? Where's your studio?"

"I share one with four other artists. We're not far from Klimt's. You know his work?"

"Of course," Jeremy said. "Is your style similar to his?"

"Not at all. I'm afraid mine is rooted more in realism."

"I'd like to see your work, Mr. Henkler," Jeremy said. "I understand you did a magnificent sketch of Lady Ashton."

"It would be my pleasure to show you." Friedrich ripped a scrap of paper from his book and scratched an address on it. "If I'm not here, I'm at the studio."

"Well, I won't come until this dreadful snow has stopped. Tomorrow, perhaps? In the afternoon? Four o'clock?"

"Very good. I'll be waiting for you."

"We need to go," I said.

"So soon?" Jeremy asked. "I've only just got warm."

"You need better boots." I pulled on my coat and hat. "Friedrich, if I don't see you here tomorrow, I'll have the duke let you know when you should come to the Imperial."

"A million thanks, Kallista. Anna and I will be forever indebted to you."

Jeremy leaned close to me as we walked towards the door. "It's unexpectedly delightful to see you mingling with the masses."

"Why would you say such a thing? Do you object?"

"Not particularly. It's just surprising, that's all. He seems like a capital chap. Where are we going now?"

"To the first address on the count's list," I said. "It's a short walk from here. I looked at my map while you were discussing your new passion for art with Friedrich."

"I'm certain I don't agree with your definition of a short walk. Should I plan to freeze to death before we reach our destination?" We'd come to the front of the café, and he swung open the door, but I paused before exiting, distracted by the sight of someone sitting near the door, his face half hidden by a newspaper: Mr. Harrison.

"Coming?" Jeremy asked. "There's going to be a snowdrift inside if I don't close the door."

I followed him out, and we crossed the street. We'd gone less than a block when I knew that we were being followed.

"This isn't going to work," I said. I looked around and saw the elaborate tiles of the Stephansdom's roof, which was the only object in sight not covered with snow; the pitch was too steep to allow accumulation. I took Jeremy's hand and pulled him towards the church. "I've always wanted to see where Mozart was married."

Chapter 13

We ducked through a side door, disappointed to find that the massive Riesentor—the Giant's Door—was closed, and walked down the nave in the direction of the high altar at the opposite end of the cathedral. I sat on an empty pew.

"What are you doing?" Jeremy whispered.

"We're being followed."

"By whom?"

"Mr. Harrison."

"Is he in here?"

"I don't know." I looked around, but did not see him. "If he's not, he's waiting for us to come out."

"So are we to spend the rest of the morning in church?"

"It will be good for your soul, Jeremy." We sat quietly for approximately three minutes.

"I'm bored," he said.

"Your attention span is astonishing. I'll ask something that will amuse you. What do you think of the countess?"

"She's gorgeous, obviously, in that devastating, self-assured, sophisticated way," he said. "Smart too, from what I hear. An experienced woman of the world."

"A nightmare." I sighed.

"You're not jealous of her?"

"Maybe a bit."

"Does Hargreaves know?"

"No! Telling him would make me feel even less devastatingly sophisticated, self-assured, and experienced than I already do."

"You've no need for worry."

"I know. It's just—" I stopped. "We've known each other since we were babies, Jeremy. Can I speak freely?"

"Of course. Shock me at will."

"You're . . . experienced. Do you ever regret the loss of a former mistress?"

"Em, this is a conversation you do not want to have."

"I can't imagine that it's possible to simply stop loving someone."

"Most mistresses are just amusing games."

"I don't think Colin plays amusing games," I said, tipping my head back and looking at the vaulted ceiling.

"He's quite good at chess."

"You're not being helpful."

"No, and I can't be on this count," he said. "He's the only one who can ease your mind."

"I don't want him to think I doubt his fidelity."

"Do you doubt it?"

"No."

"Then why do you feel threatened by the countess?"

"Not because I think he would go back to her, but because I'm afraid that in comparison, he may find me a disappointment."

"Highly unlikely, darling."

"I'd very much like to believe you." I glanced around, but saw no sign of Mr. Harrison. "Do you think it's safe to leave?"

"Impossible to say."

"Perhaps we should just return to the Imperial."

"Let's stay here," Jeremy said. "As you said, it's good for my soul, and the morbid bit of me would like to see the relics."

"They have a piece of the tablecloth from the Last Supper."

"Right. Undoubtedly purchased from some dubious medieval merchant. Besides, I'm looking for bones."

"We could tour the catacombs," I said, and took him by the hand. We walked past Saint Valentine's chapel, which held the cathedral's reliquary, and headed straight for the catacombs, which we found inaccessible to tourists. Inaccessible, that is, until Jeremy made it worth the while of a caretaker in possession of a useful set of keys. He admitted us for a fee, and we found them dank and gruesome and everything one would want such a place to be.

"I hope my bones don't wind up heaped in a stack under some church," Jeremy said. "Or maybe I do. It's rather romantic down here."

"Romantic? Hardly. And I don't think you need fear for your bones. You couldn't keep them out of the family vault if you tried."

"Unless I run through my fortune and die penniless in Vienna."

"You're not profligate enough to manage that," I said. "But if by chance you somehow do become that corrupt, I promise to see to it myself that you have a shelf of your own down here. I won't have your skull piled in a heap."

"You are generosity itself. If only you'd be so kind to me while I'm still alive. Instead you're bent on breaking my heart."

"I didn't think you had a heart, Jeremy."

"Neither did I."

I caught no sign of Mr. Harrison when we left the Stephansdom. Even so, we returned to the Imperial before continuing our mission, taking extra care to be certain that he was no longer tailing us. While Cécile and I caught up on the events of the morning,

Jeremy spoke to the manager of the hotel, who quickly agreed to increase security near our rooms. After a quick luncheon, we set off again.

Before that afternoon, I had never seen neighborhoods like those found on the count's list. As a girl, I had accompanied my mother when she visited tenants on my father's estate, but their happy, well-tended cottages did nothing to prepare me for the dire conditions in which Vienna's poor lived. The houses aspired to the finery of those in the city's best neighborhoods, with corniced windows and elaborate decorative detail. But this did nothing to hide laundry hanging from windows, garbage strewn across sidewalks, the stench of decay defying the freezing temperatures, and gardens covered with soot from the factories that surrounded the area. Children dressed in little more than filthy rags ran through the streets when they should have been in cozy rooms eating something hot.

It took several hours for Jeremy and me to find all six addresses, our task made more difficult by the heavy snow. And when we did find them, Herr Schröder's compatriots, tucked in their dingy, cold houses, proved unwilling conversationalists.

"It was naïve of me to think they would talk," I said, stepping over a pile of hideous-smelling trash in an alley. "How could these people ever trust us when we allow them to live in these conditions?"

"It's hardly our fault."

"It will be should we do nothing to improve their plight." I looked across the street at a girl who was leaning against a building. Her dingy coat barely covered a threadbare dress, and she wore no gloves.

"Looking for someone, sir?" she asked, in English untouched by the slightest hint of an Austrian accent.

Jeremy tightened his grip on my arm and walked towards her. "Do you know Franz Kaufman?"

"Maybe." She winked at him. "But you'd have more fun with me."

My breath caught in my throat as I tried to look nonchalant.

"Shock your friend, did I? Or is it your wife?" She crinkled her nose. "Imagine a *gentleman* wouldn't bring his wife to this sort of neighborhood."

"Are you English?" I asked.

"My mother was."

Without thinking, I handed her my muff. "You must be freezing." She batted it away.

"I don't need no charity from you."

"Don't be a fool." Jeremy pushed it back at her. She smiled at him, revealing a surprisingly bright set of teeth.

"Why're you lookin' for Kaufman? He in trouble again?"

"What sort of trouble is he prone to?" I asked.

"Don't know that I could say," she said, burying her hands deep in the muff's fur. She stared at me for a moment, but the hardness in her eyes did not thaw. "Thank you."

"It's nothing," I said. "What's your name?"

"Rina."

"I'm Emily."

"*Lady* Emily Ashton?" she asked. I nodded. "There's a gent been around here inquiring about you. Harrison was his name."

"What does he want?" I asked.

"Best I know, he wants to find out who you're looking for. Word's gotten around that anyone who talks to you will face a heap of trouble."

"Are people scared of him?"

She shrugged. "Not really. They're more scared of Schröder. But I guess you know that. That's why you're here, isn't it?"

"Did he send you to watch me?" I asked.

She laughed. "I hate him more than anyone."

"Why?" I asked.

"Don't see why I should tell you."

"I'm looking for information that could save the life of an innocent man in England. Will you help me?" I asked.

She pursed her lips and blew out a long breath, then motioned towards Jeremy. "Is he going to protect me if I do?"

"Of course I will. You've my word as a gentleman." Jeremy gave her a quick but smart bow.

She laughed. "Don't know what good that is, but I'll take it just the same."

"Do you know Stefan Gross?" I asked. "I'm trying to find him. Or perhaps Jacob Reisner?"

"You're wasting your time with that crew. Schröder's the only one who knows anything. Do you know a *beisl* called Ofenloch? It's a restaurant two streets from here."

"Yes, I noticed it as we passed." Jeremy tugged at his gloves.

"He goes there most every night."

"Can you find out if he'll be there tomorrow?"

"I don't talk to him," she said. "He killed my father."

JEREMY WAS SILENT as we made our way back to the Imperial. "Are you all right?" I asked.

"There was something about that girl. . . . I don't know what it is . . . she looks so familiar, but I can't place her."

"Bainbridge!" Colin stepped across the Kärntner Ring in front of the hotel and shook Jeremy's hand before kissing mine. "Where the bloody hell have you had my fiancée all afternoon?" He kissed my hand again, his eyes full of teasing warmth.

"Oh, you know Em, she's been running me around all day in search of justice. Tedious girl. Don't know how you tolerate her." He looked at my face as he spoke, but did not meet my eyes.

"You're a beast, Jeremy. But thank you for accompanying me. I don't know what I'd do without you."

He stared down at his feet, then looked into my eyes. "Right, then. I'll be off if you're quite done with me." The moment he'd disappeared into the hotel, Colin pulled me close and kissed me.

"You're lovely with the snow falling all around you," he said. "But I'd best get you inside before you freeze." As we turned to the entrance, I saw Jeremy standing in the doorway, watching us. He saw me looking at him and came back out, his face red as he rushed past us and made his way down the street. I called out to him, but he did not stop. Colin grabbed my arm when I started to follow.

"Let him go."

"But I—"

"This is difficult enough for him, Emily."

"You don't think that he—" I stopped, looked after him. "No, Colin. You're wrong."

"Believe what you want, my dear, but this is one case where I know better than you."

Chapter 14

"Maudlin," Cécile said, tossing aside a collection of Goethe's poetry. We were in the sitting room of our suite, taking tea. "I much prefer something French." Odette, singing a mournful-sounding aria, came in with our mail, which she handed to Cécile. "Nothing from England for you today?" she asked her maid.

Odette did not reply, only increased the volume of her song as she disappeared into her mistress's bedroom.

"You see what I suffer?" Cécile said. "Your butler is ruining my peace of mind."

"I can accept that so long as Klimt is keeping you happy," I said.

"I like him because he has no expectations. We're perfectly suited to each other, at least for the moment."

"What about after the moment?"

"Why would I bother to even begin thinking about that? I'm not looking for a grand passion, Kallista. I had that once and don't want to suffer through it again."

"You've never told me this," I said. "Who was it? I know not your husband."

"*Non*, not him. It was a long time ago, but not long enough that I'm ready to think about him again."

"Do you still love him?"

"*Non*."

"Not at all?"

"Perhaps a very little bit. That's the trouble with grand passions, *bien sûr*. You can never entirely cleanse yourself of them. It's best to avoid them altogether."

"So who was this grand passion?" I asked.

"Someday I will tell you the story, but no time soon. It's too frustrating."

"I don't like to see you frustrated," Colin said, coming into the room.

"You, Monsieur Hargreaves, are divine." She offered him her hand, which he kissed before sitting next to me. "Not only to say that, but to come in at the exact moment I want the subject of our conversation changed."

"I'm glad to be of service, and you, madame, are enchanting as always." He accepted the tea she poured for him. "I've figured out Harrison's game, and the stakes are higher than I thought."

"What is it?" I asked.

"He's trying to draw England into a war with Germany. A few years ago he was involved in a failed plot to persuade the crown prince to overthrow his father."

"Rudolf?" I asked. Colin nodded.

"Obviously nothing came of it. The goal had been to see the prince, who was much less sympathetic to the kaiser than his father, on the throne. Rudolf would then abandon Germany and ally Austria with England and France. Fortescue was always opposed to the scheme, so far as I can tell. Didn't think it particularly mattered who Austria is allied with."

"Did you know that Rudolf wrote pieces for *Wiener Tagblatt*?" Cécile asked.

"The newspaper?" I asked.

"*Oui*. A very liberal newspaper."

"What did the emperor think of that?" I asked.

"I don't believe he knew," Colin said. "Did he?"

"He did not," Cécile said. "Rudolf published under the name Szeps. His father would not have agreed with much, if any, of what he wrote."

"So Harrison and his crew tried to convince him to stage a coup?" I asked.

"Yes," Colin said. "But they failed."

"How would this lead to war now?" Cécile asked.

"Germany is becoming increasingly aggressive in her nationalism, and there are many who believe war is inevitable," Colin said. "Harrison seems to have abandoned his plan to gain Austria's support and is instead trying to instigate some sort of incident that will precipitate a major conflict between nations."

"But that makes no sense," I said. "First he thought we needed Austria's support, now he doesn't?"

"He knows he won't get it. So he believes we should fight now, before Germany and her allies grow more powerful."

"Are you quite certain nothing came of his earlier plot?" I told them about the letter I'd seen on the empress's desk. "From what I read, it sounded as if the French and English were involved with Mayerling."

"It's possible that Harrison has a French ally," Colin said.

"Could you ask the empress about it, Cécile?"

She sighed. "I don't think it is a good idea. She's fragile, and dredging this up will only cause her more pain."

"But if she's looking into the matter herself—," I began.

"So far as I know, she's learned nothing new in more than a year. And before that, she learned almost nothing. She's a mother grieving the loss of a child and is desperate for there to be an explanation more significant than a lovers' suicide pact."

"But what if she's right, and what if we could find the truth?" I asked.

"Right now we need to focus on Harrison and Brandon," Colin said. "If what happened at Mayerling is related, we'll figure it out. But I don't think it's necessary to disturb the empress at this point."

"Lord Fortescue controlled those around him with blackmail. If he had evidence that Mr. Harrison had anything to do with the crown prince's death—"

"—Fortescue would have absolute control over him," Colin finished for me.

"And now that Fortescue is dead, Mr. Harrison is free to pursue his agenda," I said. "How convenient for him."

"Harrison didn't kill Fortescue. He was standing next to me when we were shooting."

"He might have hired someone else to do it," I said.

"Possibly." Colin nodded, but his face revealed not the slightest hint of agreement. "But I find it hard to believe that an assassin would use a dueling pistol from his victim's house."

"Why not? It makes it look like an ordinary murder," I said.

"An ordinary murder? You're becoming entirely too corrupt, my dear."

"Isn't that why you love her?" Cécile asked.

"Among other things." He smiled.

"I've read enough sensational novels to know that it's perfectly reasonable to begin a murder investigation by ascertaining what individuals benefit from the victim's death," I said. "Clearly Mr. Harrison has benefited. Robert has not."

"They believe his motive was anger, not that he stood to gain something," Colin said.

"You don't believe that he's guilty, do you, Monsieur Hargreaves?" Cécile asked.

"Of course not. But Emily wouldn't be happy if she didn't have someone playing devil's advocate."

"No one else at Beaumont Towers stood to gain from Lord Fortescue's murder. Poor Mary's going to once again be dismissed from her home," I said. There was a small dowager's house on the estate, and it was to there that she would be banished once her husband's eldest son descended to collect his inheritance.

"Harrison is a likely suspect, but if we're to consider the murder as assassination, we need to look at all of Fortescue's political enemies."

"All of Britain and most of the Continent," I said.

"Unfortunately close to the truth." He had stopped pacing and rubbed his forehead. "I'll see what I can dig up." He kissed me quickly and nodded at Cécile. "I must go. I've an appointment I cannot miss. Will I see you tomorrow?"

As had become my habit, I went to the Griensteidl early the next morning, and spent more than an hour happily studying Greek and drinking hot chocolate. I'd neglected my studies since Robert's arrest, and even now felt pangs of guilt at being so pleasantly employed when my friend was suffering in Newgate. Friedrich was sitting with me, reading classified ads from the newspaper out loud.

"'To the exquisite lady sitting in the Café Griensteidl with a male escort yesterday: she had the kindness to hand a copy of the magazine *Kikeriki* in a most sympathetic manner to a gentleman at a neighboring table, and would do said gentleman an even more incalculable kindness by indicating to Box 672, this newspaper, when and at what café he would be allowed to hand a *Kikeriki* to her.'" He gulped his coffee. "Was it you?"

"Me? Hardly."

"I sat with you for a while yesterday. I was hoping that I'd made it into the paper—even if only as your escort."

"Did you see me hand a magazine to anyone?"

"No." He looked back at the paper, smiling to himself. I returned to my Greek until my companion jumped up from his chair. "I'll leave you to her," he said.

"What?" I asked, starting to call after him, but stopping as the Countess von Lange, dressed to stunning effect in a crimson gown, slipped into the chair he'd just left. She was holding a coffee cup full to the brim, but she moved with such grace that she did not spill a drop.

"I understand you've been meeting with my friend Gustav Schröder. I told him to speak freely to you."

"Does he need your permission?"

"No, but I've convinced him to trust you."

"That's very good of you. I owe you more than thanks."

"Your debt is already paid. You care more for your friend than I guessed."

"And you are less selfish than I expected."

She laughed. "Not at all. Colin came to me last night." I wished I could will away the color flooding my cheeks. "You are uncomfortable?"

"Not at all." She couldn't be telling the truth. I didn't believe for an instant that he'd gone to her after he'd left me. Yet even as I began running through the reasons that I would never doubt him, a nagging, searing feeling shot through my stomach. The countess was nothing short of an exquisite beauty, a person to whom Colin had, at some point, felt a strong attraction. I trusted him, but not her. Just how persuasive could she be?

"You'll find, I think, that marriages invariably wind up tedious. Best that you learn that before you march down the aisle. I can see you're pained now, but it will pass, especially if you keep yourself distracted."

"You're quite mistaken. I wouldn't have agreed to marry if I thought the result would be tedious."

"Is he amused by your naïveté, I wonder? Surely not. He's far too sophisticated for that. You are quite pretty in an innocuous sort of way. I can see that he would find you attractive, even if he is used to someone more—" She paused and smiled. "Well, no need to discuss that."

"No, there's not. Will you excuse me?" I was not about to sit and listen to more of her nonsense. I pulled on my coat and went outside. The snow had stopped, and the sun had burned away the clouds, but the air was colder than it had been since I'd arrived in Vienna, and a wicked wind nearly knocked me over. Strong arms kept me from falling.

"You must be more careful, Lady Ashton." Mr. Harrison's hat was pulled low over his face.

"Let me pass," I said. He gripped my arm tightly as he forced me across the street and into a narrow alley.

"I've been hoping to have a conversation with you. Your fiancé is asking impertinent questions."

"Is he getting too close to the truth?"

He swung me around, slamming me into the wall of a building. "If anything interferes with my plans, he will suffer for it."

"Unhand me." I spoke through gritted teeth, equal measures terrified and outraged. No one had ever touched me like this. I could not help recalling the calm manner in which Herr Schröder had admitted to killing when necessary. Would Mr. Harrison do the same? Fear seized me.

He shook my shoulders. My head banged against the brick wall, and for an instant I could hardly see. "You will stop him."

"You're a fool if you think I could keep him from his duty," I said, the very core of my body shaking.

"You're a clever girl. Find a way to distract him, or he will be eliminated." He shoved me against the wall again, then stepped away and brushed something from the sleeve of his coat. "I will be keeping a close eye on you. And don't forget that I can reach you anywhere." He flung a bullet at me and walked away.

I watched him go, but was unable to summon the courage to order any of my limbs to move and follow him. Instead, my knees buckled, and I sank along the wall until I was crouched in the snow, my teeth chattering uncontrollably, my breath coming fast and ragged, tears freezing on my cheeks.

"Emily!" Jeremy came racing out of nowhere. He lifted me to my feet, then tore off his gloves and wiped my tears with his bare hands.

"How did you find me?"

"I was looking for you in the Griensteidl. The countess told me you'd gone outside. What happened?"

"I—I—" I could not slow my breathing enough to speak.

"It doesn't matter." He embraced me, his arms clutching too tightly, and I buried my head in his chest. He smelled like tobacco and peppermint, and with my eyes closed, I could almost imagine I was a little girl, safe in my father's arms. But then he pulled away, and looked at me with wild eyes. "Em . . ."

He kissed me, hungrily, with a raw passion that terrified and excited me. I had not the presence of mind to stop him.

"Bloody hell, Em, forgive me." He pulled away, then closed his eyes and buried his face in his hands. "You can't forgive me. It's unforgivable." He rubbed his temples. "I only wanted to comfort you, I never meant—"

"It's all right." I was too overwhelmed to care, and of the affronts I had suffered that day, this was the least troublesome, at least for the moment. "Will you take me back to the Imperial?"

"Of course." He hesitated before taking me by the arm, as if he weren't sure whether he should touch me at all, and led me out of the alley, flagging down the first fiacre that passed. We did not speak until we'd reached the hotel and were standing at the bottom of the magnificent stairway that led to my rooms.

"It might be best if you took Hargreaves with you to meet Schröder tonight."

"He's working. But Cécile and I could—"

"No. You can't go into that neighborhood unprotected. I'll come." For the first time I could remember, I saw no hint of laughter or joy in his eyes.

JEREMY ESCORTED ME TO MY SUITE, insisted that I see a doctor, and waited, standing near the fireplace in one of our parlors, to hear the diagnosis. Satisfied that I was not seriously hurt—a mild concussion, but nothing to cause alarm—he left when the physician did.

The moment they were gone, Cécile rapped her fan on the marble-topped table that stood next to the chaise longue on which we were sitting. "This has become too dangerous. The man could have killed you."

"He wouldn't kill me. If I were dead, I couldn't do anything to stop Colin's investigation."

"Monsieur Hargreaves would agree with me. No unnecessary danger, Kallista. We should leave Vienna."

"Not until we've either found out who sent Lord Fortescue the warning or uncovered Harrison's plot," I said.

"Leave it to Monsieur Hargreaves."

"No, Cécile. He's been sent here for a specific reason. And though I don't know the details, I do know it's not to find information that can exonerate Robert."

"He's perfectly capable of doing that along with whatever his mission is."

"But I'm perfectly capable, too. More than capable, in fact. And

I like doing this, Cécile. I'll be careful. There's no need to worry."

"You are taking Jeremy with you to meet Schröder?"

"Yes," I said. "Although I'm not certain it's a good idea."

"What can that mean?" Cécile's talent for picking up on any sort of romantic signals was unparalleled.

"Something happened after he found me this morning." I described for her every detail of what transpired between us.

"*Mon dieu!* Well, I won't have to worry about you then. He's enough in love with you that he can be counted on to keep you from being harmed. Still, I'm going to accompany you as well. I'm curious about this anarchist. Any man with passionate beliefs is worth knowing."

"I'd wager that he's over forty, Cécile. He might even be fascinating. What would Klimt say?"

"Very little," she said, smiling wickedly.

22 December 1891
Berkeley Square, London

Dear Emily,

I've been feeling vaguely useless, stranded here in London, unable to offer Ivy much in the way of comfort or relief, horribly jealous that you and Cécile are once again charged with the interesting tasks.

For once, I have an interesting tidbit for you: I've learned that the gun used to kill Lord Fortescue has been misplaced. It somehow never made it from Yorkshire to London. Suspicious? Of course it is! Disappearing murder weapons are always significant.

How was your intrepid friend able to persuade Scotland Yard to divulge this information? Mr. Michaels (who's down from Oxford on the unlikely errand of Christmas shopping at this late date) is closely acquainted with a member of the police force who slipped and mentioned it when they were having a lunch that included several bottles of very expensive wine. Must be kept quiet, of course—it's not something they've told the general public—but I thought you should know.

The weather is dreadful here, and Robert must be suffering more than ever in Newgate. Ivy is unwell—I think you know why—and though I know she'll be all right, I'm worried, Emily. She's gaunt. I know you are doing all you can, but I must implore you to hurry. Nothing is good here.

I am yrs., etc.,
Margaret

Chapter 15

I may have reacted in the most casual sort of manner to Jeremy's kiss, but in fact it had unsettled me. My mind was so cluttered with troubling emotions I could hardly form a coherent thought. The kiss itself did little more than give me pause; it had come in a heated, raw moment, and I felt no guilt about it. Jeremy was a consummate flirt. But had this kiss meant something to him?

I had several hours before we were due to meet Herr Schröder and was desperate to talk to Colin. I hesitated to walk alone after my encounter with Mr. Harrison, so took a fiacre. Cécile offered to go with me, but I wanted to be alone with Colin, and neither of us saw danger in the trip so long as I took a carriage. As I neared the house that contained my fiancé's apartment, I saw the countess leaving the building. She chatted familiarly with the *Hausmeister* while he held the door for her. I supposed they were old friends. Not in the mood for confrontation, I ordered the driver to stop where we were, and I ducked out of the open carriage and across the street into a *Durchhäuser*, one of the many passageways that ran through the courtyards behind houses in the city. The air was still bitter cold, but I welcomed the burning as I drew it into my lungs. It felt like painful purification. I peeked out and did not see Kristiana. Perhaps she had hired the fiacre I'd abandoned and gone home.

Wanting to be certain she had left, I counted to two hundred in Greek, then paused. Another hundred, and I was too cold to delay any longer.

Colin's rooms were on the fifth floor, but I bounded up the stairs, barely noticing the effort it took. He opened the door himself when I knocked, and I fell into his arms the moment I saw him.

"What is it?" he asked, sitting me down in a singularly uncomfortable chair. I tried sitting forward, then sitting back, then teetering on the edge, but nothing made it better. "Awful, isn't it? All the furniture's that way. Apologies."

"It's fine." I stared at him before continuing, relishing every line on his face, wishing I could lose myself forever in the warmth of his eyes. This was not the first time I'd been inclined to throw myself on him and beg for assistance. Not that I wanted to stop my investigation or for him to take it over. But in difficult moments, the lure of a strong shoulder and an offer of protection are potent temptations.

"Emily?" He was standing in front of me, arms crossed. "What is it?"

"I love you because you challenge me, because you see my potential and want me to reach it." My head had begun to throb. Or had it been throbbing all along, and I hadn't noticed?

"You don't have to be strong all the time." He tugged at one of my curls. "I can, occasionally, be of some use, you know."

"I know that." I picked up his hand and kissed his palm. I would take his comfort, but I would never ask him to take care of me.

"You haven't told me what happened today."

"I had a rather serious encounter with Mr. Harrison." I described in detail everything that had transpired. The first thing

Colin did was feel the back of my head, searching for and finding the large lump that had developed on it.

"Have you seen a doctor? Let me call someone."

"I did already. It's fine. No need to worry."

"Do you feel ill?" he asked, his hand now resting on my shoulder.

"No, though I do have a rather spectacular headache."

"My dear girl." He kissed my forehead.

"I'm worried about Schröder's threat against you," I said, looking into his dark eyes.

"It's nothing. He can't harm me, and he knows it. He's only trying to scare you." He sat in a chair across from me, pulling it close so that he could hold my hand. His grip was tight, his expression serious. "I'm much more concerned about what Harrison's done to you. I can't have you hurt."

"I'll have to be more careful about going places alone."

"You'll have to stop doing it entirely," he said. "It's an unnecessary risk. Can you count on Bainbridge to accompany you when you need him?"

"Yes, of course." I spoke rather too quickly, immediately feeling nervous and wanting to redirect the conversation. "I'm still worried about you. I think you're a bit too cavalier about your own safety. Why couldn't Schröder hurt you?"

"Because, my dear, I am at least four times as clever as he, and I've dealt with adversaries more sinister than he can ever hope to be. I can take care of myself."

"But—"

"In my line of work this sort of thing falls in the realm of the ordinary. You needn't worry." I did not reply. He was unnervingly calm, not flustered in the least to have his life threatened. I couldn't imagine anyone could be so immune to such a thing, regardless of his line of work. "I'm sorry, Emily, I can see you're troubled. I can't expect that this won't be hard for you, but I don't want to have to shelter you from these things."

"I'd never want that," I said, knowing it to be true, but wishing that it weren't so difficult. "My head hurts, that's all."

"I'm so sorry." He placed a gentle hand on my cheek, leaned forward, and kissed me. "You're going to try to see Schröder tonight?"

"Yes. I've no illusions about him giving me information about his plot. I only want to determine whether it's possible he has ties to Britain."

"I've a meeting at the Hofburg, or I'd come with you. You're taking Bainbridge?"

"Yes." Jeremy again. I bit my lip, debating whether to tell Colin about the kiss. Honesty is, in theory, always the right choice. But what good could come of full disclosure in this situation? I remained silent, wondering if I was setting a bad precedent.

"Good. He'll keep you safe." The easy manner with which he said this cut, filling me with guilt. Lying, even by omission, didn't come easily to me. "I wish I could do it myself."

"So do I," I said, again feeling the urge to change the subject. "The Countess von Lange tells me she's a friend of Herr Schröder's. Do you know what their connection is?" I asked.

"I didn't know they had one."

"Are you certain that you can trust her, Colin? I say that not as your fiancée but as your colleague."

"Together we've faced difficult foes, and she's never once let me down."

"But is the situation different now?" I asked, unable to meet his eyes.

"Because I've left her? You think she's a woman scorned?"

"No, I don't think she'd allow herself to be scorned." I had to tread carefully here, or I would look like a jealous society girl. "But she knows Schröder. Why doesn't she find out for us what we need to know? She wouldn't even give me the names of his compatriots. I don't expect her to befriend me, but—"

"Did it occur to you that she might be acting like this to give you room to solve things for yourself? How would you feel if she were to swoop in and save Robert?"

"It wouldn't trouble me in the least so long as he was out of Newgate."

"I don't think that's true, Emily. Maybe she's helping you more than you know. Her husband brought you the list of names, correct?" I nodded. "Do you really believe that he got it without her knowledge? She's far too careful to allow such a thing."

"I'll defer to your judgment this time. Don't, however, expect me to make a habit of it." I wanted to ask him if he'd seen her the previous night, why she'd come to him this afternoon. I wanted to further question his faith in her. But if I were to keep my small secret from him, I could hardly expect him to divulge everything to me. I trusted him enough to allow him secrets of his own.

That said, if the countess had dropped suddenly off the face of the earth, I would have felt very little regret. A person's maturity can only be expected to go so far.

THAT EVENING WE TOOK a fiacre to the Ofenloch, leaving the classic elegance of the Ringstrasse behind us and descending into the grimy neighborhoods where Herr Schröder's associates lived. If they were dingy during the day, they were darkly terrifying at night, when the figures that stepped out of shadows would be unidentifiable until they were too close to escape from, even by running. Jeremy sat across from Cécile and me, keeping quiet and looking sullen the whole way.

"I have never seen you so dull," Cécile said, leaning forward and poking him with her walking stick. "Have you grown tired of protecting hapless females when you could be courting a mistress?"

How I wished she'd said anything but that.

"I find doing anything on behalf of hapless females tedious—

not that it stops me, mind you. But though Emily could be described as many things, hapless is not one of them."

I smiled at him, but he did not look at me. Instead, he was staring intently at his gloves.

"I cannot have you glum," Cécile said. "It is intolerable. I spent the entire afternoon with Friedrich and Anna and cannot stand even one instant more of romantic angst."

"Angst?" I asked. "I thought they were blissfully happy?"

"Oh they are, *chérie*. Until they remember that their time together is limited. Then it's all weeping and sighing and—" She stopped and shrugged.

"I can assure you, Madame du Lac, that there is no angst of any form in this carriage tonight," Jeremy said.

Cécile reached over and took his hand. "I'm so glad, *mon ami*. I was afraid you had decided to never flirt with me again." She winked at him, and he laughed.

"Far from it," he said, kissing her hand. "You're irresistible."

"And old enough to be your mother," she said. "I begin to care less and less that you are not so handsome as Monsieur Hargreaves."

"Coming from you, madame, that is a compliment of the highest order." The carriage slowed as we reached our destination. Jeremy paid the driver and helped us down from our seats. The street was filthy, and a man stumbling in an intoxicated blur nearly knocked into me as we made our way to the door of the Ofenloch. Jeremy steered me to safety with a firm arm, a thin smile on his face. I wanted to make a teasing remark about him rescuing me, but no longer felt I could do such a thing. My head hurt all the more at the realization of this.

The inside of the tavern was not at all what I had expected, particularly given its surroundings. An enormous fireplace filled the room with a cozy warmth, and boisterous laughter came from the patrons who occupied nearly every table. There was a bright energy about the place, a sort of sincerity in the atmosphere that I hadn't often felt.

"There's Rina," Jeremy said, walking towards her without pausing to make sure we were following. When he reached her, he bowed as carefully as he would have at a party at Buckingham Palace. He kissed her hand, and she blushed, her expression turning hard the moment Cécile and I reached them.

"I brought your muff," she said, grabbing it from a chair and thrusting it at me. She was wearing what must have been her best dress, a carefully constructed copy of last year's latest fashion. The material, a soft wool, claret-colored, was worn but well cared for.

"I meant for you to keep it," I said, hoping this would not embarrass her. She looked at me through narrow eyes.

"I s'pose you've got so many you won't miss one?"

"Not at all." I had no desire to flaunt my wealth. "But it looks lovely with your hair and ought to be yours."

"Then I guess I might as well keep it." She tried to glare at me, but I could see in the dim light that her eyes were shining, just a bit. "Who's your friend?"

"I am Cécile du Lac." She shook the girl's hand and sat down at the table. "What shall we eat? I'm famished."

This seemed to take Rina by surprise, as she jumped and looked at Jeremy, who sat across from Cécile, next to the chair where the muff had been. "Schnitzel, I imagine."

"It's the best in Austria," Rina said, taking the chair next to Jeremy. "I didn't think you would want to eat."

"It is rather late," Jeremy said, meeting her eyes. "But I assumed that you were sending us somewhere worth the wait."

Cécile looked at me and raised an eyebrow.

"Is Herr Schröder here yet?" I asked.

"*Ja.*" The voice came from behind me, and I suddenly wished I were seated with my back to the wall. He stepped forward. "Come sit over here with me, Kallista."

Jeremy gave me a questioning look and Rina glared at Herr

Schröder, who took not the slightest notice of her. I flashed an uneasy smile to Jeremy before sitting at a table near enough that he could keep an eye on me.

"I feel lucky to have tracked you down," I said in German.

"I'm not pleased Rina told you where to find me. I didn't think we had anything else to discuss," he answered in English.

"You're wrong." I did not switch to my native tongue. A waitress deposited tall glasses of beer in front of us. "I know about your plans, and so does the British government."

He laughed and replied in German. "I do like you, Kallista. You're full of spirit. Misguided, but entertaining nonetheless."

"So you're not hoping to assassinate the kaiser in spectacular fashion and blame England for it?" He did not reply. I'd spent no short time planning what to say to him, how to trick him into confessing something, and bluffing seemed my best—if not only—option. I'd decided it was reasonable to surmise that if anarchists were planning something during the kaiser's visit, a dramatic murder would be at the top of their agenda. "I need you to help me find out who warned Fortescue. In exchange, I will provide you with England's plans to thwart your attack."

"You have no way of learning such a thing."

"Do not underestimate women, Herr Schröder. You'd be shocked how loose a man's grip on his secrets becomes when he's with his mistress."

He laughed louder and slapped the table with his palm. "I'm to believe that you're stealing state secrets from a lover?"

"Yes." I looked at him with a level stare.

"A lover or your fiancé?"

"Does it matter?"

"It might." He drained his glass with astonishing speed and motioned for the waitress to bring another.

"I'm aware of much more than you give me credit for. You un-

doubtedly know about Mr. Harrison's escapades at Beaumont Towers? That he stole papers from Lord Fortescue's room? I believe
they had to do with your plans?"

He flinched, and I knew my deduction was correct. How I
wished I'd been able to see the papers! I was beginning to enjoy
this.

"Did you know that Fortescue accused me of taking them?" I
asked, swigging my own beer and trying to ignore its bitter taste.
"You would do better to ally yourself with me than Harrison. Harrison sought my assistance in England, then double-crossed me.
What makes you think he won't do the same to you?"

"I'm beginning to think this isn't all fantasy on your part. Harrison—"

"Harrison attacked me this morning. He wouldn't do that if I
didn't threaten him."

"He's not concerned about you, it's Hargreaves who worries
him."

"I have access to everything my fiancé knows."

"And I'm to believe you'd double-cross him?"

"The Countess von Lange is his mistress. He'd sworn to me
that he'd broken it off with her." I paused, bit my lip, and lowered
my eyes, hoping that I looked wounded. "I learned this morning
that he has not."

"Kristiana?" The familiar way her name tripped off his tongue
and the flash of anger in his eyes were telling.

"I've been told you know her well, but it seems your acquaintance is . . . closer than I realized. I do hope you've been careful. She'd
be all too willing to share your secrets with Mr. Hargreaves."

"That is none of your concern." He drained his second
beer.

I shrugged. "Everything she does is my concern so long as
he's betraying me with her." My nerves were beginning to lose
the steel I'd tried so hard to inject into them. Acknowledging in

a semi-public fashion that Colin had been unfaithful to me stung, even if it was not true, and I realized that this was partially due to my suspicion that Kristiana was doing everything in her not inconsequential power to tempt him.

My cheeks grew hot, and I feared that my companion would catch my lie. Instead, he misinterpreted what he saw.

"You're angry, aren't you? Can you prove to me that you have access to Hargreaves's information?"

"Of course I can," I said, filled with uncertainty, hoping upon hope that Colin would help me with this.

He pulled a piece of paper and a pencil out of his jacket pocket and scrawled something on it before handing it to me. "We must do this privately. I can be found at this address every afternoon between two and five. Bring me something as soon as you can that will prove you're telling the truth."

This time he spoke to me in German.

23 December 1891
Darnley House, Kent

My dear daughter,

I have heard the most outrageous thing from Lady Elliott. She claims that you visited Robert Brandon at Newgate. I tell you this not to send you scurrying to ease my mind on the subject, but to offer you a bit of amusement.

Your father and I are going to Balmoral after Christmas and I am beside myself that you will not be able to join us. Perhaps, though, Mme du Lac has arranged for you to spend time with the Hapsburgs. I am delighted to learn that you have been presented to the empress! She is an eccentric woman, but much to be admired. If she takes a liking to you, I wonder if she might be persuaded to come to your wedding. Imagine if you had her in addition to the queen! Your father once met the tsarevitch, Nicholas, of Russia. I wonder, if we set our minds to it, if we could have a guest list superior to that of Princess Louise when she married that abominable German prince last summer.

Oh, my dear Emily, you know how pleased I am at your engagement, but when I think of the tsarevitch, who is not yet married, I must say that you should have tried harder for a royal match. Such a thing is always difficult for a commoner, but a girl of your wealth and beauty could have tempted a prince. Not, mind you, that I mean any disrespect to your dear, departed husband.

Do write soon and tell me all about the parties in Vienna. Lady Paget says the atmosphere is hideous there, and that the balls are poorly organized. Hardly surprising. But I am glad you are enjoying the pleasure of such high company. It was wise of you to leave England with this scandal of the Brandons brewing. I fear for poor Ivy. No one will marry the widow of a murderer.

Prince Eddy's marriage to May is set for the twenty-seventh of February. I have already told the queen you will be there.

I am your loving mother,
C. Bromley

Chapter 16

Mr. Harrison's presence everywhere I turned had become more and more unsettling. Cécile and I were in our sitting room at the Imperial—a lovely space, furnished in Louis XVI antiques—ostensibly chaperoning Friedrich and Anna, who were leaning extremely close together on a sofa. I'd planned to work on my Greek, but was too distracted to think. When I went to my bedroom to collect my books, I found a bullet resting on top of them. When I returned to the sitting room, I gave it to Cécile, who was suitably horrified.

"What are we going to do about this, *chérie*?" she asked.

"I don't know. Obviously the hotel's increased security measures aren't enough."

"This is dreadful, Kallista," she said, the bullet still in her hand.

"Beyond imagining. But we cannot be daunted. Terrified, yes, but daunted, no."

"Robert Brandon is lucky to count you among his friends," Cécile said.

"There's no fear I would not face to save him." Strong words that were not matched by a calm demeanor. I sat on my hands to keep them from shaking.

Cécile straightened her shoulders and raised an eyebrow. "I'm going to ask Sissi to send someone from the palace. We need a better guard."

"*Merci*," I said.

"And in the meantime, I will not allow this despicable man to torment us. I will distract you. You do realize that Christmas is in two days?"

"I'm not feeling particularly inclined to celebrate," I said, wondering when Mr. Harrison would tire of leaving bullets and decide instead to shoot them.

"We will have a small party here." Cécile was holding Caesar on her lap while Brutus stared up at her with longing eyes. I took pity on the dog and picked him up, regretting it at once as he began to gnaw on my lace cuffs.

"Must we?" I returned the dog to the floor and gave him a biscuit.

"I've invited Klimt. Monsieur Hargreaves, of course, and Jeremy. Friedrich has nowhere else to go, and it might be amusing if you could convince Monsieur Schröder to join us. I was thinking of telling Jeremy to ask Rina."

"Rina?"

"*Oui*. I think he's fond of her. Do you object?"

"Of course not. I'm just surprised. Are you sure?"

"They were quite friendly when you were meeting with Schröder at the restaurant. And yesterday I overhead him having an earnest discussion about houses in a neighborhood not far from here."

"You think he's going to take a house in Vienna? Why would he do that?" I asked.

"Not for himself. For her."

"Surely not!"

"I confronted him about it. He's concerned for her safety. You've seen the neighborhood in which she lives, Kallista."

"Yes, it's dreadful," I said. "He's right to try to take her out of it. I just don't—"

"You're shocked at the thought that he might make her his mistress."

"No! I—" I paused. "Yes, I am. And I'm ashamed of myself."

"Is it because of her class?"

"No, it's just . . . such a blatant thing to do. And it ruins her while it saves her. There must be a better way."

"It is preferable to leaving her in a slum, don't you think?"

"Of course." And it was, but it did not sit well with me for a host of reasons I did not entirely comprehend. "I suppose he won't see her often. It's not as if he often travels to the Continent—"

"Are you jealous?" Cécile asked.

"Not in the least!" I said. "I just . . . I've never before known someone who's done such a thing."

"You undoubtedly know many gentlemen who've set up households for women. But until now, you were blissfully unaware of it."

"I'm not sure that makes me feel better, Cécile."

Cécile looked over at Friedrich and Anna. "What can we do to convince her parents that they should be married?"

"I don't know," I said. "I'm afraid I've given the subject sadly little thought. It's not that I don't wish to help them—"

"You do not have the luxury of focusing on such pleasantly challenging endeavors at the moment. I spoke to Klimt about the university murals. It will be two years at least before anyone will be given the commission. And the fact is, it's unlikely that it will be awarded to anyone but Klimt and his brother."

"Poor Friedrich. There must be something that we can do."

"Leave our young lovers to me. I will see them engaged before we leave Vienna."

"I'll leave you to it," I said.

——

MY FIANCÉ WAS WAITING for me when I arrived at the Griensteidl. Jeremy had come with me, but did not go inside, only checked
to make sure Colin was there. I nodded to Viktor to indicate that
I wanted my usual and dropped into a chair, beginning to feel my
nerves calm the moment I breathed in the rich smell of coffee. I
might not like to drink it, but its scent provided instant comfort,
undoubtedly because the Griensteidl had started to feel like home.

"This paper," he said, waving a copy of the *Neue Freie Presse* in
front of me. "It's outrageous the way they report on every detail of
suicides in the city, almost as if they're sport. One more spectacular
than the next."

"I wonder if it encourages people?" I asked, pulling off my
gloves and removing my hat, glad to be discussing something other
than Mr. Harrison and Herr Schröder, even if only for a moment.

"There's a strange culture of death in Vienna. You should see
the parades of people leaving flowers in the cemeteries on All Saints'
Day. The *Neue Freie Presse* runs lengthy critiques of what's left at
famous graves. Did Beethoven get better flowers than Schubert?"

"Friedrich told me about that," I said, tucking a stray curl behind my ear. "Morbid."

"Of course many of the suicides end up in the Friedhof der
Namenlosen, the Cemetery of the Nameless. A bleak, unhappy
place."

"But full of flowers and devout prayer on All Souls' Day," I said.
"Lady Paget says that even the children here throw themselves in
the Danube if they can't do their schoolwork. She's exaggerating,
I'm sure, but it's all so very different from England."

"Where none of it would ever be spoken of."

"Precisely," I said. "Though I'm not sure if that's entirely a bad
thing."

"How was your meeting with Schröder?"

"I'm afraid I got a bit carried away."

"How so?" Colin asked, and I described for him exactly what had happened. "You have quite a flair for this, my dear. You've no fear at all, do you?" He reached across the table and squeezed my hand.

"It was rather thrilling," I said, feeling a creeping flush of excitement along with a sigh of relief. I'd been afraid that he'd be angry at being put in what could be considered an awkward situation. "I hope you don't object to my giving your mistress back to you."

"I couldn't care less what Schröder thinks of me so long as it does not trouble you."

"I'll tolerate you living a debauched double life so long as it's fictional. But I'm afraid I may have overstepped my bounds, offering to give him information." The curl had fallen back in my face. Again I pushed it behind my ear, but it would not stay.

"No doubt you have, but I admire your boldness." He stared at me with an inspiring intensity.

"I'm glad to hear it." I opened my reticule to pull out a hairpin, refusing to admit defeat to a defiant curl. Instead of finding the pin, however, my hands rested on the cool surface of another of Mr. Harrison's bullets. I placed it on the table in front of Colin. "Mr. Harrison's been leaving these for me to remind me that he can reach me anywhere."

Colin grabbed both of my hands and squeezed them hard, his eyes full of concern. "How many times has this happened?"

"I don't even know. I seem to find them everywhere I go, including my hotel room," I said. His face was calm. "I admit it scares me."

"It should. I'm not suggesting it should dissuade you from continuing your work, but you must proceed with extreme caution."

"I'm being careful. We've already spoken to the hotel manager about further increasing security, and Cécile's going to have Sissi send a guard from the palace."

"An excellent idea. But . . ." He stopped and met my eyes. "It is so very tempting to order you to stop. To send you back to London. To—"

"To behave like the typical overprotective English husband."

"The role does have some merits." He squeezed my hand.

"Not for us," I said.

"No, though it would make this much easier."

"Easy does not equal worthwhile."

"So what are you going to do about Mr. Harrison and his bullets?" he asked.

"Be more vigilant," I said. "I will take every reasonable precaution."

"Don't limit yourself to reasonable ones."

I smiled. "Jeremy will keep me safe."

"I'm inclined to believe that Harrison won't harm you. It wouldn't forward his plans. But I can't be certain. Are you sure you want to continue?"

"There can be no answer to that question but yes," I said. "You must trust me to be careful."

"I will, Emily. But be forewarned. If the situation deteriorates, I will put a stop to this."

"You can't," I said.

"I can." He folded his arms over his chest.

"Well, I'd lose all respect for you if you did, so I suppose I'll have to make sure it never happens." My flip tone did nothing to lighten the mood. "Will you help me with Herr Schröder? Can you give me something for him?"

"I can draw up some correct, official, and utterly useless documents. That should secure his trust. The key is to produce something that he can verify with just the right amount of difficulty. How did you manage to take over my work for me? At this point I think you've a better chance of uncovering his plans than I do."

"Perhaps, but you may be better able to stop them than I."

"Why does this make you more irresistible than ever to me?" he asked.

"More irresistible than ever, am I? Have I mentioned that my mother's hoping to have half the royal families of Europe at our wedding? Wouldn't you prefer to elope?"

"Can you convince the queen?" He smiled.

"I'd rather work on you," I said. "I know I've no chance with her."

"I'm known for my strength of will."

"Only because I've never really tried to tempt you."

"How is it that you've managed to construct a game in which my default position requires denying everything that I want?"

"You're too loyal to your queen, my dear," I said.

"It's not that. I've already tried her patience once, when I refused the K.C.M.G. She handled it well enough, blaming my eccentricity on my family. She knows I come from a long line of gentlemen who turned their backs on royal attention. But I would hate to test her again."

"You turned down being made a knight?"

"I've no desire to be ranked above anyone else. We have not earned our positions, Emily. We hold them because of luck."

"I do, certainly, but not you. The queen wanted to knight you because of the work you do for the Crown."

"Work I would never have been able to undertake had I not been born to a privileged life. It's my duty to serve my country, but the manner in which I fulfill that obligation makes me no better than the lowest sailor in the Royal Navy. We are both doing what we can for Britain."

There is something about watching a gentleman who is not only passionate about what he does, but very good at it, too. Every nerve in my body was tingling as I listened to Colin speak.

"You're flushed," he said. "Are you unwell?"

"Quite the contrary," I said. "You're lucky we're in a public place."

"Or unlucky." He traced the rim of his coffee cup with a finger. "Though I don't believe you'd speak with such restraint were we alone."

"You underestimate me."

He shifted in his seat. "That's quite enough temptation, my dear."

"All right." I flashed him a smile. "I'll change the subject entirely. When can you get me something for Herr Schröder?"

"I'll send a set of papers to you at the Imperial. Let me know what your anarchist friend says after he sees them."

THE NEXT MORNING CÉCILE, Jeremy, and I breakfasted at Klimt's studio. Cécile had ordered the staff at the Imperial to pack up and send over a stunning assortment of pastries, fruit, and even hot dishes. The only flaw was that the hotel's coffee had not traveled well; it was entirely too cold. Undaunted, my friend prepared some herself on Klimt's small stove.

"She's all energy," Jeremy said, watching Cécile bustle about. I began to think that his manner towards me had thawed.

"You're quite right." I passed him a nut-filled pastry. "Do you want anything else?"

"No, thank you."

"Have you spoken with Rina recently?" I asked.

"Yes."

"How is she?"

"Fine, thank you."

"I—I've heard that you found a house for her. I—"

"I'd prefer not to speak with you about this. Forgive me." He stood up and walked away from the table, crossing to the far side of the studio and staring blankly at the pictures on the wall.

"You must go easy on him," Klimt said, leaving Cécile to manage the coffee on the stove.

"I haven't done anything," I said, rubbing the soft fur of the cat that had taken up residence on my lap.

"You let him fall in love with you. You can't expect there to be no consequences." He stepped back from his canvas, tilted his head to one side, and studied his work.

"Consequences?"

He did not answer for a moment, still looking at the painting in front of him. Then, all at once, he touched a brush to his palette and went back to work. "I'm an expert when it comes to such matters. It's delicious to have people adore you, but it's exhausting, too. Particularly when your own feelings don't match theirs."

"Is that how it is between you and Cécile?" I asked.

He laughed. "She would never allow that."

"No, I would imagine not." The cat slunk off my lap and stalked after Jeremy, who took no notice of it brushing against his legs.

"She and I are well suited. We understand one another," he said.

Jeremy did not speak to me for the rest of the morning. I hoped this would change on our way to Herr Schröder's house that afternoon.

"It's colder today, don't you think?" I asked once we were bundled into a fiacre.

"I hadn't noticed." He did not look at me, focusing instead on the buildings we passed. So intent was his stare I found myself following it, half expecting to find something stunning outside the coach rather than another row of elegant shops.

"It always feels colder here when the sun's out. Why is that?"

"I've not the slightest idea."

"You'd think it would warm the air." I watched him closely; he did not move, nor did he reply. "Have you plans for the evening?"

"I haven't decided."

"Are you adamant about refusing to engage me in conversation?" I asked.

"I'm tired and don't feel like talking."

We sat in silence for twenty more minutes before we reached our destination. As we approached the house, Jeremy spoke at last. "It's unlikely your friend is going to want to talk in front of me. If that's the case, I shall stand directly outside the door of the room you're in, eavesdropping in the most obvious fashion. Shout for me if you feel threatened in the least."

"Thank you, Jeremy," I said. He did not return my smile.

Herr Schröder's house was not at all what I expected. It was in a fine neighborhood, elegant and graceful, nothing like the areas in which his compatriots lived. I could have imagined myself in Mayfair until I'd knocked on the door and Herr Schröder answered it himself.

"You look surprised," he said, ushering me into a cavernous entrance hall. No carpet covered the polished marble floor; our footsteps echoed as we walked. "And you've brought your favorite chaperone. How charming."

I ought to have introduced them, but stumbled over the words. How to announce a duke to an anarchist? Our host held out his hand.

"Gustav Schröder."

"Jeremy Sheffield." They shook hands.

"*Lord* Sheffield?" Herr Schröder asked.

"I'm a duke, actually, so it would be Your Grace, if you're the sort of man who insists on standing upon ceremony. Otherwise you can call me Bainbridge."

Herr Schröder laughed. "In other circumstances I think I might like you, but as it is, I've no time to form a new acquaintance. You'll forgive me if I don't allow you to join me and your companion while we speak?"

"So long as you'll forgive me for hovering outside the door. I will not leave her alone."

"I'll get you a chair." He dragged an elaborately carved chair across the hallway and put it next to a doorway that led into a well-appointed sitting room. "We won't be long." He ushered me in and closed the heavy door behind us. The room in which we stood was furnished in the style of the Napoleonic era, much of it with an Egyptian flair, as had been popular after the Frenchman's adventures in the land of the pharaohs. I was drawn at once to a spectacular stone panel that hung on the wall.

"Is this authentic or a copy?"

My host shrugged. "For the price my grandfather paid, it had better be genuine. Do you read hieroglyphs?"

"No, but I wish I did." I reached up, longing to touch the worn stone, to feel the words carved by ancient hands. "Your grandfather was a collector?"

"I don't know. I never knew him."

"I'm sorry," I said, and turned to take in the rest of the room, full of shades of gold and green.

"You don't like my house?" he asked.

"Why would you say that?"

"You have an odd expression on your face."

"I confess to not having expected to find an anarchist living in such luxury."

"I come from a good family."

"You're a man of contradiction. It's fascinating. What do your peers think of your wealth?" I asked. "I'm surprised they haven't demanded that you renounce your fortune. Or at least divide it equally among them."

"I'll gladly renounce it the moment human beings are treated as equals in this world. Until that day, I need it to finance my work.

Enough of this. What information have you brought me?" he asked. I handed him the papers Colin had sent to me. He gave them a cursory glance, then began looking at them more closely. "This is better than I could have hoped. Does he know you took this?"

"Of course not. What do you take me for? I was . . . with him in his rooms last night and took them after he'd fallen asleep." My cheeks felt hot as I said this. "I'll need to return them before he gets home this evening. You're free to copy whatever you want."

"Are you certain he hasn't missed them?"

"He hadn't when he left this morning." I watched him sit at a table and begin scribbling furiously in a notebook. "What do you have for me?" I asked.

"I haven't yet decided. You surprised me by being so successful with your acquisition. I confess to having had very little faith that you could do what you said."

"So will you give me what I want? Did someone in Vienna order Lord Fortescue's murder?"

"I will find out what I can. My 'organization,' as you call it, was not involved."

"What about Mr. Harrison?"

"Give me twenty-four hours."

"You want to meet on Christmas Eve?"

"Have you something more important to do?"

"Not in particular. Shall I meet you here again?"

"No. Go to the Stephansdom. I'll come to you in Saint Valentine's chapel at nine o'clock."

I agreed to the meeting, then stood up and started for the door. The sight of something hanging on the wall brought me to a dead stop: a dueling pistol embellished with the image of a griffin in profile, the arms of the Baron of Beaumont. I recognized it at once as the twin of the one used to murder Lord Fortescue.

"Where did you get this?"

"This is one of the guns from the duel in which my brother was killed. I keep it to remind me why I continue to fight for justice in this world."

I WENT DIRECTLY from Herr Schröder's house to the offices of the *Neue Freie Presse*, towing Jeremy with me. He did not play unwilling companion on the journey, instead telling me in matter-of-fact tones what he'd seen while he waited for me in the hall: the Countess von Lange, wearing an evening gown in the middle of the afternoon, coming down the stairs. A friendly chat with a servant and a handful of change had confirmed his suspicion that she'd spent the night at the house.

Once we arrived at the *Neue Freie Presse*, we did not emerge for nearly two hours, but when we did, I had with me an item cut from an old issue of the newspaper, full of details of a duel fought more than ten years earlier, in which it was reported a Mr. Robert Brandon had killed Josef Schröder.

> The duel that recently took place between Robert Brandon and Josef Schröder proves once again why this barbaric practice is illegal. Schröder was mortally wounded and Brandon fled the country immediately, but that was not the end of this tragic story. Schröder's second, an Englishman, Albert Sanburne, was found dead yesterday morning, having killed himself with a single shot to the head. He used the same pistol that had ended the life of his friend. One can only suppose that the guilt he felt at not having been able to dissuade Schröder from fighting was overwhelming.
>
> But in a season of suicides, Sanburne's is unremarkable when compared to that of the woman who jumped from a car on the Budapest express, ending up a tangled mess in her bloody wedding gown and veil.
>
> — *NEUE FREIE PRESSE*, 20 SEPTEMBER 1880

Chapter 17

This is very troubling," Colin said, pacing in front of my fireplace at the Imperial, reading the article from the *Neue Freie Presse* over and over. "To have Brandon connected to this set of pistols more than once . . . Not good at all."

"No one knows but us," I said. "Unless it was part of the information Lord Fortescue was holding over Robert, and whoever is in possession of that now decides to come forward with it."

"I can't imagine that Fortescue would have missed such a detail. But unless we can find his private papers, we've no way of discovering what precisely he knew."

"He was too sharp to keep them somewhere people would search. I'm going to write to Mrs. Reynold-Plympton. She was more of a wife to him than any of his three legal ones, and so far as I can tell, she exerted a great deal of influence over him politically. They were more than lovers."

"I suppose now that Fortescue is dead she'd have no reason to keep his secrets hidden."

"Unless she's planning on using them herself," I said. "She might not be ready to relinquish her political power."

"Perhaps, but she'd have a difficult time wielding it without Fortescue."

"Doesn't that depend on how spectacular the information she knows is?"

"To a degree. But the fact is that without him, she has very little clout."

"I had one other thought," I said. "I think Fortescue was also having an affair with Flora Clavell. Could his murder be a simple case of jealousy?"

"You think Flora Clavell killed him? I seem to remember you suspected her husband at one point."

"I don't think either of them is guilty. But what about Mrs. Reynold-Plympton? She wouldn't have ever felt threatened by Lady Fortescue, but Flora's young and pretty and smart."

"An interesting theory. But she wasn't in Yorkshire."

"She was. At Highgrove, attending the Langstons' party," I said. "Jeremy was there, too."

"You're certain?"

"I remember it distinctly."

"That's a lead worth pursuing." He tossed the newspaper article onto a table. "Damn Brandon for lying about this."

"He lied?"

"He was shown the gun—held it in his hands—and denied ever having laid eyes on it before," Colin said.

"I can't believe he'd do such a thing."

"He was in desperate circumstances, Emily, and he probably assumed that no one other than Fortescue could make the connection between the guns. In theory, it shouldn't matter, but if it were to be exposed during the trial . . ." He shook his head. "What I don't understand is how the pair of pistols was separated, and how one of them wound up back in England if their owner died in Vienna."

184 ◆ Tasha Alexander

"Mr. Sanburne's personal effects would have been returned to his family, wouldn't they? And that must have included one of the pistols and perhaps their case."

"It's odd they didn't send both of them," he said.

"Perhaps Schröder stole it after his brother was killed. We can find out easily enough how he came to get it."

"Perhaps it doesn't matter." He was pacing again.

"I don't believe for a moment that Mr. Sanburne killed himself because he didn't stop the duel. Did you know about his suicide? I thought he'd died of influenza."

"That was the story circulated by the family. His sister was in dire enough straits without having the stigma of suicide to contend with."

"I've one other distressing piece of news. Would you like it now, or shall I wait?"

"May as well bludgeon me with all of it at once."

"I believe I know who warned Lord Fortescue."

"One of Schröder's men?"

"Not quite. Schröder is having an affair with a woman who is . . . connected with politics in England."

"Who?"

"The Countess von Lange."

"Kristiana?" he asked. I nodded. "How do you know this?"

"I was suspicious when I saw his reaction when I told him she was still romantically involved with you."

"But you have no firm proof?"

"Jeremy confirmed it this afternoon." Meeting Colin's eyes was difficult. I was afraid of what I might see in them. "She is not an infrequent guest at Herr Schröder's house."

If he felt any emotion at that moment, he did a superb job of hiding it. His demeanor did not change in the least, but he did stop pacing. "I'll speak to her at once. If it was she, and she's been hiding it all this time . . ." He paused. "No. I can't imagine she would do that. She's unscrupulous in many ways, but she would never stand by and send an innocent man to his death."

"I'm sure you're right," I said, but I was skeptical, and not entirely pleased that he was so quick to defend her. "But if so, it doesn't bode well for Robert unless there's another part to the story that we're missing."

"While we're on the subject of illicit loves, have you talked to Bainbridge?"

"What on earth do you mean?" I asked, hoping I looked imperturbable.

"He's in love with you, and I'm feeling a bit guilty for sending you around with him. He must be feeling supremely tortured. But I can't go myself without neglecting my own work, and I can't let you continue what you're doing alone."

"I could ask Cécile to come instead."

He shook his head. "You're treading in parts of the city that could turn dangerous in an instant. I'd prefer to know that you've a gentleman to—"

"To protect me?"

"Forgive me, yes."

"Do you want me to stop what I'm doing altogether?" I asked.

"Would you?"

"No." I stared at him, feeling more than a little uneasy.

"Good. I think it's easier that we are both embroiled in complicated messes. I don't mean Bainbridge—I mean the work. Neither of us would ever expect the other to stop."

"Of course not. But Colin . . ."

"What is it?"

I could not meet his eyes. "He kissed me."

"I know. Kristiana saw everything and was all too glad to tell me."

"I'm so sorry. I should have told you as soon as it happened, but I—"

He put three fingers on my lips. "I have never doubted your fidelity." My breath started coming more quickly as our eyes met. "Perhaps I'm overconfident."

"Not at all. No one else could be to me what you are," I said.

"I'll have to make sure you never forget that." He kissed me, slowly at first, gradually increasing the intensity and depth till I was so consumed with pleasure that were I the sort of woman who fainted, it would have required several applications of smelling salts to make me sensible enough to tend to the mundane rituals of daily life.

COLIN CONFRONTED KRISTIANA as soon as he'd left me. She admitted that she had spoken with Lord Fortescue when she saw him at Beaumont Towers about trouble brewing in Vienna. But she insisted that she did not warn him of any specific threat. Most particularly, not a threat against him. All she'd told him was that the city was like a tinderbox, ready to burst into flame at the slightest provocation.

Lord Fortescue, she said, was hardly interested. He'd commented that the Balkans were headed for disaster and that Britain would keep out of any trouble in the region for as long as possible. This, he said, was a problem for the emperor of Austria and the kaiser to address. Britain was not concerned.

But why, then, had he confided in Robert that he'd been threatened? A dark thought crossed my mind, and I pushed it away before it could fully form. It was impossible to ignore altogether, though. Robert had lied about the gun; could he have invented the conversation in which his mentor told him he'd been threatened? Or, Kristiana might have spoken to Lord Fortescue before he'd received the written warning. Someone had stolen political documents from Beaumont Towers—documents significant enough that their disappearance had merited charging Robert with treason. If Mr. Harrison was the culprit—something I did not doubt for an instant—he might have also stolen any written evidence of the warning sent to Lord Fortescue.

Snow fell all that day and through the night, leaving the inhabitants of Vienna to crawl out from under their warm covers in the morning and find their city still reposing beneath a glistening white quilt of its own. When I dragged myself from my bed, I did not get dressed, but pulled on a robe, moved a chair in front of one of the enormous windows in my bedroom, and sat, watching the snow but not really focusing on it. I had slept fitfully, plagued by troubling dreams. Meg opened the door to bring me tea, but I had no time for it. Having spent too long mesmerized by the snow, I would now have to hurry to keep my appointment with Herr Schröder.

Jeremy and I walked in silence to the Stephansdom. As we approached the cathedral, I saw Rina standing outside. Jeremy took her arm and invited her to join us; they sat together in the nave, keeping in sight of the chapel where I was to meet the anarchist. He was kneeling when I arrived, a look of such piety on his face that I could not help but laugh.

"Surely you're not a religious man?" I asked, dropping to my knees next to him in front of Saint Valentine's small altar.

"Not at all. You're as likely to get results from sacrificing a goat as you are from praying here."

"You shouldn't say things like that."

"Why not? Afraid we'll be struck down?"

"Yes, actually," I said, feeling prickles up and down my arms.

"It's all mythology. Ours is just more modern."

"I'm not here to debate religion. What do you have for me?"

He stared at me for a moment before answering. "You are a beautiful woman. It is unfortunate that you are caught up in any of this. You have not made a wise choice in deciding who to marry."

I sighed. "Herr Schröder, I've no interest in being lectured on my romantic life. I'm perfectly capable—"

"You've no idea what misery your choice will bring you."

"Is this about Kristiana?"

"No," he said. "Although I wouldn't discount the possibility of her heaping grief on you. He's in great danger, Hargreaves. You know enough about his work to understand the risks he takes."

"He's perfectly capable of taking care of himself."

"Is that what you believe?" He drummed his hands on the railing in front of us. "He's good, I give you that. But no one in his situation is ever safe."

"I know that."

"I've been asked to kill him," he said, and I felt as if the blood had stopped flowing through my body. "An easy enough assignment. He's careful, but not invincible."

"Why are you telling me this?"

"I'm feeling rather conflicted about the whole thing, actually."

"Don't be facetious," I said, trying to keep my knees from shaking, my teeth from chattering.

"I'm not being facetious. I'm being straightforward. It's a job, Kallista. He's a threat to my goals and those of my partner in a certain matter."

"Who is your partner? Harrison?"

"Very good."

"I thought you didn't trust him," I said.

"I don't."

"And he's the one who wants you to—"

"Yes." He stood up and wandered over to the case of relics. "He's paying me well. But if I eliminate Hargreaves, they'll send someone else to take over his job. Someone to whom I will not have access via you."

"So my ability to steal information from him can keep him alive?"

"As long as what you give me is worthwhile."

"I'll make sure it is." I gripped the railing, steadying myself as a wave of dizziness overwhelmed me.

"There is one problem, though. You are here to help a friend, correct?"

"Yes."

"The answers you seek are in England, not Austria. If you stay here, your friend will hang."

"I'm certain that Harrison stole some documents from Beaumont Towers. I need to know what they say and if, among them, there was a letter that contained a specific threat against Lord Fortescue."

"You're not in a position to make demands," he said.

"I will make demands when I think it necessary. You are asking terrible things of me. This is the least you can do for me."

He smiled. "I'm not ready to divulge that information. Perhaps once my own plans are complete. Of course, the more quickly you supply me with what I need . . ."

"You're abhorrent," I said.

"Far from it. Any of my colleagues would have already completed the job. You're lucky I'm sophisticated enough to see the value in keeping him alive."

WE WENT STRAIGHT from the Stephansdom to Colin's rooms, but he was not there. Without pausing to think, I looked everywhere I could: the Griensteidl, the Imperial, even the von Langes' residence, but he was nowhere to be found. In the end, I returned to his apartment and bribed the *Hausmeister* to unlock the door for me, then insisted that Jeremy leave me alone. Rina was still with us, and I did not want her to see my emotions come completely undone. It was not easy to force Jeremy out, but sincere promises that I would not leave the house unaccompanied—I would either wait for Colin or send word to the Imperial that I needed an escort—eventually worked.

As soon as they had left, I began tearing about, searching for anything that might indicate where he'd gone. It was irrational to think that he had already come to harm; I believed Herr Schröder would not kill him. Not yet, anyway. But I was taking shallow half-breaths and wouldn't be able to stop until I saw for myself that he was safe.

He had three rooms that seemed large enough when I'd first entered, but their walls grew closer and their ceilings lower as I felt an increasing sense of desperation. I found nothing of use in the sitting room and passed through his bedroom to a small chamber that contained a desk. Without hesitating, I began to rifle through the drawers, hoping to find a calendar, but stopping at the sight of a bundle of letters.

They were from me. He'd kept every word I'd written to him, even a note scribbled on a scrap of paper torn from an opera program. I'd passed it to him while we were watching *La Traviata* at Covent Garden. At once I was consumed with emotions: love, confusion, anger, and an undeniable desire to collapse in tears. Why could we not share an uncomplicated life together? Safe, dividing our time between England and the Continent. I returned the letters to the drawer and staggered back to the bedroom, where my strength left me. I dropped onto the bed and sobbed, vaguely aware of the sound of pealing church bells outside welcoming Christmas Eve.

I didn't hear him open the door or step into the room, but gradually became aware of the smell of cinnamon and tobacco and a hint of shaving lotion. He was standing in front of the window, his figure a silhouette, light spilling around him.

"I hardly know what to say. Is there an appropriate response to finding you on my bed?"

"Colin—"

"You're crying." He sat and pulled me up beside him. "What is it?"

I could not help myself. I put my head in his lap and made no effort to slow my tears. He said nothing, but rubbed my back until it had stopped heaving, then pulled me up and kissed the top of my head, so gently I could hardly feel his lips. I opened my eyes and saw his, inches from me, full of concern.

"My dear girl, what happened? What are you doing here?"

I sat up straight, took his hands, and blurted out what Herr Schröder had told me. "I'm scared," I said. He smoothed my forehead and put his hand on my cheek.

"There's no need for concern. As I've already told you, I'm accustomed to people wanting to kill me. And now that I know who's trying to do it, it will be that much easier to avoid."

"I cannot treat this with casual disregard," I said, my stomach burning. "Of course there's need for concern."

"You must trust that I know what I'm doing, Emily. That I'm capable of handling this. I understand how shocking it all seems to you." He ran his hand through his wavy hair. "This is why I've always been loath to marry. It's a terrible situation to expect a wife to bear. But I cannot hide it from you."

"I would not want you to," I said, my voice so low I could hardly hear it myself.

"For the moment we must deal with the situation at hand. But then, my dear, you are going to have to consider whether you still want me, knowing that this sort of thing will almost certainly happen again."

"Does it have to?" As soon as the words escaped my lips I regretted them, and I shook my head, which had begun to throb again. "Yes, of course it does. I would not love you so well as I do if you were capable of compromising all that's important to you."

He did not look at me, and I realized that this was perhaps the first conversation we'd had where his eyes were not fixed on mine.

Even when we'd first met, his ability to maintain eye contact had been striking, almost unnerving. I took his face in my hands and turned it to me, but he removed my hands and rose to his feet. The bitter taste of fear stuck in my throat.

"The very nature of what I do compromises your happiness."

"Don't start pacing," I said.

He didn't listen and began taking slow, measured steps back and forth in front of the window. The snow was still falling. "There will be no easy joy for us."

"I'd rather share bursts of joy with you between weeks of unease than years of meaningless comfort with anyone else."

"We'll see if you still believe that at the end of all this." He took me by the hand. "Come. I'd better give you something more for your friend. I'd prefer not to die before New Year's."

24 December 1891
Berkeley Square, London

My dear Emily,

I feel terrible to be so selfish at this time of year, thinking of nothing but my own dreadful situation, consumed with gloom. You, my friend, are my only hope, and I know that writing and saying that does nothing but make you feel pressure. But I do not know what else to do.

My world has fallen apart.

Robert still refuses to allow me to visit him. I can hardly bear it. It's become increasingly clear that no one holds out much hope for my dear husband. Nearly all our friends are in the country for Christmas, but of those who came to town to shop, very few came to see me. The ones who did might as well have been making calls of condolence. They speak in hushed tones about only the safest, most trivial subjects, all the while looking afraid that I will mention my husband's plight. I'm sure that were I to raise the subject, they would race from the room.

And I'm ashamed to admit, Emily, that I've hardly any hope myself. It's as if I'm betraying Robert too.

I've not the courage to write to him about the baby. Wouldn't knowing make his present situation that much worse? I'm not good at being this alone.

Forgive me for sending you such uneasy Christmas greetings.

I am your most devoted friend,
Ivy

Chapter 18

Mon dieu!*" Cécile dropped the gingerbread cookie she was
holding. I had met her coming out of the Imperial on
my way back from Colin's and agreed to go with her to
the Christkindlmarkt, a Christmas market in the Am Hof square.
So it was while we were surrounded with dolls, toys, candy, and all
things festive that I told her of Schröder's revelation. "You cannot
allow Monsieur Hargreaves to continue this."

"I will not ask him to stop." We passed by an enormous Christmas pyramid and a row of beautifully decorated fir trees.

"Oh, *chérie*, you are right, *bien sûr. C'est très difficile.* What can
I do to help you?"

"I don't know."

"Do you believe he will be safe so long as you're giving Monsieur Schröder what he wants?"

"Can you trust a man who admits to killing?" She did not answer my question, so I continued. "I'm almost beginning to hope
that whatever this dreadful plan of his is comes off without the
slightest hitch."

"You don't wish that."

"I might." I frowned. "We must find out what it is."

"Isn't that what Monsieur Hargreaves is trying to do?"

"Yes, but perhaps we can beat him to it," I said. "I want to determine whether the destruction they're planning would be worse than losing him."

"And if it isn't?"

"I'm not prepared to answer that question at the moment." I'd been tugging at the trim lining the cuffs of my coat, and it was beginning to unravel. Meg would not be happy with me. "I need you to find out if the empress can be of any service to us."

"She has completely removed herself from Austrian politics."

"But she may be able to find out if there's concern for the safety of anyone in the royal family. This is not like dredging up her concerns about Mayerling."

"You think your anarchists are planning an assassination?"

"Possibly."

"I will speak to her after Christmas."

"I can't wait that long. Can you see her today?"

"Impossible. She's with her family."

"You could write her a note."

CÉCILE HAD ORDERED our maids and several members of the hotel staff to decorate our rooms for Christmas, and the end result was stunning. We had an enormous tree covered with candles and ornaments, a garland hung across the mantel, wreaths on every door. But despite this, our holiday celebrations lacked any heartfelt enthusiasm. Friedrich was sullen because he couldn't see Anna. Rina had refused our invitation without explanation, and of course I had never invited Herr Schröder. Jeremy did all he could to avoid speaking to me, and Colin appeared to have taken up brooding as a hobby. The only person with anything to say was Klimt, who proved immensely amusing when discussing the merits of his cats.

"I'm so glad you managed to smuggle this in," I said, taking another bite of the Sacher torte Friedrich had brought for us. The specialty of the Hotel Sacher, its dark chocolate icing and apricot filling perfectly complemented our vintage port.

"I wouldn't say I smuggled it. I don't think the staff at the Imperial would dare stop anyone from bringing whatever they'd like to this suite," Friedrich said. "Even if it does come from a rival hotel."

"I prefer the Imperial to the Sacher," Klimt said, his eyes meeting Cécile's. "I've a better time here."

"I would hope so," she replied. "From what I've heard, the rooms here are much more comfortable."

"Let me assure you, they are."

I began to feel that I was watching a conversation that ought to have been private. Colin drained his glass and rose from the table. He looked as if he was going to begin pacing. Cécile must have noticed this, too. She rose from her chair, whispered something to Klimt, and then threaded her arm through Colin's.

"Come," she said. "We're overdue for a game of chess."

Once they were gone, Friedrich turned his attention to Klimt. "I very much admire the murals you did in the Court Theater."

"*Dreck! Schweinsdreck!*" the painter exclaimed. "I do not wish to discuss them."

"Apologies," Friedrich said, the slightest quaver in his voice.

"Cécile tells me you are an artist," Klimt said. "Do you have a sketchbook with you? I'd like to see it."

"It's in the other room," Friedrich said, leaping from his seat and racing towards the door. Klimt followed, leaving me alone with Jeremy, who was idly swirling the port in his glass.

"Do you need me tomorrow?" he asked.

"I don't know. Jeremy, I—"

"I've plans for the afternoon. If you want me to cancel them, could you please let me know before two o'clock?"

"You don't have to do any of this," I said.

"But you know I will. I must tell you—" He stopped as Colin came back into the room.

Colin handed me a small envelope. "This was delivered for you."

I opened it at once. Inside were two articles clipped from newspapers. The first was Albert Sanburne's obituary as it appeared in the *London Daily Post*. The second, the article I'd already seen from the *Neue Freie Presse* about the duel and suicide. Across the top of the obituary someone had scrawled, "Answers hide where lies are told."

"This is Sir Julian's paper," I said, holding up the piece from the *Post*. "I wonder what he could tell us about Mr. Sanburne's death. Would he know who fabricated the story of the influenza?"

"Anyone in the family might have done that." Jeremy pulled out a cigar and lit it. "Standard operating procedure to protect his sister."

"But there was no one left in the family," I said. "His title reverted to the Crown."

"There was no heir, but there were relatives through the female line," Jeremy said. "Why does it matter?"

"I'm not sure." I looked at the articles again. "I wonder who Robert's second was in the duel. Perhaps Margaret can find out, if only he'd agree to see her."

"He's a fool if he refuses to talk," Colin said. "But I'm not convinced any of this is relevant to his current situation."

"Perhaps not. But I wonder . . ." I grasped at the elusive strains of a thought trying to take cohesive shape in my head. "It's easy to believe that Fortescue's death was political. Who stood to lose more than Robert at Fortescue's hand?"

"It's time you return to England," Colin said. "Harrison's plans may have been set in motion in Vienna, but the answer to who killed Fortescue isn't here. You've found what Robert wanted to learn, but there's no testimony that Kristiana can offer that's going to help him. It's time to go home."

"You know I can't do that," I said.

"You must." His eyes met mine, but they were cold.

SUNLIGHT POURED OVER the streets on Boxing Day, but the cold air was too much for Cécile, and she insisted that we take a fiacre to the Hofburg, where Sissi had summoned us after reading my friend's letter. She met us in a dark sitting room, the curtains drawn, hardly a lamp lit. She crossed directly to Cécile and they embraced, her thin, fragile body looking as if it might snap.

"I don't know that I can be of any help to you," she said, wafting to a papier-mâché chair inlaid with mother-of-pearl and sitting with the lightness of a dragonfly. "I'm not allowed to have useful information. They won't even tell me how my son died."

Cécile took her hand. "You know enough."

"I don't." Her face, her shoulders, and her neck appeared perfectly placid, but her fists were clenched so tightly that her nails could have drawn blood from her palms. "My husband knows more."

"And his knowledge will change nothing, *chérie*. You must not upset yourself." Cécile bent close to her and whispered something in her ear. The tight fists relaxed.

"You want my help, dear Cécile. I've spoken to my husband—no, I did not tell him why—I let him think I was curious about our official schedule. He told me nothing of particular note. Once the Fasching balls start, it's party after party."

"Was there anything, Your Highness, that if disrupted could cause a considerable commotion?" I asked.

"Aren't the Fasching balls commotion enough?" she asked.

"Perhaps," I said. "But what of political meetings? Will you be hosting any state visits?"

"Kaiser Wilhelm will be here in a few weeks, but not for a state visit. He and the emperor will meet privately, but I've no idea what they'll discuss. You'd do better to ask Katharina Schratt if you want detailed information."

It was an open secret that the actress had become the emperor's closest confidante. They breakfasted together daily, and he'd gone so far as to have his villa connected to the one belonging to the woman with whom he shared what he called a "soul friendship." Because she was not of high rank, her presence caused no political difficulties. She cooked for Franz Joseph, gossiped with him, kept him happy in a grounded, bourgeois way. "I'm sorry, I never meant—"

The empress waved a slender hand. "It is nothing. I'm pleased he has her."

"Did he tell you anything else planned for the kaiser's visit?" I asked.

"Nothing of significance. Wilhelm will only be here a few days. They're going to attend mass, and then a reception for the boys in the court choir."

"An unlikely spot for anarchists," Cécile said, shrugging.

I opened my mouth to speak but stopped myself, and was instantly horrified by my motivation. A reception with innocent choirboys sounded like a perfect target for anarchists to me. But I wasn't about to tell the empress that. If I did, she might do something to cancel the engagement and derail Herr Schröder's plans. I could not risk that, could not risk losing Colin.

"How I long to return to Corfu and be away from all this," the empress said, her voice heavy with exhaustion. "Anarchists, violence, suicide. This city reeks of death."

"I can't think of a happier escape than Greece," I said.

"Yes, you study Greek, do you not, Kallista?" the empress asked.

"I do. I've only just finished reading the *Odyssey* in Greek."

"Do you know the modern language as well as the ancient?"

"Not so well as I would like. I've a villa on Santorini, and my cook's son does his best to teach me, but I haven't spent the time necessary to become fluent."

"It's a wonderfully passionate language. How long will you be in Vienna? Perhaps we could meet and practice our conversational skills while you're here."

"That would be lovely," I said.

"My instructor in the ancient language, Monsieur Rhousso-pholous, is incomparable." She fluffed her skirts, a flighty gesture that was at odds with the rest of her. "And the best classicists in the world come to me. Although not so often as they used to."

"You have been entirely negligent of your needs since the death of your son," Cécile said.

"Isn't it enough that I manage to stay alive? Even that requires more effort than I'm inclined to expend. My poor dear boy. I miss him terribly."

"I can't imagine a pain greater than that felt by a mother who has lost her child," I said. "I'm so very sorry."

We all sat very still, no one speaking, until the empress shook her head. "I will never believe that he killed himself." She looked at Cécile. "You know he and his father had radically different political views. The French and the English both would have been happy to see Rudolf on the throne instead of my husband. He might have been persuaded to transfer Austria's allegiance away from Germany."

"Which means they would never have wanted Rudolf dead," Cécile said. "This is a fruitless line of thought, Sissi. You must stop."

"I'm sorry if we've distressed you," I said.

"I no longer remember what it is not to be distressed." She closed her eyes and said nothing further for a long moment. "I do have one other thing to tell you," she said, opening her eyes and looking directly at me. "I've a friend who's still . . . active . . . in political matters. He knows about you, and told me that you're in danger."

"Did he say how he knew?" I asked.

"No, only that you've drawn the attention of one of your countrymen, a very undesirable man."

"Mr. Harrison," I said.

"You must tell Monsieur Hargreaves at once," Cécile said. "He will arrange to have you protected. He can—"

"No, Cécile. It's fine. I'll be careful. Don't worry. Please let's not discuss it any further right now. Tell us about Klimt. Are you going to see him tonight?"

"YOU THINK THEY WILL STRIKE against these children?" Cécile asked after we'd left the palace.

"How did you know that's what I suspect?"

"You entirely abandoned questioning her once she'd told you about the emperor's plans. You would never have let go of the topic if you were not satisfied with the information before you."

"I shall have to learn to be less obvious," I said. "But yes, I do think that's where they'll attack. Mr. Harrison wants to start a war. If he could assassinate the rulers of Austria and Germany simultaneously, as well as a group of innocent boys—"

"People would be angry, but I do not see how that would lead to war."

"What if it leaked out that the attack was supported by the British government?" I asked.

"*Mais ce n'est pas possible.*"

"Mr. Harrison is part of the government."

"You must inform Monsieur Hargreaves at once."

"Yes." I was paying attention only to the snow falling outside the window.

"Kallista? Are you listening? We must do something about this threat at once."

"We don't have credible information about a threat," I said.

"All we've done is trust that the empress knew what to look for in her husband's diary. She could have missed something."

"You don't believe that. Be careful, Kallista. You will never feel right if you sacrifice even one life in an attempt to save Colin's."

"You're quite wrong about that. For him, there is nothing I would not sacrifice."

27 December 1892
London

Dear Lady Ashton,

I was quite taken aback by your letter. Although I suspect your condolences were not heartfelt, they were appreciated nonetheless. My dear Basil was a man of incomparable talent, and all of Britain will feel the loss of him. He was not well understood by his peers—that, I suppose was the price levied on him for greatness.

I was rather amused by your request. Surely you are not so naïve that you would believe, even for an instant, that I would share with you such sensitive information? But I will admit that after you drew my attention to Robert Brandon and his family difficulties last summer when you were investigating the murder of David Francis, I found myself growing more than a little fond of the man, although he lacks the callousness required to be a truly extraordinary politician. Even without this scandal, he would never have survived in politics.

He'd already been cut from Basil's inner circle, and knew that his career was hopeless. Regardless, I don't believe he committed murder. Mainly because he's not cold-hearted enough to do such a thing.

There is very little I can offer you in assistance other than to tell you candidly that Brandon was not the only man with political aspirations on the dueling field in Vienna the day Schröder died. But Brandon is, unfortunately for him and his lovely wife, far less significant to the government than his colleague.

I am sorry to say it, but it seems utterly unlikely that any verdict other than guilty will be returned when at last he goes to trial. So far as I have learned (and you know my connections enable me to learn whatever I want), there is no evidence that would exonerate Brandon or lead the police to consider another suspect. I'm afraid it's a hopeless business.

I do feel, however, that I should warn you before you delve further into all of this. Basil's enemies were an unsavory bunch. Should it be that any of them was involved in his murder and you came close to exposing the truth, your own life would be at risk. Harrison in particular is not someone with whom you should trifle.

I am yrs., etc.,
D. Reynold-Plympton

Chapter 19

Herr Schröder was not waiting for me in the Stephansdom at our appointed time the next day. I knelt at the altar railing for a quarter of an hour, wondering what saint to petition for protection against hired assassins, but could conjure up no one save Saint Jude, patron of hopeless and desperate causes. My knees began to hurt. I moved to a pew and opened the battered copy of the *Odyssey* that I'd brought with me.

"Reading pagan authors in a Christian church?" Herr Schröder slid along the bench next to me. "You would make a lovely martyr."

"You've reversed things entirely. It was the Christians who were martyred."

"Until the Crusades." His arm rested uncomfortably close to me along the back of the pew. "I saw your chaperone in the nave. Does he like following you?"

"Not particularly," I said.

"What do you have for me today?"

"You're enjoying this rather too much." I handed him a slim envelope. "He knows about the kaiser."

"What about the kaiser?" Herr Schröder would never be

Colin's equal in the realm of spying; he lacked the ability to freeze emotion out of his eyes.

"The visit, the reception . . ."

He opened the envelope, read the contents, and handed it all back to me. "How does he know?"

I shrugged. "I can't imagine. You've assured me repeatedly that your 'organization' is sound."

"How is he planning to stop us?"

"For today you must be content with knowing that he's aware of your plan."

"I need more." He leaned too close, and I pushed back from him. "*You* need more, unless you're fond of widow's weeds. Although you're not his wife. A funny position, that of fiancée. Nothing official, nothing real. If he were to die before your wedding, it would be as if you'd never been connected."

"An entirely irrelevant observation," I said.

"You're overconfident. If he is in a position to stop what I am planning, I will kill him." His arm was once again inching closer to my shoulder. "You, Kallista, must do more than bring me information. You must convince him that my plot is something altogether different."

"That's ridiculous. He'd never believe I would have knowledge of such things."

"He knows you're an intelligent, resourceful woman."

"Who he does not expect to begin playing spy," I said, gripping my book.

"I don't trust you." He was almost touching me. "You love this man. Perhaps you are double-crossing me, not him."

"He's betrayed me."

"Kristiana tells me he's come to her only once since he's been back in Vienna."

Words that I didn't believe ought not to have stung so much. "She's lying."

"Undoubtedly. Theirs was a passion not so easily sated." His eyes narrowed. "This makes you uncomfortable?"

"Should I enjoy hearing about his past loves?"

"Past?"

I looked him dead in the eyes and leaned towards him, then lowered my gaze. "I keep trying to convince myself that if it were only the past, it wouldn't matter. But that's not quite true, is it?"

"You have a history of your own. You were married to his best friend, were you not?"

"Yes."

"So you are no stranger to betraying those you love."

"You can't betray the dead."

"You couldn't be more wrong." He dropped his arm from the bench and rested a hand on his knees. "But that does not concern me at the moment. I see the jealousy on your face when you hear Kristiana's name. I'm inclined to believe that you are upset enough to betray Hargreaves. And if not . . ." His lips parted in a wide smile that in any other context would have charmed the most cynical soul. "It doesn't matter. You love him enough to want to protect him. So now convince him that the attack on the emperor will come at a Fasching ball."

"How am I to do that?"

"That, Kallista, is no concern of mine. You're the one with a vested interest in seeing him alive at the New Year."

I HAD NO INTENTION of hiding any of this from Colin. But with each step I took from the cathedral to his rooms, my legs grew shakier and my stomach lurched, until Jeremy suggested we find a fiacre. Driving, we reached the house quickly. Though the frigid temperatures ought to have made it impossible, sweat beaded on my forehead as I burst through Colin's door. Jeremy, who had been ten paces behind me, caught up at the instant my fiancé, taken aback by my appearance, took me in his arms.

"It doesn't appear you have any further need for me," he said, nodding at Colin, who reached for his hand and shook it.

"I'm much obliged, Bainbridge."

Jeremy left without another word. Colin turned to me, his face full of concern.

"You are unwell. Let me get you some wine."

"I don't want wine." I lifted my lips to his and kissed him so fiercely that he started to lose his balance.

"What brings this on?" he asked.

"Need I have an excuse?"

"Never." He took my face in his hands and kissed me gently, then dropped one hand to the back of my neck, pulled me closer, and abandoned any pretense of softness.

I would have happily continued on in this manner for the remainder of the afternoon and into the evening had I been able to ignore the fear stabbing at me. With effort, I slowed my breathing and stepped away from him. "I've learned something significant."

"About Robert?"

"No. About Schröder's plans." I bit my lip. "I know I must tell you everything, but I'm finding doing so unexpectedly difficult."

"Why is that?"

"Because if you know his plans, you'll thwart them. And if that happens, he'll kill you."

"You give him far too much credit." His untoward smile troubled me.

"I fear your confidence will make you careless," I said.

"You must tell me what you know."

"You could at least pacify me by insisting that you'll be careful."

"Honesty is more important to me than pacifying you, Emily. My work requires confidence—and boldness—that would not be possible if I were overly concerned with being careful."

I stared at my hands.

Then at his boots.

Then back at my hands.

And finally I mustered the courage to meet his eyes.

"I understand and respect your work. I know that it's dangerous. That does not trouble me. But I will not lose you to arrogance."

"What would you have me do?"

"Consider carefully the threats against you. Do not assume you are invincible."

"I would never be so foolish," he said.

"Yet you seem so very cavalier about knowing that someone has been hired to kill you."

"I am well trained to take care of myself, Emily. You must trust in that."

"I'll ask nothing of you that you don't ask of me: No unnecessary danger."

"Fair enough." His answer came too quickly. "So what have you learned?"

I looked into his eyes and for an instant knew what it would be to never see them again. "It will happen during the kaiser's next visit here, after the Fasching has begun."

"The kaiser is not scheduled to be in Vienna until the summer."

"It's an unofficial visit."

"How did you learn this?"

"The empress."

"And how did you confirm that the attack will take place then?"

"Schröder."

"Is there anything else?"

"At the moment, no." My heart was knocking against my ribs. Surely this was enough. He would figure out the rest, but not so easily that it would alarm Herr Schröder. But what then? While Colin solved his puzzle, I would have to figure out a way to render Mr. Harrison powerless. And somehow, in the midst of all this, find whatever he might have stolen in Yorkshire. I felt Colin's finger on my lips.

"I'm curious to know what inspired your amorous greeting this afternoon."

"I'm not sure. It took me by surprise. I was so scared after talking to Herr Schröder, and every nerve in my body seemed . . . I don't know."

"More alive?"

"Yes, but I was terrified."

"Invigorating, isn't it?" He was kissing my neck.

"Inexplicably, yes."

"Almost makes the fear palatable."

"Almost."

"You'll have to redirect the emotion." And he proceeded to act in a manner perfectly designed to do just that.

AFTER LEAVING COLIN, I set off for the von Langes' house. My courage did not wane even when I was ushered into the countess's too-hot sitting room. The last time I'd been in it, I'd welcomed its warmth; now I found it cloying. I peeled off my coat, dropped into a chair, and pulled a fan out of my reticule.

"Warm, Lady Ashton?" The countess glared at me as she came into the room.

"Terribly. I don't know how you bear it." I snapped open the fan and began waving it.

"Why are you here, Lady Ashton? I'm not bored enough to have even the slightest inclination to pretend to be your friend."

"Do you love Colin?"

Her eyes flashed. "Why don't you ask him?"

I stared at her a moment before continuing. "I suppose love is irrelevant. You still long for him. That's obvious."

"I have a connection with him that will never fade."

"What precisely is your relationship with Schröder?" I asked.

"That's none of your business."

"Harrison has hired him to kill Colin."

"He told me. Thought I'd find it amusing," she said.

"Did you?"

She met my stare. "I did not."

"I've already admitted that I don't like you," I said. "When I'm near you I feel awkward, inept, and inexperienced. I look at you and wonder how he could have loved both of us."

"We're not so different," she said.

"Your sophistication puts me to shame."

"Colin's had more than his share of beauty, and it never made him happy. I was always able to offer him more, as are you." She lit a cigarette. "Not that I take any pleasure in saying that. I'd hoped to find you nothing more than pretty and vapid."

"I'd hoped never to find you at all."

She blew smoke towards me and laughed, then drew deeply on her cigarette. "Your naïveté is almost touching."

"You're Schröder's lover, aren't you?"

"Sometimes. He tells me you're providing him with information that's making it worth his while to delay completing the job."

"Yes, but I may have to return to England soon. And if I do, I need to know that there's someone here in a position to influence him."

"You would trust me to do that?"

"I trust that you don't want Colin harmed. Can I count on you? For this, at least?" I asked.

"*Ja*. But not for anything else."

"I'm not so naïve as you think," I said.

"Perhaps not."

I stood to leave, but before I'd crossed to the door I stopped and turned back to her. "Why didn't you marry him?"

"Because I knew that the responsibility of having a wife would weigh on him, and the distraction might make him careless in his work. I didn't want to lose him, but I couldn't let him know that I loved him. He would have kept proposing if I'd given him any hope of that. And so you see, Lady Ashton, that is the difference between us. My love for him is selfless. Yours will kill him."

"KALLISTA, *CHÉRIE*! Why have you kept this from me all this time?" I'd found Cécile in Klimt's studio and pulled her into a quiet corner while he mixed paint.

"I don't know. I feel so insecure and hopeless and foolish."

"There's nothing foolish about it. Tell me about this Kristiana. You are not truly concerned that she could pull Monsieur Hargreaves away from you?"

"No, it's not that. I just worry that after loving a woman like her—so sophisticated and experienced, with so much knowledge of the world—he'll find me lacking."

"He would never have proposed to you if that were the case. He knows you better than anyone, Kallista."

"Yes, but—"

"I know what you are worrying about." She looked at me, her gray eyes serious. "I have no doubt that he will be pleased. It is not a difficult thing. But you already know this."

"To a very small degree."

"That is enough. Your passion will take care of the rest."

"I wish I knew why he stopped wanting her," I said, tugging my bottom lip with a nervous hand. "Can emotions be so fickle?"

"They almost always are, *chérie*."

"He proposed to her, Cécile. She turned him down."

"That was years ago."

"Turned down whom?" Klimt had finished with his paints and come over to us.

"No one," I said.

"Kristiana and your fiancée?" he asked.

"Does everyone in Vienna know their history?" I asked, petulant.

"*Ja*, pretty much. It was quite a story at the time."

"All that matters is that he's with you now," Cécile said.

"More or less," Klimt said.

"You're not exactly inspiring confidence," I said.

"Love is not a static thing." He rolled a paintbrush between his hands. "You have him now, and that should be enough. Don't worry about what came before or what will come after."

"I can't imagine something coming after. I can't imagine not loving him," I said. "Or feeling it with less intensity, regardless of our circumstances, regardless of how much time goes by."

"Hold on to that," Cécile said. "Don't let it slip away from you."

"Is it something over which we have control?" I asked.

"I don't know, *chérie*. I don't know."

"There's no controlling love," Klimt said. "It comes when it comes and goes when it goes."

"I don't want to believe that," I said.

"Then close your eyes, Fräulein. You'll need to."

28 December 1891
Berkeley Square, London

Madam:

I felt I should inform you that the difficulties Mrs. Brandon faces are increasing daily. Newspaper reporters are hovering on the front steps day and night, daunted only slightly by the footmen emptying buckets of dirty water directly above them. They follow Miss Seward and Mrs. Brandon whenever the ladies leave the house. Miss Seward and I have developed any number of complicated schemes to throw them off, but unfortunately we've met with something less than success. Tomorrow she plans to wear a maid's uniform and exit through the servants' entrance.

It is an admirable plan, but I'm afraid that even a newspaperman can tell the difference between a maid and a lady. I find that I don't have the heart to tell Miss Seward this. She's quite consumed with excitement.

Mrs. Ockley has informed me that Odette has a tendency to suffer in cold weather and suggests that she take a tincture—recipe enclosed—before bed every night. I should hate for Mrs. du Lac to lose the services of so capable a maid even for a short time.

Berry Bros. & Rudd have delivered the port you ordered and I wonder if you would prefer that I send it directly on to Park Lane. I cannot imagine any circumstances in which you and Mr. Hargreaves would not be married before it is ready to drink.

I am your most humble and devoted servant,
—Davis

Chapter 20

Cécile finished sitting for her portrait the next day. I wondered if she would continue to see Klimt, but she had very little to say on the subject. We spent the afternoon at the Imperial, hosting Friedrich and Anna, and I must say that being in the proximity of such eager love made me feel nearly as cynical as the Countess von Lange. I turned my back to our guests (who weren't paying us the slightest attention anyway) and read my mail, laughing when I came to Davis's letter.

"You're quite diverted," Cécile said.

"My butler is concerned that your maid will suffer in the cold weather."

"It is essential we keep them apart, or one of us is going to lose a servant."

"You could move to London," I said, bending down to scratch Brutus's head.

"I've already been away from Paris longer than I can bear."

"But you're providing so many valuable services in Vienna," I said. "Look how happy Friedrich and Anna are. Do you think her parents will ever come around to accepting him?"

"Herr Klimt was impressed with his sketches. He will help the boy. But whether that makes him acceptable to her parents . . ." She shrugged. "If he could get a commission to work on the murals in one of the Ringstrasse buildings, he would be in a much better position."

"He'll never allow us to arrange such a thing, and I respect him immeasurably for it. But there must be something. The empress doesn't allow her image to be taken any longer, does she?" I asked.

"*Non.* She's adamant about it."

"But what if he were to draw her—you've seen the vitality in his work—she could not help but be charmed. Even if the piece were never exhibited, so long as word got out that he'd sketched her . . ."

"*Très intéressant.* This is something that perhaps I might arrange. I will convince her to call on me here at the Imperial and have Friedrich arrive at close to the same time."

"Could you do that?"

"She's desperate to leave the palace. It would do her good to get out. I can persuade her to come to us."

"But will she object to meeting Friedrich?"

"Not if I tell her he is a friend of mine."

I glanced at the watch hanging from my lapel and called out to our guests. "It's nearly time to go, Anna. I'll take you home." Cécile and I turned our heads so she and Friedrich could bid each other a proper farewell. I pulled on my coat and waited at the door until Anna joined me, her eyes shining.

"He's so perfectly lovely," she said as we made our way out of the hotel. When we'd reached the bottom of the stairs to the lobby, I tripped and slammed into a gentleman in front of me. "Jeremy! I'm so sorry." His hand gripped my arm, and our eyes met only for an instant.

"Lady Ashton—apologies."

"Jeremy, don't be so formal. I—"

"Are you going somewhere? Do you need an escort?"

"Oh, you're so sweet, Your Grace," Anna said. "But we need privacy. Ladies often have much to discuss, as I'm sure you can imagine."

He looked at me, questioning with his eyes.

"We'll be fine," I said. "We'll get a fiacre."

"Very good." He kept walking.

"The poor duke," Anna said, looking after him. "He's so sad these days. I wonder why?"

"It's not always simple to be happy in love."

Anna grinned. "Can we walk home? I want more time to chat with you than driving would allow."

"I suppose so," I said, smiling. "It won't be dark for a while. But you must speak to me in German. Cécile has no need to practice her idioms, but I'm not so lucky."

"I think we should speak French if we're discussing love."

"German," I said with a smile. "You're supposedly here as a language tutor."

"Do you think the duke will be married soon? He's awfully handsome."

"Yes, I suppose he is handsome." My voice was slow, measured. I'd never before given Jeremy's appearance any thought. "I have a hard time seeing him as anything but a little boy." I explained to her that we had grown up together, and found myself filled with sadness as I remembered days spent with him fishing, climbing trees, and racing our horses.

"What a pity you never fell in love with each other. It would be such a touching story."

"You're a hopeless romantic."

Something caught my eye as we crossed the street. We were being followed. "It's colder than I thought. Let's get a fiacre." I increased my pace, hoping we would find a carriage quickly.

"You're walking too fast," Anna said.

"It's the only thing keeping me warm." We went another block without seeing an empty coach. Harrison, skilled at slipping into shadows, was hard to see, but I knew he was close behind us. I took Anna by the arm. "Tell me more about Friedrich."

"He's found a perfect house for us near his studio. It's so charming that not even my mother could find fault with it. If he gets a few more commissions—"

"Let's cross to the other side of the street." I pulled her to the curb. "A few more commissions, you say?"

"That's all he'll need to be able to afford it. I can't think of anything sweeter than struggling together."

"It will be lovely, I'm sure." Harrison waited until we were at the end of the block, then crossed to the other side.

"Things are more simple when you're not swimming in money, don't you think? Sharing a snug little house, eating soup all the time. It's so romantic I can hardly bear it."

"Poverty isn't a game, Anna." My voice was throaty, harsher than I'd intended. I glanced backwards; he was still following us.

"Of course not. But we wouldn't really be in poverty. It would be more like Marie Antoinette in her little rustic village at Versailles. Papa would never let me starve."

"I've seen the circumstances in which the poor are forced to live. It's appalling. And for either of us, who've never known real hardship in our lives, to speak lightly of their plight . . . I can't abide it."

She fell silent. The footsteps behind us quickened.

"Come, I didn't mean to upset you." I increased my pace, and soon was all but pulling her alongside me.

"Please, Lady Ashton, can't we slow down?"

"I'm sorry. I'm just so cold." We were only two blocks from her house. "Has Friedrich painted your portrait?"

"No, but I'm going to sit for him next week. If, that is, you and Madame du Lac will help me come up with an adequate excuse to escape from my house."

"That shouldn't pose a problem."

Harrison had crossed the street again and was walking directly opposite us, his top hat pulled low over his face, hands in his pockets, and shoulders hunched. The cold air could not compete with the chill I felt at finding myself so close to him. Another block to go.

"I can't begin to express how grateful I am for all that the two of you have done for us. I'd nearly given up hope."

"Never abandon hope." We had reached the beginning of her block. Her father's house stood in the middle, and though I breathed a sigh of relief as soon as I saw it, I did not slow my pace until we'd reached the stoop. I ducked inside with Anna and asked for the family's carriage to be ordered for me, but when I exited it after arriving back at the Imperial, I realized that Mr. Harrison was not so easily deterred.

"You will not escape from me unless I allow it," he said, stepping out from behind the carriage and gripping my arm so hard I knew it would bruise. I twisted to get away from him, but he released me. "And this time I will allow it. But remember, Lady Ashton, that I know where you go, who you see, what you say. It would be remarkably simple to eliminate you."

He had scared me, but now I was angry, and I spun around to face him. "Then why don't you?"

"Only because I think you may yet be of some use to me."

"Highly unlikely, Mr. Harrison."

"I hear rumors that you're planning to return to England."

"Idle gossip," I said.

"The best kind." His hands were in his pockets, and I could see he was fingering something in one of them. "I've never doubted that you'd choose Hargreaves over Brandon."

"I've no need to make such a choice."

"Yes, you do." He handed me a piece of paper. "But you should understand that the likelihood of your saving either of them is negligible at best. Brandon's case is all but hopeless, and Hargreaves . . . though he's capable of taking care of himself, I share your concern that his careless arrogance may prove his undoing."

I held up the paper. "Shall I read this now or later?"

"It makes no difference. Either way I'll know your reaction."

"I'm going inside before you grow even more tedious," I said. "I do hope you enjoy gauging my response to your missive." I marched into the hotel and doubled back through the lobby to make sure he hadn't followed me. He did not reappear, but I found Jeremy sitting on a couch in the smoking room, cigarette in his hand.

"What are you doing still down here?" I asked, taking the seat next to him.

"Nothing."

"I've had an adventurous afternoon," I said.

"Is that so?" He studied his cigarette as if it held the secrets of the universe.

"Another encounter with Mr. Harrison."

He bristled. "Did he harm you? I shouldn't have let you leave the hotel without me."

"I'm perfectly fine. A bit scared, if I'm honest, but more angry than anything."

"Do you need something from me, Em?"

"I can't stand this silence between us. I need your friendship. I miss you, Jeremy, and I hate feeling so distant from you. Will you never laugh with me again?"

"I've behaved abominably," he said, tapping his cigarette on a crystal ashtray.

"You behave abominably nine-tenths of the time. What makes this instance so different?"

He dropped his head against the back of the seat and blew a stream of silver smoke towards the ceiling. "I suppose there's no use hiding the truth from you."

"There's nothing you need hide from me."

"Oh, Em . . ." He groaned. "I love you. I suppose I always have. But when I kissed you . . ." He sat up straight and at last let a smile escape, then shook his head. "You've ruined me."

"Jeremy, I—"

"Don't say it. I know you love Hargreaves, et cetera, et cetera. Spare me the romantic details, will you?"

"You'll meet someone else, these feelings will—"

"No, I won't have it. Don't tell me to look elsewhere, that my feelings will change. I don't want them to. You know what an obstinate brat I am."

"You only feel like this because I'm unattainable. You've never wanted to marry," I said.

"I'll admit there's some truth in that, but you needn't point it out so callously. I may be a cad, but I do have some feelings. You could at least acknowledge the terrible pain I'm suffering." I could hear the beginnings of a smile in his voice.

"Now you sound like your old self." I stopped myself from reaching across and patting his arm.

"I see what you're doing. Afraid to touch me now, are you?"

"I only—" I sighed. "I don't want to make things worse for you."

"Things couldn't be worse for me, and you can blame yourself not only for my own broken heart, but for the demise of the House of Sheffield. I shall never marry."

"You always were a master of melodrama."

"We all must have some skill. But my uncle will thank me. If I lead a dissolute enough life, I may die early. He's always coveted my estate, and even if I should outlive him, his idiot son will inherit. And you, my dear girl, will have single-handedly destroyed one of the oldest families in England."

"Mmm." I smiled. "I see now why you don't want to marry. This makes for a much better story."

"I shall forever be known as the Bachelor Duke."

"I can already hear the mothers of every eligible girl in England keening."

"What's the provision for bastard children? Perhaps I could father some, and they'd challenge my cousin for the title."

"They'd never be allowed to inherit."

"How disappointing. I've quite a wonderful vision of them laying siege to Farringdon. Whose side do you think my tenants would take?"

"How generous are you with them at harvest time?"

"I love your cynicism." He released a long breath. "I feel much better having this out in the open. You don't despise me for having kissed you?"

"I could never despise you. Besides, this wasn't the first time."

"Em! I may be a monster, but I do make a point of remembering which ladies I've kissed."

"I was ten years old. We were by the lake on my father's estate. I'd fallen out of a tree. You picked me up off the ground, made sure nothing was broken, and kissed me."

"So you're suggesting that I make a habit of kissing women I've rescued?"

"Yes. And I've problems more pressing than your debauched methods of consolation."

He lit another cigarette and studied my face, a wicked gleam in his eyes. "Tell me—did you enjoy it? Just a bit?"

"Maybe a very little bit." I couldn't help smiling. "Your . . . technique has improved over the years."

"You're very bad. I shall live on that for the next five years. After that, take heed, I have every intention of kissing you again."

"And I every intention of avoiding it."

"You're right, Em, this is why I love you."

Chapter 21

I had glanced at the paper Mr. Harrison had given me as soon as I'd walked into the lobby, and looked at it again now as I sat with Jeremy. It contained a single sentence:

I will take great pleasure in destroying all your happiness.

"What are you going to do?" Jeremy asked, leaning over to read it with me.

"I don't know," I said, and quickly recounted for him all that had happened.

"You don't need to worry about Hargreaves. No one's going to kill him."

"I'm not certain that's a subject on which I can trust you." I smiled.

"Well, I might kill him, certainly, if the circumstances were right. But seriously, Em. You can't spend your life trying to save him from his work. You have to trust that he knows what he's doing."

"Schröder will assassinate him if I stop bringing him information."

"Do you trust Kristiana to help you?"

"To a degree." I rubbed my temples. "I'm just afraid. How can I leave him?"

"Harrison wants you to stay in Vienna. That's why he's orchestrated all this," Jeremy said. "Have you forgotten that he's your prime suspect for Fortescue's murder? Don't you think he wants you far away from any evidence that could implicate him?"

"Then who is trying to lure me back to England?" It all sounded reasonable when Jeremy said it, but I could not shake the feeling that he was absolutely wrong.

"I've not the slightest idea." He let his eyes meet mine for a beat longer than he ought to have, then looked down. "I can hardly bear to look at you. I'm never going to forgive you for bringing angst to my life, Em."

"Perhaps it's the punishment you've earned for living such a profligate life."

"It would help if you'd stop being so bloody charming." He kissed my hand.

"I think my new mission will be to find you a wife. I can't think of anything that would make me less appealing to you. Let's see . . . whatever happened to Lettice Frideswide? She's not yet engaged, is she?"

TWO DAYS LATER, Sissi came to us at the Imperial for tea. As one might imagine, the arrival of an empress at a hotel caused a furor. She came with two bodyguards, who stood at her side while the manager made an impromptu speech and presented her with an Imperial torte. She gave a faint smile to the crowd that gathered to watch (Meg alerted us to the excitement so that Cécile and I didn't miss it) and looked relieved when we whisked her upstairs.

"I'm so tired," she said, once we were ensconced in our suite. "But it's such a relief to be out of the palace."

"We're glad you could come," I said. "I can't thank you enough for sending your guard."

"I hope it's helped," she said.

"We've not been troubled inside the hotel since his arrival." I had poured tea for all of us and was now cutting the Imperial torte.

"I can't have that," Sissi said, shaking her head at the piece I offered her.

"What's your current slimming plan?" Cécile asked. "Are you eating nothing but celery broth?"

"Does it even matter? It's clearly not working."

"You're ridiculous as always," Cécile said. "You're wasting away."

"You're too kind," the empress said.

"It was not a compliment, Sissi." Cécile put a plate with a slice of torte in front of her. "Eat."

She took a single bite, but no more. "What is the amusement you've planned for me this afternoon?" she asked. "I was all curiosity when I read your note."

"I've asked a friend to join us. I think you'll find him excessively charming," Cécile said. "He's an artist, and I want you to let him sketch you."

"Absolutely not," she said. But half an hour later, when Friedrich at last joined us, Cécile had very nearly changed her mind with an artfully delivered series of cajoling compliments combined with a moving account of the obstacles the stood in the way of our young friends' love.

"I do wish you had ironed your coat," Cécile said as Friedrich sat down next to her. "How did you expect to make a good impression?"

"I had no expectation of Her Highness—Her Majesty—" He looked at Sissi, eyes full of confusion. "Forgive me, ma'am, I don't even know how to address you."

"There is something charming about him," Sissi said, leaning towards Cécile. "You really think it will make a difference in his career if I do this?"

"*Oui*," Cécile said. "Let him make your likeness and then give the picture to me. I want something to remember you by other than portraits from your youth. You were beautiful then, but you've character now." Her hair—said to be ankle-length—was still thick and surprisingly free of gray, though not as lustrous as I suspected it had been in her youth. An olive complexion that must have once glowed was now dull and pale, but this did not detract from the delicate beauty of her chiseled features and wide eyes. Cécile looked at her closely. "I much prefer this version of you. Perfection, *chérie*, is not so charming as people believe. It's bland."

"I've no energy to argue with you." Her voice was listless, but her eyes showed the slightest hint of a sparkle. "Go ahead. Do I have to sit still?"

"I'd rather you didn't," Friedrich said. "I need to see the life in you to capture it." So we ate Imperial torte—layer upon layer of the most exquisite chocolate cake and almond paste—and drank tea while his fingers flew. He worked quickly, charcoal gliding over the paper with remarkable speed. It was like watching someone dance. Before long, he stopped, placed his pencil on the table, and held his sketchbook at arm's length. "*Ja*. It is you."

He stood and crossed over to Sissi, handing her the pad so that only she could see it. She looked at it, and tears streamed down her pale face. "I am no longer this lovely."

"You are to all who see you," he said. "It is not always wise to believe mirrors."

"I think I will give this to my husband." She had not taken her eyes off the paper. "He will recognize me in it."

"Will you show it to us?" I asked.

"No." She handed it back to Friedrich, who rolled it into a tube and tied it with a bit of string that he pulled from his jacket pocket. "*Danke*," she said.

"*Bitte*," he replied.

"I almost wish I were wearing a gown that showed off my tattoo," she said.

"Tattoo?" Friedrich asked.

"Yes. An anchor. On my shoulder." Then she laughed, and the smile that moved from her lips to her eyes made her face come alive and I saw, just for an instant, how beautiful she had been before grief ravaged her. She rose from her chair, and as I watched her prepare to leave us, I found that I could not resist approaching her.

"Your Highness?" My voice was tentative as I stepped close to her. "May I speak to you privately?"

"I suppose. What is it?" She had switched to speaking Greek.

"I share your suspicions about Mayerling." My command of the modern language was lacking; I hoped that she could make sense of what I said. "There is an Englishman in Vienna right now who may know something about your son's death."

"Who?"

"A man you're already familiar with. Mr. Harrison."

"What does he know?"

"I'm only suspicious of him. I don't know details."

"I know that there was a plot—I know they assassinated my darling Rudolf."

"Have you any evidence that I might be able to use to convince him to speak to me? Even a small fact might make him think that I know more than I do."

"I've had everyone I can think of looking for evidence. It was all destroyed. But I do know this: the gun that killed my son was fired six times. He was an excellent shot. Why would it have taken so many attempts for him to kill the Vetsera girl and then himself? It makes no sense. And there were bruises on his body. He must have been struggling with someone." She clutched my arm. "If you can learn anything, you must tell me. I'm certain my husband knows more than I do, and I must find out what he's hiding."

"I will do all I can," I said.

"What were you discussing?" Cécile asked after Sissi had left, surrounded by the bodyguards who had waited for her outside the door.

"Mayerling," I said. "She deserves to know the truth."

NEW YEAR'S EVE HAD ARRIVED, and the entire city was in a festive mood. People all but waltzed as they walked through the town, anticipating the evening's balls. Musicians lugged their instruments, ready for a long night, while florists delivered heaping mounds of flowers to fill the city's ballrooms, the occasional stray petal floating to the snowy street, a bright spot against dirty gray. Young ladies beamed, heads tilted together, laughing voices predicting full dance cards and stolen kisses. The streets even smelled festive: pine garlands left from Christmas mingling with baking bread and mulling spices.

Colin's work had taken him to a small town outside Vienna, and he would not return until the next day, but Cécile, Jeremy, and I had tickets to the opera, where Strauss's *Die Fledermaus* would be performed. After that, we planned to go to the Imperial Ball. But before I could give myself over to revelry, I had to meet Herr Schröder.

"I don't know how I'm going to manage to stay awake tonight," Jeremy said as we walked down the stairs at the Imperial.

"You look exhausted. You should take a nap."

"This city is taking its toll on me. I'm thinking of wiring my uncle and telling him to start planning what he'd like to do with my house once I'm dead."

"After we're done at the cathedral, you should take a nap. I will not tolerate you dozing during the opera."

"Perhaps I'll go to the Griensteidl. I could use some coffee."

"Nap."

"It's useless to argue with you."

"I'm glad you've finally realized that," I said. We were about to exit the hotel when the concierge called to Jeremy.

"Sir! This was just delivered for you." He handed my friend an envelope that Jeremy opened at once, squinting as he read it, his hand reaching up to his forehead.

"Is something wrong?" I asked.

"It's Rina. She's asking me to come to her at once. Something terrible has happened. She gives no details, only says that Harrison is involved and that she's in immediate danger."

"You must go to her," I said, seeing the hesitation on his face.

"I can't leave you alone. Perhaps we could go to her first?"

"We'll get a fiacre. You'll drop me off at the Stephansdom. Schröder won't wait for me if I'm late, and I can't risk missing him."

"I won't leave you alone."

"I'm perfectly safe with Herr Schröder. Mr. Harrison's the one who's dangerous. You can escort me inside if you insist, make sure that he's there, and then continue on." I buried my hands deep in a fur muff as we stepped out of the hotel. The temperature had been warmer yesterday, melting a great deal of the snow, but a cold night had hardened what was left to ice.

"I'll have the driver wait for you outside the cathedral," Jeremy said, helping me into the carriage.

"And how will you get to Rina?"

"I'll be able to hire another one easily enough. But I don't want to risk you not finding one the moment you need it."

Jeremy did not relax for a moment on our drive. He tapped his walking stick rapidly on the floorboard and was too distracted to meet my eyes. I squeezed his hand, surprised to find it trembling. When we reached the Stephansdom, he insisted on accompanying me inside. The church was eerie in its silence, the nave empty. The stream of tourists that ordinarily filled it must have been in search of more secular delights for the New Year. As we approached Saint Valentine's chapel, I could see Herr Schröder sitting on a pew in the back row, head bent forward, clearly asleep.

"I think I'm safe," I whispered to Jeremy, smiling. "Go, Rina needs you." He kissed my cheek and rushed out, disappearing into the light that spilled through the church's door when it opened. I turned back to the chapel and walked towards Herr Schröder.

"I do fear for your soul," I said as I came up behind him. "First blasphemy, now sleeping in church. You really ought to—" I stopped. Something was wrong. He hadn't moved at all when I started talking. I reached the edge of the pew and saw a thick liquid pooling on the bench, soaking his clothes. I felt light-headed, but stepped closer and saw that the liquid—blood—was coming from his throat.

I could not bring myself to look any further. I did not want to see his face. I turned and started to run from the chapel, calling for Jeremy, only to find my exit blocked.

"Is something wrong?" Mr. Harrison asked, gripping my wrist.

"Unhand me." I'd never been so frightened, yet was surprised to find my limbs perfectly steady. It was as if my body recognized the gravity of the situation and was able to steady itself in spite of my spinning brain.

"Unfortunate that Schröder chose to end his life. But then, Vienna is a city of suicides."

"You murdered him."

"Can you prove it, Lady Ashton? It seems you're having trouble enough trying to exonerate Robert Brandon. I shouldn't waste my time on Schröder if I were you."

"You're despicable," I said. The words rang hollow, not nearly strong enough. I looked around, hoping that someone would come to my aid.

"There's no one here. Don't think you'll be rescued. I cleared the cathedral before Schröder arrived. Told everyone the church was closed until mass tonight. Locked all the doors after your friend left. You're in a rather bad situation, Lady Ashton." He stepped closer to me. "Give me the papers you brought for Schröder."

"No." I tightened my grip on the notebook I was carrying with the papers folded inside.

"You should worry more about your fiancé." He wrenched my arm and tore the notebook out of my hand. "After I'm done with you, I'll go straight for him."

I know not how I managed to form a coherent phrase at that moment, only that suddenly I was speaking. "I know what happened at Mayerling. I know about the six shots, the bruises on the crown prince's body. He struggled, didn't he? Did you kill them yourself, or do you prefer to hire out your unpleasant jobs?"

"If you were a man, I'd call you out for saying that. As it is—" He raised his hand and slapped me. Pain exploded through my cheek. I could hardly see, but resisted the urge to bring my hand up to my face. "It was a mistake to tell me you know these things. I've nothing further to say. Now I only have to act."

He started for me, a knife in his hand. "I think I may enjoy this." My heart felt as if it would explode, my lungs paralyzed. The only part of my body over which I still had control was my eyes, and I kept them focused on my enemy. I steeled myself, certain that death was upon me. I'd like to say I faced it bravely, but the truth is, I was seized with terror, unable to form a clear thought. I tried to picture Colin's face, wanting it to be the last thing I remembered, but I could see nothing save Mr. Harrison's knife.

Knowing there was no hope of overpowering him, I decided to run. He grabbed for me as I started, managing only to get the sleeve of my coat. He jerked me towards him, hard, then let go as we both heard the sound of the church door opening and voices filling the nave. Three priests and two altar boys walked in, the oldest priest, keys in hand, wondering aloud why his cathedral was locked.

Harrison twisted my arm violently, then let it go. "I will come for you," he said, then stalked away.

The instant he was gone, I started to shake. I ran towards the priests, shouting for help, feeling with every step I took that Herr Schröder was right behind me, soaking my clothes with his blood.

25 December 1891
Berkeley Square, London

Dear Emily,

*What a Christmas this has turned out to be. When I woke
this morning, Ivy was gone. She'd taken it upon herself to send
for the carriage and set off for Newgate, bent on seeing Robert.
She returned in tears. He'd refused, again, to come to her. But the
warden, taking pity on her, offered to bring him a note from her.
She sat in his office for nearly an hour writing him a five-page
letter. The warden delivered it and waited for a reply. And what do
you think dear Robert sent our poor girl?*

"Happy Christmas to my darling wife."

*He's lucky he's behind bars. If I saw him, I would throttle him
myself.*

*So it was a miserable morning. Robert's parents spent the day
with us— and heavens, they are deadly dull—but I suppose that's
to be expected given their son's circumstances. Things did improve
steadily over the course of the afternoon, though. Your cook stuffed
us with an obscene meal—I don't think I've ever had superior roast
beef—and Davis clearly liked his gift. He very nearly smiled when
he opened it. I suggested that he try it out with one of Philip's cigars,
but he said that would be presumptuous and that he'd never do such
a thing without the express permission of the lady of the house.*

*I'm thinking that it would be amusing if you were to wire him
and give him permission.*

*Mr. Michaels was with his mother today—she lives near Kew
Gardens—but he stopped by this evening unannounced to bring
me a small present. I was caught completely off guard and had
nothing for him. So forgive me, Emily, I took a copy of the Aeneid
from your library, wrapped it in newspaper, and gave it to him.
I'll replace it next week. I'd rather hoped he'd give me a book—the*

package looked promising—but it was note cards instead. Still, the sentiment, as it were, is appreciated.

 I do hope you've found some joy this holiday, Emily, and that you'll be able to come home soon.

 Margaret

Chapter 22

I can hardly recall what happened next. Everything swirled around me, pulling me down to murky depths of terror and sadness. The police came, and someone tried to bundle me off to the British Embassy, but I refused, preferring instead to return to the Imperial. I wanted neither to be alone nor in the company of others, and the crowded streets of the city called to me, offering an uneasy sort of anonymous comfort. I asked the sturdy officer who had carefully written down my answers to his questions about finding the body and Harrison's threats if he would walk me there.

He refused, insisting that we take a carriage. He rode with me back to the hotel, escorting me all the way to my room, where Cécile reached for me the moment she saw my face. I think she spoke to the policeman, but I didn't particularly notice. I walked over to the window and stared out of it, focusing on nothing. The door closed, the officer was gone, and my friend embraced me.

"Kallista, we must leave this city."

"I have to find Colin," I said. I wanted to cry, to scream, something. But all I felt was an enormous void engulfing me. Cécile rang for Meg and Odette and ordered them to begin packing our things.

I did not leave the window.

I didn't hear Jeremy come in. He'd found Rina curled up at her house, reading a book. She had not sent him the note and was completely astonished to see him. Knowing instantly that he'd been tricked, he returned to the Stephansdom, only to learn that someone had been murdered inside. I hardly heard him speak as he told the story.

My friends did not try to convince me to come away from the window. Eventually, Jeremy pressed a glass of port into my hand, guiding it with his up to my mouth. I drank, but tasted nothing. I handed the glass back to him and dropped into a chair.

"We will leave on the Orient Express tomorrow," he said, sitting across from me. "Do you know where Hargreaves is? We can send him a wire if you'd like. I've no doubt he'll return before our departure."

COLIN DIDN'T COME BACK. I had not the slightest idea of where he'd gone—only that he'd traveled by train, wasn't terribly far from Vienna, and had expected to return before the end of the day. We waited as long as we could, sending our baggage to the station ahead of us and not leaving until we were in danger of missing the train. The last thing I did was write two letters: one to Colin and one to the empress.

The trip was a hideous one. I did not sleep at all, images of Herr Schröder and Harrison's knife haunting me whenever I closed my eyes. I did not want to know how much worse my dreams would be. I staggered onto the ferry at Calais, and was barely cognizant of anything around me when we arrived at Victoria Station the next morning. The yellow fog was back again, shrouding London in an unholy veil. Margaret was waiting for us at the platform—Jeremy must have wired her—and the moment I saw her, I snapped out of my morose trance.

"Are you all right?" she asked almost before I'd stepped off the train.

"I wouldn't know how to even begin to answer that question," I said. "But I'm glad you're here." She looped her arm through mine, and we bent our heads together. A silent friend can offer untold comfort. I knew not how to begin to cope with what had happened, only that I could not bear to stop and think about it. Keeping occupied was the only solution. Robert's trial was fast approaching; I could not let him run out of time. I would focus on him and later think about the rest. Margaret understood this well.

Once outside the station, our party split. Jeremy took a cab to his club while Cécile, and the maids returned to Berkeley Square in my carriage. Margaret and I had other plans: we were going to Windsor to descend unannounced on the estate of the Reynold-Plymptons.

If the lady of the house was surprised to see us, she hid the emotion with the skill of an artisan. She welcomed us into her drawing room, which was filled with souvenirs from the time she and her husband, who had been an ambassador, spent abroad: ivory from India, Egyptian glass bottles, an elaborate Turkish coffee set. On the walls were stuffed and mounted animal heads—the ambassador must be a hunter—most of them African, all of them staring down upon us with looks of reproach.

"What a lovely room," Margaret said, the corners of her mouth twitching as she tried not to smile. "I understand that you've quite a flair for home redecoration."

"It's always been a hobby of mine," Mrs. Reynold-Plympton said.

"I recognized your touch at Beaumont Towers," I said. "I particularly liked the *Merchant of Venice* murals in the drawing room."

She gave me a catlike smile. "You did not come here to discuss the drawing room at Beaumont Towers."

"No, I did not. You were kind enough to tell me that there was someone else on the dueling field in Vienna with an interest in British politics. Would you please tell me who?"

"Lady Ashton, you know that I, more than anyone, want to see my dear Basil's murderer brought to justice. But I have looked into this matter of the second—a man for whom I have no personal liking. Regrettably, he was not involved."

"Tell me his name," I said.

"It's irrelevant."

"I'd still like to speak with him."

"Emily is incorrigible," Margaret said. "She'll never rest unless she finds out for herself. Can't you humor her?"

"I don't see what good could come of it." Her smile was implacable.

"But surely it would lead to nothing bad. I'm not going to accost him in public."

"I simply don't see the point," she said.

"You should have no objection to me wasting my time," I said.

"You are remarkably persistent, a quality I admire." She put on a pair of spectacles and peered at me. "I did not much like you when we first met, but I should perhaps excuse your naïveté as a thoroughly unoriginal sin of youth."

"I admit freely that we started off in a less than desirable manner."

This made her laugh. "You accused me of having an affair with Robert Brandon."

Margaret leaned forward in her chair. "I've always thought Emily should write fiction. She has such a flair for narrative."

"Yes, well, I assure you my decision to confront you stemmed from the best of intentions," I said. "But what has always impressed me about you, Mrs. Reynold-Plympton, is that you have forged for yourself real political power. I can't think of another lady of my acquaintance who's managed to do such a thing. It's common knowledge that Lord Fortescue depended on your advice."

"An astute observation." She pulled her shoulders back just a bit and sat taller in her chair.

"And one that should be shared by gentlemen in the government." I was gambling. Was she sensitive to the fact that the majority of men would have dismissed her expertise?

"Hmpf." She whipped off her spectacles with a flourish. "We ladies are forced to operate entirely behind the scenes—and that's unlikely to change in my lifetime."

"I have . . ." I paused, smiled, and wrung my hands, hoping that I looked like someone in search of a mentor. "I've taken some steps to assist my fiancé in his work. I confess that you've been my inspiration. I know I'm an absolute novice, but perhaps someday you and I could combine forces."

"Are you trying to manipulate me?" she asked.

"No, of course not."

"Of course you are." She studied me for a moment and then laughed again. It sounded like music. "I may have just begun to like you, Lady Ashton. It's possible you would make a useful ally."

"Will you tell me his name?" I asked.

"James Hamilton. He works in the office of the chancellor of the exchequer and is very likely to be prime minister one day."

"Thank you."

"I'm hoping that you're a more dependable confederate than the typical gentleman. I don't like being disappointed."

"You've no cause for worry on that count," I said. "I'm at your disposal should you require my assistance."

"Of course you are." She returned her spectacles to her face. "You owe me. I won't forget that."

"Can I beg one more favor?" I asked.

"You can beg anything you'd like," she said.

I told her, as succinctly as possible, about Mr. Harrison's threats towards Colin. "Lord Fortescue was able to keep him in check. Can you do the same? You don't have to tell me how, just please, please stop him."

She shook her head, her eyes lowered. "He never showed me what he had on Harrison. It was too sensitive even for my eyes. I'm sorry. You'll have to hope your fiancé is capable of avoiding the worst. I know Harrison's methods well enough to be afraid for you."

"I NEVER SUSPECTED you ladies of being so debauched," Jeremy said. "Drinking port in the middle of the afternoon? Hedonistic."

Margaret and I had returned from Windsor, and we were all in my library at Berkeley Square. Davis had decanted a port for us, and I'd insisted that he returned Philip's cigars to the room so Margaret could smoke them. He did this not so much because I ordered him to, but because Odette was back in the house. It could never be said that Davis was giddy, but there was an extra crispness in his efficiency today, and I had no doubt what emotion was fueling it.

"It's never too early for port," Margaret said.

"You must tell us what you learned in Windsor," Ivy said. "I can't say that I'm much fond of Mrs. Reynold-Plympton."

"Well, I certainly don't trust her," Margaret said.

"Nor do I," I said. "I can't help but wonder whether Lord Fortescue ever disappointed her. He was quite devoted to her for years and years."

"And what did his wife think of this?" Cécile asked.

"Which one?" Margaret asked, choosing a cigar from the box. "Not that it matters. I don't think any of their feelings much concerned him."

"He wouldn't have cared, but regardless, she—his second wife, that is—never seemed to mind it in the least," I said. "After all, the more time he spent with his mistress, the less his wife had to deal with him. As I remember it, theirs was a marriage completely devoid of emotion."

"A happily matched couple, then?" Margaret asked.

"Apparently." I held up my glass towards the fire. The tawny liquid glowed in front of it.

"I never would have guessed ladies could be so cynical," Jeremy said, lighting a cigar. "I'm astonished. I feel like I'm in possession of an invaluable secret."

"You are," Margaret said. "And if you ever disclose it, we'll murder you."

"What of Fortescue's current wife?" Cécile asked.

"Widow. I don't know her well at all, but she seemed content enough," I said.

"They'd been married less than a year," Ivy said. "Certainly she's grateful to have been returned to her family's estate, but beyond that, I've no idea what her feelings are." There was no hint of her usual rosy hue left in my friend's complexion. "I did think it was odd, though, that Mrs. Reynold-Plympton was not at the party. Lord Fortescue always used to make a point of insisting on her presence. Would refuse invitations if she weren't invited."

"He was clearly carrying on with Flora Clavell at Beaumont Towers," I said. "I wonder if Mrs. Reynold-Plympton knows what was going on between them?"

"Oh, I can't imagine!" Ivy said.

"Of course she knew," Margaret said. "She would have made it her business to."

"Margaret is right," Cécile said.

"You don't think she was involved in the murder?" Ivy asked.

"She was at the party at Highwater with me," Jeremy said. "She could have come to Beaumont Towers as easily as I did."

"I can't believe she would have harmed him," Ivy said. "Despite their . . . immorality . . . she loved him."

"Ivy, you are too good," I said, glancing up at the clock. "I'm off to the Treasury to see Mr. Hamilton."

"Want me to come with you?" Jeremy asked. "I rather miss skulking about with you on nefarious errands."

"And I very much enjoyed having you with me, my dear, but it won't be necessary today," I said. "Perhaps another time."

Ivy snapped to attention. "Hamilton! Of course. That's why it seemed familiar. Isn't his mother Mr. Reynold-Plympton's mistress?"

"I thought he was ancient," Margaret said.

"He is. But you're right, Ivy. My mother told me that they were childhood sweethearts and weren't allowed to marry," I said. "She's been taking care of him in his old age."

"Rather sweet, really," Ivy said. Margaret rolled her eyes.

"Does it matter?" Cécile asked. "Apart from Monsieur Reynold-Plympton being pleased that someone's tending to his needs as he reaches the age of infirmity? I don't see how any of it's relevant to Lord Fortescue's murder."

"Perhaps it's not. Mrs. Reynold-Plympton was awfully quick to give up his name despite her initial refusal," I said.

"And here I thought it was simply a matter of you cleverly convincing her to trust you," Margaret said. "I'm crushed."

"I wasn't even there, and I'm devastated," Jeremy said.

"You know I adore your confidence." I finished my port. "But she set it up beautifully, didn't she? Made us think that she was telling us something valuable."

"So you think Hamilton is useless?" Margaret asked.

"I think Mrs. Reynold-Plympton is as capable as anyone of overlooking a significant detail."

Chapter 23

Of course I was distressed more than you can imagine when I heard about Brandon." Mr. Hamilton's office in the Treasury was a comfortable one, full of furniture so elegant I would have expected to find it in the chancellor's room, not a junior minister's. "We were at university together, you know."

"I'm more interested in the time you spent together in Vienna," I said.

"It was so long ago I hardly remember. We toured the Continent after we'd left Oxford—the usual sort of Grand Tour. I suppose Vienna was one of our stops."

"I'd think the visit would be rather more permanently fixed in your brain. Or have you so frequently witnessed fatal duels that you're blasé about such things?"

"H-how do you know about that?" Gone was the lazy Oxonian drawl. His voice became rough and lost its confident tone. He picked up a pen and began tapping it on the edge of his desk.

"I've just come from Vienna, where I made the acquaintance of a man called Gustav Schröder." Mentioning his name immediately conjured up the image of his body in the Stephansdom. It was all

I could do not to shudder. "His brother was the one killed in the duel."

"Yes, well, it was a terrible business. Brandon never intended to kill the poor chap."

"Then perhaps he ought not to have shot him."

"Of course not. But he was young and hotheaded, and Schröder had insulted a woman of whom he was fond."

I could not picture Robert Brandon as hotheaded. "He wasn't arrested, though?"

"No, we fled the country at once. What choice did we have?" Now he was twirling the pen in his hand. "Not an honorable decision, I suppose, but Brandon had his whole life ahead of him. I told him he'd be a fool to stay and face charges. Duels may be illegal, but the fact is, no one's much concerned with them. He would've received little more than a slap on the hand, but that would have been enough to keep him out of public life."

"So did Lord Fortescue hold your involvement in all this over you?"

"I'm not sure what you mean, Lady Ashton." He pulled his brows close together and returned the pen to an elaborately carved cup on his desk. "What has Lord Fortescue to do with any of this?"

"He was blackmailing Mr. Brandon over the duel, a fact that will undoubtedly come into play during his trial," I said. "I wonder if perhaps you, too, were being blackmailed."

"My role in the fiasco wasn't worthy of blackmail. I didn't kill anyone. But what are you suggesting? That I was involved in Fortescue's murder?"

"Of course not." I smiled sweetly. Mr. Hamilton's eyes flashed bright, and I knew at once that he was a man who could be charmed in under half a second. "But Lord Fortescue had files on everyone. He was a staunch supporter of yours, and I don't believe he bestowed that distinction on anyone over whom he did not have power." I pulled my chair closer to the desk and leaned forward. "I do hope I'm not offending you."

He picked up the pen and began twirling it again, faster this time. "I . . . I can't say that I'm accustomed to ladies discussing these sorts of things with me."

"You seem to me enlightened enough to welcome lively discussion." It was appalling, but I actually fluttered my eyelashes.

"I—I certainly hope so."

"So what did Lord Fortescue hold over you?" I asked.

"It has to do with my mother. I will say nothing further."

"Then I will not press you on the subject," I said. This revelation made me even more disgusted with Lord Fortescue. I ran over the facts of the duel in my head again, grasping for anything that might help Robert's case, although it seemed an increasingly unlikely prospect. "One more question. It strikes me as odd that Josef Schröder chose an Englishman as his second. Were he and Albert Sanburne close friends?"

"I wouldn't say that." Now he leaned forward. "Sanburne had only been in Vienna a week or so before the duel. He'd left London on the heels of a scandal. All very hush-hush, of course."

"What sort of scandal?"

"Oh, dear. Well, I never heard the details, and it was only a rumor at any rate." He stopped and tugged at his collar. "It's not the sort of thing to which a lady should be exposed."

"Come now, Mr. Hamilton, you can tell me." He did not respond immediately, so I tilted my head and gave him a look of earnest, sweet interest that I'd not pulled from my arsenal since the first season I was out in society.

"Well." He coughed. "You've perhaps heard some mention of the Cleveland Street scandal? More than two years ago, I think."

"I can't say that I'm familiar with it." It must have occurred when I was in deep mourning for Philip, before I'd begun reading the newspaper on a regular basis.

"If I may be candid, Lady Ashton, I'm relieved to hear that."

I could find out the details of the scandal on my own. "So what was Mr. Sanburne's connection to Josef Schröder?"

"Suffice it to say that Schröder was sympathetic to Sanburne's involvement in the scandal. Please don't ask me to say more."

I did not think it possible that my opinion of Lord Fortescue could be lower than it was, but knowing that he had held over Mr. Hamilton his mother's relationship with a man she'd loved since childhood sickened me. I had no interest in tormenting the poor man, so I thanked him effusively and excused myself, amused by the way he tripped over himself to escort me from the building. From the Treasury, I went directly to the offices of the *London Daily Post* and asked to see Sir Julian Knowles.

The burly newspaperman greeted me with effusive affection and paraded me through the building as if I were a trophy he'd won in a sporting contest. "Lady Emily Ashton, boys. Aspire to earn a formal introduction to a person of her stature." He ushered me into his office, a cozy room full of walnut paneling and leaded glass windows, the unmistakable odor of pipe tobacco oozing from every corner. "To what do I owe the honor of this visit?"

I perched on the edge of a leather chair. "It's a bit embarrassing, really. I was hoping you could give me some information about the Cleveland Street scandal."

His eyebrows shot up, and he burst into a fit of coughing. "Not a topic fit for a lady." But then he leaned forward. "Why do you want to know? Have you learned that someone connected to you was involved in it?"

"No, not that. But . . ." I hesitated, wondering if I should continue. "I have some information that's related to it that may be significant to Robert Brandon's defense."

"How so?"

"First you must tell me the nature of the scandal."

"Well." More coughing. "It was . . . you see . . . the Metropolitan Police shut down a . . . er . . . house of ill repute that counted several high-ranking aristocrats among its clients."

"Oh. Is that all? Doesn't that happen with alarming frequency?"

"Not quite in this manner, Lady Ashton. And how would you know about such things?"

"I read your paper, Sir Julian."

"Yes, well . . ." He coughed again.

"What made Cleveland Street different?" I asked.

"The . . . er . . . establishment was staffed by . . . telegraph boys."

"I don't . . ." I paused, not entirely understanding.

"A brothel. Staffed by telegraph boys." He covered his mouth with a handkerchief and turned an astonishing shade of red.

"Oh," I said. "I'd assumed it was something much worse."

"Worse?"

"Sir Julian, I've read all the Greeks. I'm not so easily shocked."

"I do like you, Lady Ashton, very much." He wiped his forehead with a handkerchief and began to warm to his subject. "Lots of rumors about the Duke of Clarence connected with Cleveland Street."

"Prince Eddy?"

"The one and only. He managed to wriggle out of it, though. Lord Arthur Somerset and the Earl of Euston weren't so lucky. What has any of this to do with Brandon?" he asked.

"A gentleman called Albert Sanburne was involved in a similar scandal."

"How do you know about that?"

"Surely you can't expect I'd reveal a source?"

"Touché, Lady Ashton. I do remember Sanburne, though. And I think I see why you believe there's a connection with Brandon."

"Do tell."

"Sanburne was arrested in a similar raid. The papers all kept quiet about it. Lord Fortescue made it worth our while. But I'm afraid that's nothing to do with his murder."

"He bribed you?"

Sir Julian shrugged. "It's not a question of money, Lady Ashton. The story wasn't particularly interesting anyway, so it didn't hurt us to focus on other things. The participants weren't nearly so high-profile as those at Cleveland Street."

"Was Fortescue involved?"

"No, no, he'd never be so careless as to let himself get caught in any sort of compromising position. Sanburne worked in his office. Main reason I can recall the story at all is because although Fortescue kept it out of the papers, Sanburne was ruined anyway."

"So the scandal did become public?"

"'Public' isn't perhaps the proper word. But someone leaked it, and Sanburne's engagement was called off. The girl's father humiliated him. Chased him all the way to Vienna, if I recall."

"Who was Mr. Sanburne's fiancée?" I asked.

"Oh, I don't remember. It must have been ten years ago. And these scandals, they come and go so quickly, who could keep track of any of them?" He poured tobacco into a battered pipe.

"I imagine those whose lives were ruined don't forget so quickly."

"Now don't go spoiling my fun, Lady Ashton. If you aristocrats are going to behave badly, you've got to expect consequences."

I HARDLY SLEPT THAT NIGHT, tossing fitfully in a state of semiconsciousness. I was no closer to finding out who had killed Lord Fortescue, nor had I even a sliver of evidence that might exonerate Robert. But while all this troubled me deeply, it was not what kept me awake. I'd heard nothing from Colin since leaving Vienna, and I could not shake from my head a series of horribly imagined images of what Mr. Harrison might do to him.

At one o'clock, I rose from my bed and paced. At two forty-five, I lit a lamp and tried (and failed) to finish reading *The Picture of Dorian Gray*. At three thirty, I gave up and scrawled a note to Colin. If he was back in Vienna, he'd have found the letter I'd left detailing Schröder's plans. The message I wrote now was a simple declaration of love. Before five o'clock, I'd lost the sense of human decency that had kept me from waking my butler. I marched through hallways and upstairs to the servants' quarters, where I rapped on Davis's door.

"Madam?"

"You're already dressed," I said, surprised.

"It's nearly five o'clock."

"Heavens. I'd no idea you get up so early."

"The household, madam, does not run itself."

"Well, I shall have to send you to bed earlier. I can't have you running yourself into the ground." I passed him the paper I'd brought with me. "Would you please have this wired at once to Mr. Hargreaves in Vienna?"

"It will be my pleasure." He bowed neatly.

"And, Davis?"

"Madam?"

"You may take the afternoon off. I'm sure that Odette would appreciate seeing some of London before she and Madame du Lac return to Paris."

"Madam, let me assure you that I am not—"

I raised a hand. "That's a direct order, Davis. Don't disappoint me."

I returned to my bedroom, but there was little point in trying to sleep now. I rang for Meg, soaked in a hot bath for an obscene length of time, and dressed for the morning. None of my friends was yet awake, and I didn't want to disturb them, so I breakfasted alone, kept company only by the worry I felt for Colin.

Alone, that is, until my mother stormed through the door.

"Lady Bromley, madam," Davis called over her shoulder, not bothering to come into the room.

"Mother, I thought you were in Kent," I said, suddenly feeling even more exhausted than I had before.

"I came the moment I heard you were back in England. You did go to Newgate. I've had it confirmed by an unimpeachable source, so don't bother trying to deny it. Whatever could you have been thinking?"

"Robert asked to see me." I was too tired to come up with an excuse that might be more palatable to her.

"How dare he try to compromise you with such a request? Where is Ivy? I want to speak to her."

"She's still asleep, Mother, and I'll not have you bothering her. She's upset enough."

"Well, she ought to be. Made a very poor choice of a husband, if you ask me—"

"I didn't."

"Emily!" She rapped her umbrella on the floor. "I will not have you speak to me in such a manner. It's unconscionable that you—"

"Ivy has trouble enough to contend with. She doesn't need you to add more."

"Her situation is—"

"More dreadful than you think." I measured my words carefully, looked at my mother and raised an eyebrow.

"Really?" She spoke slowly; I nodded. "Poor, dear girl! What will become of the child? This is too awful!"

"Robert is not guilty, Mother. He will be exonerated."

"I wouldn't say that with such confidence if I were you," she said. I could see her mind working, going through the ranks of unmarried men. "There must be a respectable widower out there who would be willing to take her on. An older gentleman, perhaps. By the time she's out of mourning she will be somewhat less tainted by the scandal, but—"

"Mother! Robert is not dead."

She sighed. "Of course not. But it never hurts to plan ahead."

"Now that you've mentioned scandals, though, I've a question for you." This piqued her interest, but she waited until a maid had poured coffee for her and left the room before asking me to elaborate. "Do you remember Albert Sanburne?" I asked.

"Sanburne . . ." She looked towards the ceiling for approximately fifteen seconds before bringing her attention back to me. "Oh, yes. Sanburne. Such a tragedy that he died so young. And his poor sister! How we all despaired for her. She was left without even enough money for a dowry. None of her relatives wanted to take care of the girl—as I recall, she moved from house to house every six months or so. To lose a brother so soon after the deaths of both her dear parents. Too awful for words."

"To put it mildly," I said.

"I must say, Emily, that I did fear for your health while you were in Vienna. The influenza is worse there than anywhere. I'm convinced Sanburne would never have died had he contracted the disease somewhere else."

"Why had he gone to Vienna?" I asked. "I understand there was some to-do over his engagement."

"Oh, yes. I believe the girl's father went all the way to Vienna to break the betrothal."

"That's strange, isn't it?"

"Fathers are protective of daughters. It was said that his objections to Mr. Sanburne were very strong indeed."

"What were they?"

"I don't know. It was never discussed."

"Who was the girl?"

"Helen Macinnis. She was heartbroken at the time, but wound up marrying a captain in the Horse Guards. It was an excellent match." She poured a second cup of coffee. "To return to the reason for my visit, I cannot allow—"

"Did you know, Mother, that Mr. Sanburne did not actually die of influenza?"

"What can you possibly mean by that? Of course he did. It was in all the newspapers."

"He committed suicide in Vienna. It was in all the papers there."

"Is that so?"

"I'm absolutely certain. Have even confirmed it with Sir Julian Knowles." As I spoke, I saw in her eyes an admiration that had never before been directed to me. But then I'd never before given her such stunning gossip.

"Did I tell you that your father and I have been invited to Sandringham for Prince Eddy's birthday dinner next week?" she asked. "Perhaps I could ask the queen if the invitation might be extended to include you."

"I wouldn't want to impose. Particularly when she's been so gracious about the wedding."

"Oh, I suppose you're right. Now, have your servants prepare a room for me. I may as well spend a few days with you before I return to the country."

2 January 1892
Vienna

Dear Kallista,

How sorry I was to call at the Imperial today and find you had left Austria without so much as a good-bye! So I must write to commend you and Cécile on your brilliance. Word about my drawing of the empress leaked out almost the moment she left the Hotel Imperial. It was reported yesterday in the newspaper that she was so pleased with the image that she gave it to the emperor, just as she'd told us she planned to do.

Since then, I have been flooded with portrait commissions—funnily enough, no one wants me to paint them—only to do a charcoal as I did for the empress. Sketches are now all the rage in Vienna.

Best of all, however, is that the dreaded Frau Eckoldt is thawing towards me. She wants a drawing of her own, and I have agreed to do hers before anyone else's. She told me that if she likes my work, she will invite me to tea at her house. I am certain that it is only a matter of time before my darling Anna and I are engaged. I owe you multitudinous thanks, especially because the assistance you provided would have had no effect if the empress did not truly appreciate my skills. So I emerge from this with pride intact.

On a sadder note, I should tell you that we've lost a mutual friend. Gustav Schröder committed suicide on New Year's Eve. I know you will be as sorry as I was to hear this news.

I hope this letter finds you well and am wishing you much happiness in the New Year. Please tell your friend Bainbridge that I've sent the sketch of you he requested to his London address.

One last thing. I've just come from Klimt's and saw his finished portrait of Cécile. It's stunning, but surprising, too. He gave her your eyes.

Friedrich Henkler

P.S. I am enclosing a set of poems that Viktor asked me to forward to you. They are from Hugo von Hofmannsthal, who I'm told regrets very much that he was not able to meet you before your hasty departure from the city.

Chapter 24

I tried to persuade my mother that she would be much happier back in Kent with my father, opening her own house in Grosvenor Square, visiting my late husband's family, being anywhere but Berkeley Square—but she would not be swayed, and in fact left me in mid-sentence to ensconce herself in one of my bedrooms.

I could not leave my friends to wake up unsuspecting and find her with us, so I knocked on Cécile's door to warn her of the addition to our party. I was greeted by enthusiastic barks from Caesar and Brutus, who were vying with each other for prime position to attack my skirt from the moment I stepped into the room. I scooped them both up and dropped them on Cécile's bed.

"Your pets are the most ill-mannered I've ever known."

"They are terrible little things, aren't they?" She scratched Caesar's head and patted Brutus.

"I'd wager Friedrich and Anna will be married before next Christmas," I said, handing her the letter from our friend.

"*Magnifique!* But what is this about Jeremy wanting a sketch of you?"

"I'm afraid to ask."

"I feel for the poor man."

"Don't. I can assure you that I am attractive to him only because there's no chance I'll try to force him to marry me." Brutus sniffed at my hand, and I scratched his ears. "Here are your letters. One looks to be from Klimt."

"How odd. I shouldn't have thought he would write. But then, we weren't able to have a formal farewell."

"Will you see him again?"

"Perhaps. Does it matter?"

"I would hope so."

"I must admit it does." She smiled, but said nothing further.

"On a wholly unrelated topic, I've come to warn you. My mother is here, and I'm abandoning you to her."

"Ah! She is always entertaining."

"You'll find yourself exhausted within twenty minutes of sitting down with her."

"So why are you leaving me alone with her?" she asked.

I told her about Albert Sanburne and Helen Macinnis. "I've got to speak to her father."

"You know where to find him?"

"Davis sent a footman to his house this morning. The family is not in residence, but Mr. Macinnis is in town, staying at his club." I sat on the edge of her bed. "And while I'm on the subject of Davis, you'd best give Odette the afternoon off."

"*Pourquoi?*"

"Because I've directed Davis to give her a tour of London."

"Must you encourage them, Kallista? Nothing good can ever come of it."

"Not for us, maybe, but certainly for them."

I HAD NO INTENTION of showing up unannounced at the Carlton Club. Instead, I'd sent a note to Mr. Macinnis and had the boy who delivered it wait for a reply. He agreed to meet me at the British Museum at eleven o'clock. No sooner had I stepped inside the magnificent building on Great Russell Street than a sense of calm melted through me. The familiar galleries welcomed me, and as always, I felt a mythic enchantment at finding myself surrounded by so much history.

Mr. Macinnis was waiting for me in front of the Judgment of Paris vase my husband had donated to the museum shortly before his death. I'd suggested this location because the Rosetta Stone seemed too obvious.

"I can't thank you enough for agreeing to see me," I said, giving him my hand as he approached me.

He bowed and kissed my hand. "Your note took me by surprise. Sanburne's name is not one I'd hoped to hear again."

"I can well imagine, and I apologize for dredging it up. I must start by saying that I know all about the scandal in which he was involved. Please don't feel any need to protect me from unsavory information. I'm here because what happened all those years ago may pertain to the murder of Lord Fortescue."

"You're absolutely on the wrong track, Lady Ashton. Fortescue was the most upstanding man in the empire. Capital fellow. I feel like I owe him my life. Or at least my daughter's."

"How so?"

"It was Fortescue who alerted me to Sanburne's deviant nature. Had he not, I can't imagine the life my Helen would have led."

I cringed at this harsh assessment of Albert Sanburne. "Lord Fortescue told you?"

"Yes. Sanburne had fled to Vienna, and I went after him, wanting to confront him in person. Helen was deeply in love with him. Ending the engagement broke her heart. Frankly, I wanted to kill him."

"It must have been awful. What did he say?"

"Very little, actually. It was a pathetic scene. He cried and begged my forgiveness. Killed himself the next day. Only honorable thing the man did in his life."

And just then, my heart broke more than a little for Albert Sanburne. I found myself unable to speak for a moment. "Does anyone else know this?"

"We kept it as quiet as possible. Helen had suffered enough, and I didn't want the fingers of scandal to touch her. Furthermore, I saw no reason to put Sanburne's family through more grief. I knew that his sister, Mary, would have a difficult time finding somewhere to live after his death. I circulated the story that he'd died of influenza, although I imagine it didn't make things all that much easier for the girl. Still, better than if people knew there'd been a suicide in the family." He shifted his weight uncomfortably.

"I appreciate your telling me all this," I said.

"I nearly refused to talk to you," he said. "But I've never felt good about how things turned out with Sanburne. Despite the fact that—well, the less said about it the better."

I thanked Mr. Macinnis and made my way back through the fog to Berkeley Square, as the beginnings of a most unwelcome thought started to weave their way through my brain. And though I would have liked more than anything to ignore them, I knew I could not.

MARGARET MET ME at my front door. "Any word from Colin?" I asked.

"No, I'm sorry. Nothing," she said. "But your mother! Heavens!"

"Oh, dear." I removed my hat and handed it, along with my coat, to a waiting footman. "What has she done?"

"She's got Ivy upstairs and refuses to allow her out of bed, let alone to come downstairs. And she's bent on marrying me off to one of Lady Elliott's sons."

"Not Henry?"

"Yes, Henry."

"No, he's all wrong for you."

"How long is she going to be here? I've always considered your house a safe haven, Emily. This is intolerable."

"You don't need to explain, Margaret. I lived with her for years."

"What happened with Mr. Hamilton?"

"Emily! Are you back?" My mother was calling down the stairs. "Come up here at once."

I heaved a sigh and started up the steps, Margaret following behind. "I want to hear about Hamilton," she whispered.

"It will have to wait."

My mother led us to the yellow bedroom, where Ivy was perched in bed, her feet propped up on a towering stack of pillows.

"You've not yet finished your broth, child." My mother picked up a bowl from the bedside table and thrust it at Ivy. "You must apply yourself to it if you want a strong boy."

Ivy did as she was told, her eyes wide. Mother turned to me. "I've told your cook she needs at least six bowls of beef broth every day and a strong glass of red wine. She must not be exposed to anything unpleasant during her confinement—"

"Her confinement?" I interrupted. "Mother, you can't possibly expect that she's going to stay in bed for the next . . . I don't even know how many months."

"Six." Ivy's voice was barely audible.

"Finish your broth." My mother turned to me and spoke in a low voice. "I've removed all the inappropriate materials from this room."

"Inappropriate materials?" I asked.

"That pile of papers, of course. What were you thinking, giving her Oscar Wilde to read? I fear for your common sense, Emily."

"You mean the script of *Lady Windermere's Fan*? Where is it? What did you do with it?"

260 260 ♦ *Tasha Alexander*

"I threw it directly in the fire. Appalling man, Wilde. Not an ounce of restraint in him."

"The fire?" I leaned back against the wall and rubbed my forehead. "Tell me you didn't."

"Stand up straight, Emily. Have you no concern for your posture? Of course I put it in the fire. What else would you have me do with such a vile thing? I opened it up. 'I can resist everything but temptation'? What sort of a person says such a thing?"

"I found it rather amusing," I said.

"Don't be ridiculous. It's wholly inappropriate for a lady in Ivy's condition, and you, my dear, aren't even married."

"But I *was* married," I walked to the fireplace and knocked the logs with a poker, but every trace of the script was gone.

"And Miss Seward! What if she were to get her hands on such a thing?"

"Oh, Lady Bromley, I would never give it so much as a passing glance," Margaret said, a broad smile on her face.

"Now there"—my mother nodded at Margaret—"is a girl with good sense."

"Where is Cécile?" I asked.

"She's bathing," my mother said, doing her best not to frown. "The French do have different habits than we English. But Madame du Lac is from an excellent family. Did you know, Miss Seward, that I believe they may have connections to royalty?"

"Fascinating," Margaret said. "I always thought I saw something regal in Cécile's manner."

"I am looking so forward to getting to know you better while I am here, Miss Seward. I'm beginning to think my initial impression of you was entirely wrong."

"Will you excuse me, Lady Bromley? I'm going to the library to try to find something inspiring for Ivy to read." Margaret winked at me as she backed out of the door.

"Go with her, Emily," my mother said. "Ivy needs to rest. You

may come up in a few hours and say a quick hello, but you must
not bother her."

I threw a sympathetic glance Ivy's way as I left the room. Margaret was waiting for me in the hall, sitting on the floor, laughing
silently.

"What on earth are you doing?" I asked.

"I've decided to befriend your mother."

"You're awful," I said, pulling her to her feet and heading back
downstairs. "Be careful, or she'll have you engaged by the end of
the month."

"There's no danger of that happening. I'm perfectly able to
take care of myself."

"Is Cécile really bathing?"

"She is. Meg was assisting her. Odette and Davis left together
hours ago. Everyone belowstairs is buzzing about it."

"How do you know?" I asked.

"Because after I watched them leave, I went downstairs myself
to see what everyone was saying. You've a charming group of servants."

"Would you expect anything else?"

"No. They're awfully protective of you. And terrified to learn
who will go with you to Park Lane and who will be left behind once
you're married."

"I've not even begun to think about that."

"Hearts will be broken. Depend upon it."

Just as we reached the bottom of the steps, someone knocked
loudly on the front door.

"I'll play Davis," Margaret said to the footman who'd stepped
forward to answer it. He bowed and returned to his post while she
swung open the heavy door to reveal a distinguished-looking gentleman. "Mr. Michaels!" Margaret grinned. "What a surprise to see
you. Come in. You remember Lady Ashton?"

"Of course." He nodded at me, started to reach for my hand,

then stopped and turned to Margaret. "I was concerned when you did not reply to my last note."

"So you came back to London?"

"I thought you might have taken offense to my most recent comments on *Ars Amatoria*."

"No, far from it. I thought they were quite brilliant," Margaret said. "Shall we go to the library?" My mother came down the stairs just as we started for the hallway, and I hung back to wait for her.

"Who is that?" she asked.

"Mr. Michaels. He's a don at Oxford."

She wrinkled her nose.

"I understand he's from a very wealthy family," I whispered. "Have you heard the stories about Henry Elliott?"

"No. Do tell."

"I will as soon as I return. I've an appointment I must keep." I felt a wicked smile on my face. "Could you chaperone them for me?"

"With pleasure."

Margaret turned back and winked at me. She had no idea what was in store for her.

I MADE MY WAY to Paddington Station and caught the first train to Windsor, where I found Mrs. Reynold-Plympton in her animal-filled drawing room sewing a black mourning band onto a handkerchief. She hardly looked up when her butler announced me.

"How did you find Mr. Hamilton? Was he of any use to you?"

"In a way," I said.

"Do you want tea?"

"No, thank you. I want to ask you a question that's undoubtedly inappropriate."

She tossed aside the handkerchief. "My favorite kind. What is it?"

"Why did Lord Fortescue propose to Mary Sanburne?"

"It does seem an unlikely match, doesn't it?" she asked. "She brought him no money, and she's certainly no beauty."

"And it does not appear there was much affection between them."

"There was enough to make the arrangement palatable to both of them."

"But he adored you," I said.

"In his way, yes." Her smile was thin.

"Why did he choose her?"

"It was odd, really. Quite unlike his usual decisions. Basil told me in no uncertain terms that he'd always felt bad about what had happened to her family, especially after the queen gave him her father's title and estate."

"So he married her in an attempt to make up for all that?"

"Essentially, yes."

"Did she know that?"

"I believe he told her when he proposed."

I rested my hand on my chin and bit my lip. "I can't imagine how difficult it would be to watch the man you love marry someone else."

"Marriages are just a form of doing business," she said. "It never troubled me."

"I can't believe that. You love him."

"Loved him. He's gone now, and I can't even mourn him openly." She closed her eyes, one hand clutching at her knee, the other clenched in a fist brought to her mouth.

"He shouldn't have married her," I said. "He should have waited until . . . until he could have had you."

"Yes, well, Basil was never the sort of man to bow to anyone else's wishes. We got along well precisely because I could accept that."

"But it's so sad."

"Yet much better than nothing." She folded her hands in her lap and straightened her back. "It was the right thing to do, marrying her. How could I fault him for it? It was the only thing I've ever known him to do that was completely selfless."

Chapter 25

Two more days passed without a word from Colin. Without knowing even the name of the town where he had gone, there was no way I could reach him, or even send an inquiry to the authorities. The kaiser would arrive in Vienna tomorrow and attend the court choirboys' performance the following day. I should have told him everything I'd learned from the empress, not just skeletal facts. Withholding the information hadn't accomplished anything positive, only put innocent people at risk. But surely he'd figured it out.

If he were still alive.

A sentence that I couldn't bear to say aloud. Not to Margaret, or Ivy, or Cécile, or even to myself. I tried to focus on Robert in Newgate, hoping that would push thoughts of Colin from my mind. This was futile, of course, but also unnecessary. I should have realized that my mother's presence would serve as its own monumental distraction.

"I'm not sure what to think of this don of Miss Seward's," she said, accosting me in my bedroom as I was dressing for dinner. "He's well-mannered and decent enough looking. A bit old for her, perhaps, but she's the sort of girl who could stand a firm guiding force in her life."

I raised my eyebrows and looked in the mirror, watching Meg expertly win another struggle to force my hair into submission. "They are very well suited to one another, but I'm not sure that Margaret has any intention of getting married."

"You talk such nonsense, Emily. The girl needs to be married. Mr. Michaels has a decent income. Not spectacular—I certainly wouldn't want you to settle for such a thing—but she is American, after all, and she does have a fortune of her own. It's a pity she and the Duke of Bainbridge were never able to work out their differences, but really, she may be better off where she is."

"Can it be, Mother, that you're contemplating the arrangement of a love match?"

"Love's all well and good, so long as it doesn't distract from what's really important. You never did tell me why you object to Henry Elliott for her."

"Well . . ." I watched her in the mirror. "It's not so much that I've an objection to Henry. But I've heard that there is a certain young woman with an impeccable background and egregious fortune who's set her cap for him."

"Really? Who?"

"I'm not at liberty to reveal a confidence." Particularly when it was entirely fictional.

"Does Henry know this?"

"If he doesn't, he will soon."

"How interesting. I shall tell Lady Elliott to keep her ear to the ground. Perhaps I should speak with Mr. Michaels this evening."

Already I felt sorry for Mr. Michaels. He did not stand a chance.

I missed Ivy that night. Cowed by my mother, she was keeping to her bed, but I was beginning to think she was enjoying herself. I'd slipped her my copy of *Lost and Saved*, Caroline Norton's sensational novel of Beatrice Brooke, who is tricked into believing that her lover has married her after she falls ill while they're on an illicit trip to Egypt. Melodrama at its best.

I paid only the slightest attention to my friends that evening. After dinner, when we'd retired to the library, I sat at my desk and started to write a letter to Colin, balling up the paper before I'd finished three sentences and beginning again.

"That's your fifth fresh start," Margaret said half an hour later, carrying the decanter with her and refilling my port. "What are you writing?"

"Apparently nothing," I said.

"I wish someone would spend half that time crafting a letter for me," Jeremy said.

"You'd have to be less of a cad to earn such treatment," I said.

"You needn't be so cruel." He sipped his port.

"Emily's horribly cruel," Margaret said and then lowered her voice. "But I'm having more fun than I would've thought possible playing with her mother. She's unexpectedly amusing."

"You say that now," I said. "I wonder if you'll still believe it next week when she's started planning your wedding."

"It will never happen. Besides, I'd have to get married in New York. I'm safe."

"No one is safe from Lady Bromley," Jeremy said. "I've known that since before I could walk."

Margaret circled the room, filling everyone's glasses and only briefly joining Cécile and Mr. Michaels in an animated conversation before stopping in front of my mother. "Now, Lady Bromley, you must humor me and try some port."

"I categorically refuse," my mother said. "It's unseemly."

"Do you really think so?" Margaret asked, her face a mask of mock sincerity.

"There's no question." She dropped her voice to her favorite and overly loud stage whisper. "What would Mr. Michaels say?"

"Oh, I wouldn't worry about that. He thinks it's an excellent vintage." She pressed a glass into my mother's hand. For a moment it appeared as if she would drink it, and I prepared myself to be overwhelmed with awe for Margaret. But alas, it was too much to hope. My mother deposited the glass on a table and asked for sherry. I was about to ring for Davis when he entered the room.

"This was just delivered," he said, handing me a wire. I tore it open at once, hoping it was from Colin. It was not.

> *Meeting soon with someone who may be persuaded to help me stop*
> *H. No sign of C. which means he's hard at work. No cause to worry.*
> *—Kristiana von Lange*

THE COUNTESS'S SUGGESTION that I ought not worry had precisely the opposite effect on me. I had an appointment with Sir Julian the following morning, the first day he was back from a brief jaunt into the country. I felt so lethargic that I sent for my carriage instead of walking to his office and spent the entire drive pulling at my gloves, wondering what was happening in Vienna.

"I do hope you'll make a regular habit of calling, Lady Ashton," Sir Julian said as soon as I'd arrived at his office. "Your charm is devastating, and it gives the boys a lift to see you."

"I'm not sure that's an appropriate compliment, but I shall accept it with grace nonetheless."

"You are too kind, Lady Ashton, too kind." He slammed his hand down on his desk. "Now! What can I do for you? Do you need more information about the debauched failings of your peers?"

"No. Do you remember, at Beaumont Towers one evening before dinner you were talking to Lady Fortescue, and she excused herself rather suddenly?"

"Yes, I think I do. It was a bit strange, but she's an odd sort of woman. An exceedingly poor conversationalist."

"What were you talking about when she ran out?" I asked. "I heard you say something about scandals delighting us."

"Yes, let's see . . . I was telling her about her husband's penchant for controlling the newspapers."

"Did you tell her about Albert Sanburne?"

"Of course not. Though I suppose I did make an oblique sort of reference to his case and said that her husband had paid to keep the story out of the paper."

"She might have known to whom you were referring."

"Impossible. Only someone with a very close connection would have caught the reference."

"You don't know who she is, then?" I asked. "Albert Sanburne was her brother."

"Yes, yes, but I can't imagine anyone would have told her the details of the affair. She was just a girl. She couldn't possibly have known."

I knew at once that Sir Julian couldn't have been more wrong.

I RACED BACK to Berkeley Square to collect my friends, but Margaret and Cécile were out, and my mother was reading to Ivy from the Bible; there was no chance I could steal her away and take her to Yorkshire with me. I just made the train I needed, and as I sat in my compartment, I felt nothing but anxious dread. Ordinarily, a book would have served as a welcome distraction, but instead of a novel, I'd brought with me the Greek grammar that Colin had given me more than a year ago; the volume he'd used in school. I paged through it idly, not really reading, certainly not studying, simply taking slim comfort in the fact that he had held the book himself.

I'd wired Lady Fortescue to alert her of my arrival, and she had a carriage waiting for me at the station. The drive along the moors was shorter than I remembered it. All too soon I was looking up at the edifice of Beaumont Towers. I'd never liked the house—it was an architectural nightmare—but now it had been imbued with a feeling of piercing sadness that prevented me from casting upon it a critical eye.

Inside, the clocks were all stopped, the windows covered with heavy drapes. The household was in deep mourning. Lady Fortescue received me in a small chamber, the same one where I'd found her worrying about dinner with the prime minister on my previous visit.

"Forgive me for disturbing you," I said. "This is a lovely room."

"It's where my mother did all her work," she said. "I loved coming in here when I was a girl."

"I can see why."

"You said it was urgent that you see me." Her face was strained, but she looked as if she had more strength than when I'd last seen her.

"Yes. I wanted to speak to you about your brother and your husband."

She blanched. "Why?"

"I know what happened."

"What could you possibly mean?" she asked.

"You know exactly what I mean," I said. "I pieced it all together."

"How?" She clutched at her chair. Her eyes clouded, and blotches of color stained her cheeks as her arms began to shake.

"The other pistol is in Vienna."

"Where? I've tried to find it but couldn't."

"The guns were used in a duel. The brother of the man who was killed kept the other one."

"He can have it. I understand the need for bloody prizes. I knew that Albert bought the set in Vienna—he'd mentioned in a letter having them engraved—but I'd no idea they'd been used."

"When did you learn of your husband's involvement with your brother?"

"At the party that weekend you were here." She hugged herself as if trying to stop the shaking. "And I couldn't believe it. That this man who had offered me kindness, who had brought me home, that he was the person responsible for all the misfortune in my life. And my dear brother"—she started to weep—"he was so hopeless. His letter broke my heart."

"He sent you a letter?"

"Yes, from Vienna before he killed himself."

"But how old were you?"

"Twelve."

"He told you what he was going to do?"

"Not specifically. Just that he'd met with certain ruin and wouldn't be coming home. He said that one man had destroyed him."

"But he didn't say who?" I asked.

"Not by name. Only that the man who'd bought his freedom turned on him." She took the handkerchief I offered her. "When Sir Julian told me Albert's story—I recognized it, of course—I knew at once that my husband was responsible."

"Did you confront him about it?"

"I did. He laughed at me, Lady Ashton. Laughed. Told me not to worry about the past now that I'm so comfortably settled. Had I the means, I would have killed him on the spot."

"So what did you do?"

"I got Albert's gun." She pressed the handkerchief to her mouth, making her words difficult to understand. "One of his friends in Vienna sent his possessions to me, including the gun and its case."

"I—I'm so sorry," I said.

"I'm not. Only exhausted. Do you know what it is like to have everything taken from you? Your house, your possessions, your very position? To be passed around, never welcome anywhere? To know that your best hope for happiness is to be little more than a servant? For ten years I've lived in grief. There's nothing left for me to suffer."

"How did you . . . ."

"Shoot him? It was simple. I'd always excelled at archery, so Albert decided to teach me to shoot after my parents died."

"What did you do?"

"I got the gun out of the library—I wanted to use the same pistol that had ended my brother's life. I walked out to where the gentlemen were, hid in some brush a short distance away, and fired when I knew the sound would be muffled by their own shotguns."

"It must have been awful."

Her eyes filled with tears. "It was. But I could not let him live."

I reached for her hand. "And you can't let Mr. Brandon be hanged for a crime he didn't commit."

"I can't . . . I just can't . . . I know it's wrong of me, but I can't face it."

"You have to, Mary," I said, reaching for her hand. "I know what happened. I'm going to tell the police. Please understand that I have no choice."

"No." She shook her head, over and over.

"I must. But surely there's some way to gain mercy for you. Anyone could understand what you've been through. Your circumstances, the fact that your own husband betrayed you in such a way . . . There must be some way for me to help you."

She rose from her chair, and for a moment I was scared. Not that she could have overpowered me, but suddenly I imagined that she had the dueling pistol in her hand. Ridiculous, of course. She hadn't known what to expect when I arrived. But emotions play funny tricks.

"Think of Mrs. Brandon. She's expecting a baby, Mary. Don't take away its father."

"A baby?"

I nodded.

"Another child with a ruined life," she said, her voice flat.

"I will help you, I promise. There are very few gentlemen in Britain who haven't feared being destroyed by Lord Fortescue. Could you tell me exactly what your brother's letter said? I think that so long as we can prove you were certain your husband was instrumental in Albert's downfall, we may be able . . ." I didn't want to make false promises. She would spend the rest of her life in prison, but that would be better than facing execution. I would visit her, bring her books, do whatever I could to ease her pain. "Well, we may be able to make things easier for you."

"I've never shown anyone his letter."

"Please, please, Mary." I took her hand. "Let me help you."

"You really think it will make a difference?"

"I do," I said, hoping that I was right.

"I'll let you read it. If you'll excuse me for a moment, I'll bring it to you."

"Of course."

Almost as soon as she'd left, I realized what she was doing. I ran out of the room, calling for her, desperately rushing down hallway after hallway as quickly as possible, hoping that I could find her. I was too late.

A single shot rang out before I reached the door of the library.

Chapter 26

It took all of my will to force my hand to open the door. Mary was sprawled on the floor, her brother's dueling pistol less than a foot from her hand, a star-shaped wound in her forehead, a thin line of blood running down her face. I forced myself to go to her, to see if she was still alive, but of course she was not. Almost without realizing what I was doing, I reached out and closed her eyes, unable to bear the vacant sadness in them.

Servants burst into the room, and someone pulled me up from the floor, but I did not require assistance. I maintained my composure, feeling detached, almost as if I were watching the scene through a window, but at the same time knowing that when I found myself alone, I would be overwhelmed with what I'd seen. On the table next to where Mary had fallen was the mahogany box that had contained the pistol. It was closed, and placed on top of it was a letter. I unfolded it, expecting it to be Albert's. Instead, it was written in his sister's shaky hand:

I, Mary Fortescue, confess to the murder of my husband, Lord Basil Fortescue.

DATED THIS 5 JANUARY 1892.

There was no sign of Albert's letter. I pulled out the velvet interior, hoping there was something else in the box, but there was nothing. I looked back at Mary and fell to my knees next to her. I hesitated to touch her, but forced myself, and gently opened her clutched hand. She was holding the charred bits of paper I'd seen the first time I'd looked in the case.

For the first time in my life, I felt more than a little inclined to faint, but managed to stay calm and called for help, directing the servants to send for the police, who arrived with astonishing speed. Or perhaps I was unaware of how much time had passed. An officer tried to remove me from the room, but I refused to be sent away until I could be certain every detail of the case had been addressed, certain that Robert would be released, and certain that someone other than one of Lord Fortescue's children would arrange for Mary's burial.

I kept my voice steady as I answered the policemen's questions, holding my hands tightly together so they wouldn't shake. They said it was obviously a suicide, that they would check the handwriting on her note against other letters she was known to have written, that they would interview the servants again to ascertain whether she'd been seen leaving the house before her husband's death. This was all perfunctory, of course, but procedure must be followed.

Soon enough, they were satisfied. The body was removed, the servants set to cleaning the carpet. But I stood, still wondering how Mary came to possess the pistol. After Lord Fortescue's murder, the police had put the murder weapon in the room they'd used to interview everyone in the house, locking the door whenever they left. Mary, who had keys to all the rooms, would have seen the gun when they questioned her—they'd shown it to each of us. She could easily have slipped back into the room to steal it. No one noticed it was missing until they'd been ordered to send their evidence to Scotland Yard.

As I watched the servants bustling to bring the house back to an ordinary state, I realized I was not capable of returning to mundane thoughts as quickly as those around me. I was relieved that Robert would be released and returned to Ivy, but could take only limited joy in the resolution. I should never have let Mary leave the room alone. I should have followed her, should have done a better job convincing her that I could help her. I could not accept the idea that to stop her would have been impossible.

And although I knew that I was not culpable—not really—this was an instance when knowledge brought no comfort. Justice was being served, but in a most painful manner. Mary's face wouldn't stop haunting me.

Chapter 27

I left Beaumont Towers as soon as I could, and within a few hours of my return to London, Robert was released from Newgate and came to Berkeley Square. My friends, understanding my melancholy, had left me to my thoughts in the library, where I was sitting alone on the window seat, staring out across the foggy park, when Robert opened the door.

"Emily . . ." He hesitated, then stepped forward and embraced me. "I shall never be able to thank you for what you've done."

"Dear Robert," I said. "I didn't do it for thanks."

"But you look sad. There's no need for that now." He was clearly exhausted, but the joy in his eyes knew no measure. He was radiant.

"I've still had no word from Colin."

"Colin? Where is he?" he asked.

"Didn't Ivy tell you?"

"I've not yet seen her. I thought I should come to you first because I owe you my life."

"Go to your wife!" I stood up and practically pushed him out of the room.

"First tell me about Hargreaves," he said. "You must let me help you now."

As briefly as possible, I explained all that had transpired while he was in prison.

"I'm not sure that I've contacts in the government anymore. We will go to Vienna ourselves and find him. Let me speak with Ivy, and then I will arrange everything."

He rushed off to see his wife, but I did not begin preparing for a trip. Whatever Mr. Harrison had planned would have happened today. I could not get there in time. And even if it were possible to do so, what could I do once there? I stayed on the window seat, trying to read a translation of Ovid's *Ars Amatoria* that Margaret had left in the library, while my friends rejoiced in Robert's return.

"Madam?" Davis opened the door. "Mr. Brandon said to inform you that he's booked you tickets to Vienna. You'll need to be ready to leave within the hour. Meg has already packed your bags, but Madame du Lac and Miss Seward are arguing as to who will take the third ticket."

"Why on earth would you go back to Vienna?" My mother followed close on Davis's heels. "Mr. Hargreaves will come here as soon as he's able. Emily, it is time that you stop gallivanting about the Continent. If you must travel, come to Sandringham with your father and me. Prince Eddy's birthday dinner is tomorrow."

"No, Mother, I've no desire to go to Sandringham. Nor Vienna, for that matter."

"And that is the first sensible statement I've had from you in I know not how long." She stepped close to me and leaned into my face. "Good heavens, child, are you merely exhausted, or are you getting lines at the corners of your eyes?"

I backed away while she pulled out her spectacles. "A bit of both, I imagine. But perhaps it's time my face began to show some character. Perfection, I'm told, is tedious."

"Don't be ridiculous. We must take action at once. Where's Meg? She must make up a mixture of—"

"No, Mother. I've no time for such things."

"And I've no time to argue with you if I'm to make it to Sandringham."

"Mother—" I knew the expression on her face well. There was no winning this battle. I handed her a piece of paper and pen from my desk. "Write down what I should do. I'll take care of it tonight."

"See to it that you do. You don't want Mr. Hargreaves seeing you like this. He'd be appalled."

"Yes, Mother."

Despite her insistence that she was in a hurry, she did not rush when writing the directions for whatever this miracle of beauty was. Every letter on the page was perfectly formed; she could never tolerate anything less. "Now, I'm off, but I must tell you that I'm quite concerned about Ivy. She tells me her parents are still in India, and I think that until they get back to England, she should come stay at Darnley House. I can make sure she's getting the care she needs."

"I'm certain Robert's perfectly capable of taking care of her."

"Child, I fear for you. Your expectations for husbands are positively wild. I've already arranged for her to come to me. Robert's welcome as well, of course, now that this dreadful business of his is finished."

"I don't—"

"Nothing more. I must run." She kissed me on the forehead and left for the train station. Not much later, Robert was back, holding my coat.

"We must go, Emily. Bainbridge is coming, too. He'll meet us at the station."

THE ARGUMENT OVER who would go to Vienna was a heated one. In the end, Cécile agreed to stay in London with Ivy, who obviously was in no condition to travel into such dangerous circumstances. Margaret, who felt it keenly that she had missed the finales of my last two adventures, insisted on accompanying us. She did, however, send a wire to Mr. Michaels in Oxford before we left.

Robert's parents came to the station with us, clearly displeased that their son was bent on traveling. Ivy clung to her husband's arm, sorry to lose him again so soon after his return, but there was no trace of anxiety on her face. Her porcelain skin was perfectly smooth. She knew he would come back to her.

"You must be delighted to be out of bed at last," I said, hugging her as I was about to board the train.

"It is a relief, I confess. But your mother was very kind to me in her way."

"Be careful, my dear," I said. "She's prepared to watch over you for the next six months."

"Wire us as soon as you have news," Ivy said. "I don't think I'll be able to sleep until we hear from you. I hope—" She stopped.

"So do I," I said.

"I don't know why you're all so worried." Cécile kissed me on both cheeks. "Do you forget that Monsieur Hargreaves is not only devastatingly handsome, but exceedingly clever, too? This Harrison is no match for him. And keep your eye on Jeremy. I expect you to send me news of what is transpiring between him and Rina."

We'd barely reached our compartment when a telegram boy burst in, holding an envelope. My heart leapt, certain that it was news of Colin.

It was not.

It was for Margaret, from Mr. Michaels. She did not tell me what it said, but it made her blush, and after she read it, she buried herself in some poem of Ovid's she was translating.

My stomach lurched as the train started, and it felt as if every nerve in my body was charged with a nervous, biting energy. When I thought about how long it would take for us to get to Vienna, it seemed intolerable, and I wondered how I would survive. Jeremy had drifted off almost before we left the station. I envied him. If only I could sleep.

Then Robert handed a book to me: *Gerard; or, The World, the Flesh, and the Devil* by Mary Elizabeth Braddon. "I believe it is her latest," he said.

"When did you have time to get it?" I asked.

"I sent one of your footmen out while Meg was packing your things."

"Dare I hope that you've begun to see the value of popular fiction?"

"Not as such. Worthless drivel, all of it, and quite corrupting. But you have convinced me that there are times when that's precisely what the mind requires, and I think, my friend, that for you this is one of those times."

"You enjoyed *Lady Audley's Secret*?" I asked.

"Immensely." He leaned close and spoke in a low voice. "But I'll never admit that to anyone but you."

"There's hope for you yet, Robert."

He squeezed my hand.

THE CROSSING TO CALAIS was stormy, but the churning water had little effect on me. I was too lost in my thoughts and worries to take notice of anything short of a biblical gale. When we reached France, it was raining, a cold winter rain that with very little encouragement would turn to sleet. I stepped carefully down the ferry's gangplank, grateful for Robert's steady arm, Margaret and Jeremy walking in front of us. We were standing on the dock, prepared to head for the train that would take us to Vienna, when I saw him.

He was walking with purpose towards the ferry, carrying a satchel, a book tucked under his arm. All of it clattered to the wet ground when he looked up to see me running towards him.

"Colin!" I threw my arms around him, nearly knocking him over. His embrace engulfed me, and he kissed every inch of my face before pulling back to look at me. "You're hurt," I said, gently touching a ragged gash next to his eyebrow.

"Kristiana is dead."

Chapter 28

I 'm so sorry."

I seemed unable to stop repeating the words. We had all gone straight back onto the ferry and were on our way to England, Margaret, Jeremy, and Robert leaving Colin and me alone in my cabin.

"I am too," he said, his voice low and husky.

"Was it Harrison?"

"Yes. She had persuaded Kaufman—one of Schröder's associates—to talk to her. When she went to meet him, Harrison was there instead." He ran a hand through his hair. "The most awful part is that I already knew the details of their plans. She needn't have met him at all. She didn't know."

"It's not your fault," I said, pulling his head onto my shoulder.

"When I left Vienna before New Year's, it was to divert the shipment of explosives that was going to Schröder. His plan was to set off a series of bombs while the emperor and the kaiser were attending a performance of the court boys' choir. I learned the details from the explosive carriers."

"How?" I asked.

"When I realized I could infiltrate the group, I decided not to return to Vienna. The town we were in was remote. I couldn't wire her."

"Colin—"

"I hadn't planned to be there so long, but it became clear that if I stayed, I'd have the opportunity not only to uncover the plot, but to sabotage the explosives."

"And did you?"

"Yes, not that it mattered in the end. We were able to stop them before they planted the bombs. But I always like to take deeper measures of prevention when I can—a double layer of subterfuge, if you will. If I hadn't this time, though—"

"You can't think that way," I said.

"No, I can't." His expression was imperturbable, marked by the calm that I'd seen every time he faced difficult circumstances. "She went to my rooms and took the letter and the wires you sent me. Karl found them in her room and gave them to me, afterwards. If she'd only opened the letter, she would have seen that you already knew the plot."

"I should have told you everything as soon as I learned it. I—I—was so scared. Scared that if I did, you'd take dramatic measures to stop Harrison, and that Schröder would kill you."

"You must learn to trust my instincts when it comes to things like this," he said. "But I'm glad you left the letter for me detailing Schröder's plans."

"If I'd shared what I knew earlier, Kristiana wouldn't have died."

"You just told me not to think that way. It's time to take your own advice." He touched my lips. "You did a marvelous job for Robert."

"And you did a marvelous job saving the world."

"A bit dramatic," he said.

"Maybe." I kissed him on each cheek. "Or not."

"Harrison had arranged it to look as if the British government was involved in the attack. We prevented something that could well have instigated a war. But there's something tugging at me. There was a small measure of truth in what Harrison believed: if we went to war with Germany today, there's no question that we'd be victorious."

"But there'll be no war," I said.

"Not now, but what if it comes later? What if it is inevitable? He's right about the kaiser wanting to strengthen his navy."

"Which doesn't mean that he's bent on fighting with Britain."

"Of course not. But if he does, and he builds an army and navy that could threaten ours, it could mean the deaths of tens of thousands of our men. I've stopped an attack on innocent victims, but in doing so, have I left the door open for even more death in the future?"

"No, no," I said. "The kaiser is the queen's grandson. He'd never go to war with England."

"I'm afraid the era of gentlemen's diplomacy may be coming to an end, Emily, and I wonder what it will mean for us. For our world." He gave a weak, closed-lip smile. "But let's talk no more of that. I'm concerned about you. You've faced horrors in these past weeks."

I met his gaze but did not speak. He pressed his hands to my face, his skin cool against my cheeks.

"I don't know which is worse," he said. "The terror you feel the first time you witness such things, or the numbness that comes after it starts to become ordinary."

"I can't imagine any of this becoming ordinary."

"Do you want to stop?"

"I didn't realize I was starting."

"You've proven your investigative abilities to me repeatedly, Emily. I think I may be able to use you as a partner, not just a wife."

286 ♦ Tasha Alexander

"For your work?"

"Yes."

"Will the queen approve?" I asked, at once shocked and delighted and full of more than a little pride.

"I find that I care about her opinion less and less." He leaned forward and kissed me, his lips soft and light.

"How much less?" I asked, returning his kiss. "Enough to have the ship's captain marry us?"

Laughter stopped his kisses. "Brandon's right. You do read too many sensational novels. No, not that much."

"A great loss for both of us," I said.

OUR RETURN TO ENGLAND should have been filled with unchecked exultation—and it was for Ivy and Robert, Margaret and Cécile. But Colin and I could not fully give ourselves over to celebration until we'd washed away the memory of death, something that would only come after months had passed. Of all my friends, Cécile understood this best, coming to me at night, when dreams brought me to tears.

This is not to say, however, that we were consumed with melancholy. London was quiet, nearly everyone still in the country, and we felt as if we had the best parts of the city to ourselves. Lord Salisbury called for Robert, and by the end of the meeting, it was decided that his political fortunes, while not perhaps as stellar as they'd once been, were not irrevocably damaged. I paid another visit to Sir Julian, who was easily persuaded to run a story lauding Robert and presenting him as a victim in a hideous drama. And while victim was not a role to which he aspired, it was preferable to that which he'd played while he was in prison.

After little more than a week had passed, my mother, swathed in black, returned to Berkeley Square.

"I come with the most dreadful news," she said, her voice full of anticipatory pleasure.

We were all gathered in the library. Robert had been reading poetry to Ivy—Shakespeare's sonnets, an obvious but sweet choice. Margaret and Mr. Michaels were arguing loudly about a passage from Ovid, while Colin and Cécile played chess. I was reading the book Robert had given me, glad for mindless distraction.

My mother smiled, her eyes gleaming, pleased to have found an audience. "Dear Prince Eddy, who ought one day to have been our king, has succumbed to pneumonia."

"Oh, dear," Ivy said. "How awful. His poor mother must be devastated."

"The Princess of Wales is taking it very poorly," my mother replied. "But you, Ivy, should not be out of bed. Robert, what can you be thinking to allow her to exert herself this way?"

"Lady Bromley, let me assure you—" Robert would not be permitted to finish his sentence.

"Send someone to pack your things immediately. I'm bringing you both back to Kent with me."

"You're too kind," Ivy said. "But it's entirely unnecessary. We—"

"I'll not hear another word on the subject. There's no sense in your staying in London, and who are your neighbors in Yorkshire? No, no, no. You're coming with me. Unless, of course, you've already decided to stay with your in-laws. I hadn't thought to speak to Robert's mother—"

Now it was Ivy's turn to interrupt. "No, no. Thank you, Lady Bromley. I shouldn't think of refusing your hospitality."

My mother gave a smug smile and turned to me; I couldn't help but flinch. "As for you, child, I don't know what will happen with your wedding now. Perhaps it would be best if you hold off on plans for the moment."

I was about to say that, in fact, it would be best if we were married quickly and with little ceremony, but Colin spoke first.

"Of course," he said. "We will proceed however you and Her Majesty feel is appropriate."

"I shall consult with the queen at the earliest possible time. It's too soon now—"

"Far too soon," he said. I could hardly believe he was agreeing to this. "But I know that you'll figure out the proper way to navigate all this, and I thank you, Lady Bromley, for all that you've done."

"Oh, Mr. Hargreaves, it is my pleasure." She beamed, then started for the door. "I will go oversee your packing, Ivy. Robert, ring for a footman and have a wire sent to Yorkshire. Your trunks can be sent directly to Kent. Miss Seward, why don't you come assist me?"

Margaret stammered something that resembled muffled laughter more than it did a reply, but followed, her eyes flashing apologies to Mr. Michaels. The don excused himself almost as soon as she'd left.

"Why are you so eager to go along with my mother's plans now?" I asked Colin, sotto voce, pulling him into a corner.

"There's nothing else to be done at the moment, so why cause her alarm?"

"Alarm?"

"I think it would be good for us to spend some time alone—together—but away from our friends. I . . . I need to mourn, Emily. I want you with me. And I don't want to be here. Not in London, not in England." The pain in his eyes cut me as I saw all that she'd meant to him. His feelings, even if they were in the past, were still significant, and though this was painful, it also offered hope to me, because I did not want to believe that any love could be so fully abandoned.

"Of course." I touched his arm. "Whatever you need."

The door opened and Davis came in, holding a letter. "This just arrived express, madam." He put it in my hand, and I tore at the envelope at once. It was from Sissi:

Dear Kallista,

I am most appreciative of your letter. Although I'd hoped for more information, you gave me enough to bring a small measure of peace to my heart. I realize that you were careful to say you had no proof, but the reaction you saw when you confronted him is enough for me. It fits with everything else I know. I hope you do not mind that I shared what you told me with a select associate—a man of action—who, shortly after learning my suspicions, was kind enough to bring me news of the suicide of an acquaintance of yours, Mr. Harrison.

Another of Vienna's victims.

I send greetings from your friend, Friedrich. The emperor was so taken by the sketch he did of me that he asked to meet the boy. I understand his engagement is to be announced any day.

Do tell Cécile I long to see her again.

Elisabeth

I passed it to Colin. "She shouldn't have done it," he said, then handed it to Cécile, who shrugged.

"There are a lot of suicides in Vienna," she said.

"I can't say I feel much of a loss." I folded the letter and slipped it back into its envelope after Ivy and Robert had read it. "Despite Jeremy's earlier admonition that 'it is not right to glory in the slain.'"

"It's not so much that we're taking pleasure in the news," Ivy said. "Simply that we knew his character well enough to feel that justice has been served."

We sat in silence for a while, and though we may not have been grieving for Mr. Harrison, we had all faced too much death in the past weeks to recover quickly from news of still more.

"You're a grim lot," Jeremy said, entering the room. "I'm astonished. Given the scene in your entrance hall, I should have thought you'd all be drinking champagne."

"Champagne?" I crossed to the door and peered into the hallway. Margaret and Mr. Michaels were caught in a tight embrace, my mother standing not five paces away, a smug smile on her face. As soon as she saw me watching, she poked Mr. Michaels's back with her parasol.

"That's quite enough, sir. Why don't you tell your friends the news?"

"News?" I asked, coming out into the hall, the rest of our party following me.

"Mr. Michaels and I are engaged," Margaret said.

"Margaret!" I confess I was shocked.

"Your mother is implacable, Emily. I could resist no longer."

"I knew you were no match for her," I said, hugging her. Congratulations rained down on the couple, and Davis, of his own accord, brought both champagne and cigars and did not balk in the slightest when the bride-to-be began puffing on one.

"Odette is being very good to him, I think," I said to Cécile.

"I am most concerned," she replied. "And ought to return to Paris posthaste."

"Speaking of travels . . ." I pulled Ivy away from the group. "You don't really want to go to Kent with my mother."

"It's already set in motion, my dear," she said. "And I've neither the energy nor the inclination to fight it. Besides, at the moment, all I care about is having Robert at my side. Not even your mother can take away my joy."

Chapter 29

The weather on Santorini was far from perfect. The sky and the ocean were gray, and rain whipped the white walls and blue shutters of my villa. Colin and I had arrived separately, planning this as a clandestine sort of meeting. We might be engaged, but we could not travel without a chaperone unless we wanted to court gossip, and certainly it could not be known that we were staying together, unsupervised and unmarried. He had come to the island five days before me, but when I reached the house, I could not find him. My cook, Mrs. Katevatis, pointed me outside, saying that, untroubled by the weather, he'd gone for a walk.

I took the umbrella she offered, but it was barely useful. The wind tugged at it, bending its ribs, and the rain, coming at me horizontally, soaked my coat as I walked along the path that skirted the edge of the island's cliffs. It was here that twice Colin had stood before me and proposed, here that I now found him, his back to me as he stared out over the caldera. I turned him around and saw his dark eyes, red-rimmed, devoid of warmth, full of sadness. He fell into my arms and cried.

More than a quarter of an hour passed before he raised his head. "I don't have to explain this to you, do I?"

"Not at all." I knew his pain too well. It was the same I'd felt when at last I'd mourned my husband, two years after his death.

"It doesn't have to do with you—you must understand that. What we have, Emily, it's everything. I did love her, years ago, but that was different. It wasn't . . . she didn't . . ."

"She loved you," I said. "She told me. She only refused you because she thought having a wife would distract you and put you in danger."

"She told you this?"

"Yes."

"I—"

I put my hand up to his lips. "Colin, it's all right. She loved you. You have to know that."

"I always believed her when she said it was just play," he said. "I never thought she loved anyone."

"She was good at being covert."

"Too good."

The smell of the wet earth rose all around us. A smell I usually welcomed, something that reminded me of childhood days playing on my father's estate. But today it caught heavy in my throat as I breathed. I could feel a trembling start in my core, and I could not stop it.

"I don't want to disappoint you." I hated the words the moment they escaped my lips.

"Disappoint me?"

I dropped my head against his chest, embarrassed. "I'm afraid I may suffer in comparison to your past."

"You have a past too, my dear, one that's not always been easy for me to accept."

"My past? My past hardly even existed."

"I knew you as someone else's wife. My best friend's wife."

"Yes, but—"

"But you loved him. Eventually you loved him. And he adored you from the beginning. You were his."

"Colin, I—"

"You're not a girl who's out for her first Season, and I'm not just down from Cambridge. We come to each other with fully lived lives, Emily." The rain was falling harder, and we were both drenched. "We must accept that. I don't think there's anything more to be said."

My eyes filled with tears. He pulled me close to him.

"You're shaking," he said. "It's cold. We ought to go inside."

Part of me wanted to stop him, wanted to insist that we talk about this more. But the rest accepted—begrudgingly, perhaps, but accepted nonetheless—that there was no need to speak further on the subject. Our pasts had brought us to where we were now, and without them, we might never have come together. He took my hand and slipped it, along with his, into his jacket pocket.

"I love you," I said, looking up at him.

He smiled. "Such simple words, yet they sing."

"How soon can we be married?" I asked, a smile creeping onto my face.

"I'm free this afternoon if you don't have other plans."

"If only," I said.

"You wouldn't dare refuse me. Not now."

"What would the queen say?"

"I've no interest in anyone's opinion but yours," he said, and I knew at once how serious he was. There was no hint of flirtatious teasing in his voice.

"Does Mrs. Katevatis know?" I asked.

"She's making spanakopita and *kreatopitakia* even as we speak."

"Then I don't see how I could say no," I said. He brushed a wet curl away from my eyes and took my face in his hands, kissing me gently. I felt every barrier to happiness dissolving inside me.

"Shall we go straight to the chapel?" he asked.

"We'd need a license."

"I've already arranged for that."

"We're soaked," I said.

"I don't mind being soaked. Do you?"

"No." I looked at him, memorizing his face so that I'd always be able to recall this moment in perfect detail. "Strangely, I don't."

How could I mind? We'd already waited long enough.

Acknowledgments

Myriad thanks to. . .
Jennifer Civiletto and Anne Hawkins, whose guidance and insight made this a better book.

Danielle Bartlett, Shari Newman, Buzzy Porter, and Tom Robinson, publicity gurus.

Dr. Vincent Tranchida, New York City medical examiner, for telling me exactly what to expect from a gunshot to the head.

Mark Smith, The Man in Seat Sixty-One, whose breadth of knowledge about the history of rail travel is staggering.

Mike Campbell, provider of boundless insider information on Vienna and title-concept master.

Joyclyn Ellison, Kristy Kiernan, Elizabeth Letts, and Renee Rosen, fiercely talented writers and partners in daily authorial neurosis.

Brett Battles, Laura Bradford, Rob Gregory Browne, Jon Clinch, Karen Dionne, Zarina Docken, Bente Gallagher, Melanie Lynne Hauser, Joe Konrath, Dusty Rhoades, and Sachin Waikar, for keeping me sane, grounded, and entertained.

Laura Morefield and Linda Roebuck, who are simply the best.

Christina Chen, Tammy Humphries, Carrie Medders, and Missy Rightley, friends I can't imagine being without.

B.S.R., who always knows exactly what I need and makes sure I get it without having to ask. You've turned me into a beach girl.

Gary and Stacie Gutting, for boundless support.

Matt and Xander Tyska, for everything.

THE HISTORY
BEHIND
THE STORY

On Writing *A Fatal Waltz*

A city ahead of its time—literally, Vienna time in the 1890s was five minutes ahead of the rest of the Central Europe zone—the Austrian capital was a sophisticated froth of high culture, political drama, and intellectual discourse. It was the perfect stop on a grand tour, the city of Strauss's waltzes, glistening with beauty. But Vienna also possessed a seamier side, rife with anti-Semitism, poverty, and the highest suicide rate on the continent.

After I finished writing *A Poisoned Season* and sat down to consider what Emily might do next, I knew that I wanted to take her out of England, away from the places she felt most comfortable. In *And Only to Deceive*, she underwent an intellectual awakening and discovered the importance of academic pursuits. In the sequel, she had to reconcile her newfound interests with a society that did not much approve of them. And, tempting though it may seem through contemporary eyes, it wasn't reasonable to think she would simply reject, out of hand, the world in which she lived.

Instead, carefully, one step at a time, she has to broaden her horizons and push the boundaries forced upon her. So with the third book in the series, I decided to bring her to Vienna, a wonderfully complicated city where she would be able, for the first time, to associate with and befriend people who were neither her class nor her servants. In the Victorian period, a person could read about the difficulties faced by the lower classes—today, we can easily view vivid images of poverty and disease. For Emily, stepping into this stunning, snow-capped city, it's the easiest thing to fall in love with the place: the Ringstrasse, the balls, the museums, the opera, the coffee houses. Seeing the difficulties faced by Friedrich and, especially, by Rina makes it impossible for her to ignore harsh realities, and gives her the beginnings of a social conscience.

One of the pleasures and challenges of writing a series is constructing a narrative arc that moves from book to book. Emily's journey from naïve widow to worldly, independent woman can't happen in a single volume. There are moments in which I wish I could push her ahead more quickly, but the fact is, the daughter of an earl who has spent her life in the most sheltered sort of circumstances cannot change overnight. It has to happen gradually, and there are bound to be speed bumps along the way.

The story of Emily and Colin's romance is one that I didn't want to drag on and on through the series, partly because I'm impatient, and partly because it infuriates me to read too many volumes of "Will they? Won't they?" Emily's first marriage stemmed from a willful and immature decision—and she was incredibly lucky things turned out as well as they did. Her love for Colin is worlds apart from that she felt for Philip, and it makes her reconsider her views on marriage. What if, instead of being subjugated by her husband, a woman were a respected equal?

To me, it's fascinating that, even in this sort of Victorian relationship, it is the man who wields the ultimate power—he is the one who must decide how to treat his wife. And again, it's here that as a writer I have to resist the urge to make Emily more modern than she ought to be. She can be strong and centered, but she must also remain a woman of her time. Colin is enlightened and wonderful, but Emily knows that, as a husband, he will have control over her—and it's only when she begins to trust him fully that she's willing to relinquish any of her hard-earned independence.

Getting into the Writing Mode

There are many, many pleasures to writing a book, not the least of which is being able to work in pajamas. I've written each of my novels in different locations: *And Only to Deceive* in an attic apartment in New Haven, Connecticut; *A Poisoned Season* in the Five Points Starbucks in Franklin, Tennessee; *Elizabeth: The Golden Age* on my couch (I'm not sure I got up more than once a day, if even that often, while working on it). *A Fatal Waltz* is the only one composed where it was "supposed" to be: my office. The book I'm working on now was drafted in bed—while I leaned back against an enormous heap of pillows. And, yes, I stayed in pajamas as much as possible. Indulgence at its best.

But there is more to a book than just the writing; there is also loads of research. One of the most fun bits of doing *A Fatal Waltz* was submersing myself in Viennese food and culture. I listened to Strauss and made Austrian feasts: schnitzel and spaetzle (with the assistance of the fantastic spaetzle maker given to me by my dear friend, the brilliant writer Kristy Kiernan), strudel, and Sacher torte. Well, not precisely Sacher torte. After more attempts at making the famous pastry than I'm comfortable admitting (there were problems with tempering the chocolate), I finally abandoned it in favor of Julia Child's Reine de Saba, which, strictly speaking, is French, but is such an elegant dessert I'm sure no one in Vienna would object to being served it.

I covered the walls of my office with old maps of the city and pictures of locations that appear in the novel, spent days and nights reading everything about the city in the 1890s that I could get my hands on, and was amazed by the rich setting I'd chosen for the book. The Court Theater's façade was lit by four thousand electric lights. The newspapers published reviews of the flowers left on graves of the famous (Beethoven, for example) on All Souls' Day. The fairy-tale Ringstrasse, of which it was said, "one came here to wait, as it were, in style," enchanted all who walked along it. Two thousand guests would descend upon a ballroom, consuming almond milk, lemonade, and hundreds of bottles of champagne.

And in the morning, the partygoers would awake to newspaper accounts of spectacular suicides:

> An elegant young woman had boarded the Budapest express, taken a small suitcase into a toilet, emerged in a bridal gown with veil and train, opened the car door, and leaped out of the speeding train. She was found dead by the rails, her snowy lace brilliant with blood.
> —Frederic Morton, *A Nervous Splendor*

Vienna. A city of contrast.

Suggestions for Further Reading

Life in the English Country House, by Mark Girouard

The English Country House Party, by Phyllida Barstow

Culture and Adultery: The Novel, the Newspaper, and the Law, 1857–1914, by Barbara Leckie

A Nervous Splendor: Vienna 1888–1889, by Frederic Morton

The Road to Mayerling: The Life and Death of Crown Prince Rudolph of Austria, by Richard Barkeley

Hotel Imperial Vienna, by Andreas Augustin

The lighter side of HISTORY

* Look for this seal on select historical fiction titles from Harper. Books bearing it contain special bonus materials, including timelines, interviews with the author, and insights into the real-life events that inspired the book, as well as recommendations for further reading.

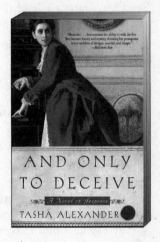

AND ONLY TO DECEIVE:
A Novel of Suspense
by Tasha Alexander
978-0-06-114844-6 (paperback)
Discover the dangerous secrets kept by the strait-laced English of the Victorian era.

ANNETTE VALLON:
A Novel of the French Revolution
by James Tipton
978-0-06-082222-4 (paperback)
For fans of Tracy Chevalier and Sarah Dunant comes this vibrant, alluring debut novel of a compelling, independent woman who would inspire one of the world's greatest poets and survive a nation's bloody transformation.

BOUND: A Novel
by Sally Gunning
978-0-06-124026-3 (paperback)
An indentured servant finds herself bound by law, society, and her own heart in colonial Cape Cod.

THE CANTERBURY PAPERS: A Novel
by Judith Healey
978-0-06-077332-8 (paperback)
Follow Princess Alais on a secret mission as she unlocks a long-held and dangerous secret.

CASSANDRA & JANE: A Jane Austen Novel
by Jill Pitkeathley
978-0-06-144639-9 (paperback)
The relationship between Jane Austen and her sister— explored through the letters that might have been.

CROSSED: A Tale of the Fourth Crusade
by Nicole Galland
978-0-06-084180-5 (paperback)
Under the banner of the Crusades, a pious knight and a British vagabond attempt a daring rescue.

DARCY'S STORY
by Janet Aylmer
978-0-06-114870-5 (paperback)
Read Mr. Darcy's side of the story—*Pride and Prejudice* from a new perspective.

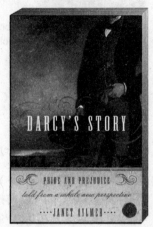

A FATAL WALTZ: A Novel of Suspense
by Tasha Alexander
978-0-06-117423-0 (paperback)
Caught in a murder mystery, Emily must do the unthinkable to save her fiancé: bargain with her ultimate nemesis, the Countess von Lange.

THE FIREMASTER'S MISTRESS:
A Novel
by Christie Dickason
978-0-06-156826-8 (paperback)
Estranged lovers Francis and Kate rekindle their romance in the midst of Guy Fawkes's plot to blow up Parliament.

THE FOOL'S TALE: A Novel
by Nicole Galland
978-0-06-072151-0 (paperback)
Travel back to Wales, 1198, a time of treachery, political unrest . . . and passion.

JULIA AND THE MASTER OF MORANCOURT: A Novel
by Janet Aylmer
978-0-06-167295-8 (paperback)
Amidst family tragedy, Julia travels all over England, desperate to marry the man she loves instead of the arranged suitor preferred by her mother.

KEPT: A Novel
by D. J. Tayler
978-0-06-114609-1 (paperback)
A gorgeously intricate, dazzling reinvention of Victorian life and passions that is also a riveting investigation into some of the darkest, most secret chambers of the human heart.

PILATE'S WIFE: A Novel of the Roman Empire
by Antoinette May
978-0-06-112866-0 (paperback)
Claudia foresaw the Romans' persecution of Christians, but even she
could not stop the crucifixion.

A POISONED SEASON: A Novel of Suspense
by Tasha Alexander
978-0-06-117421-6 (paperback)
As a cat-burglar torments Victorian London, a mysterious gentleman
fascinates high society.

PORTRAIT OF AN UNKNOWN WOMAN: A Novel
by Vanora Bennett
978-0-06-125256-3 (paperback)
Meg, adopted daughter of Sir Thomas More, narrates the tale of a
famous Holbein painting and the secrets it holds.

THE QUEEN OF SUBTLETIES: A Novel of Anne Boleyn
by Suzannah Dunn
978-0-06-059158-8 (paperback)
Untangle the web of fate surrounding Anne Boleyn in a tale narrated by
the King's Confectioner.

THE QUEEN'S SORROW:
A Novel of Mary Tudor
by Suzannah Dunn
978-0-06-170427-7 (paperback)
Queen of England Mary Tudor's reign
is brought low by abused power and a
forbidden love.

REBECCA:
The Classic Tale of Romantic Suspense
by Daphne Du Maurier
978-0-380-73040-7 (paperback)
Follow the second Mrs. Maxim de Winter
down the lonely drive to Manderley,
where Rebecca once ruled.

REBECCA'S TALE: A Novel
by Sally Beauman
978-0-06-117467-4 (paperback)
Unlock the dark secrets and old worlds of Rebecca de Winter's life with investigator Colonel Julyan.

REVENGE OF THE ROSE: A Novel
by Nicole Galland
978-0-06-084179-9 (paperback)
In the court of the Holy Roman Emperor, not even a knight is safe from gossip, schemes, and secrets.

THE SIXTH WIFE: A Novel of Katherine Parr
by Suzannah Dunn
978-0-06-143156-2 (paperback)
Kate Parr survived four years of marriage to King Henry VIII, but a new love may undo a lifetime of caution.

TO THE TOWER BORN: A Novel of the Lost Princes
by Robin Maxwell
978-0-06-058052-0 (paperback)
Join Nell Caxton in the search for the lost heirs to the throne of Tudor England.

VIVALDI'S VIRGINS: A Novel
by Barbara Quick
978-0-06-089053-7 (paperback)
Abandoned as an infant, fourteen-year-old Anna Maria dal Violin is one of the elite musicians living in the foundling home where the "Red Priest," Antonio Vivaldi, is maestro and composer.

THE WIDOW'S WAR: A Novel
by Sally Gunning
978-0-06-079158-2 (paperback)
Tread the shores of colonial Cape Cod with a lonely whaler's widow as she tries to build a new life.

THE WILD IRISH:
A Novel of Elizabeth I & the Pirate O'Malley
by Robin Maxwell
978-0-06-009143-9 (paperback)
Hoist a sail with the Irish pirate and clan chief
Grace O'Malley.

Available wherever books are sold, or call 1-800-331-3761 to order.